Alison Johnson was born in 1947 and was brought up in Aberdeen. She has an MA in English from Aberdeen University and a B.Phil. in Medieval Studies from Oxford University. In 1973 she and her husband moved to the Isle of Harris. Having taught in the local school for a few years, they bought a derelict manse and renovated it themselves before opening as Scarista House, a small country house hotel that quickly achieved a reputation as one of the most highly acclaimed hotels in Scotland and received accolades from all the major food and hotel guides. Since selling the hotel in 1990, they have been partners in the White Horse Press, publishing academic books and journals on broadly environmental subjects, and now spend part of the year living near Cambridge. She has published one novel, under the name A. Findlay Johnson, *Children of Disobedience* (André Deutsch, 1989; Mandarin, 1990) and three books that tell the story of Scarista House: *A House by the Shore* (Gollancz, 1986; Macdonald, 1987), *Scarista Style: A Free Range and Humane Approach to Cooking and Eating* (Gollancz, 1987; Macdonald, 1988) and *Islands in the Sound* (Gollancz, 1989).

D1574946

The Wicked Generation

❖

ALISON JOHNSON

THE
BLACKSTAFF
PRESS

BELFAST

417915

MORAY DISTRICT COUNCIL
DEPARTMENT OF
LEISURE AND LIBRARIES
F

First published in 1992 by
The Blackstaff Press Limited
3 Galway Park, Dundonald, Belfast BT16 0AN, Northern Ireland
with the assistance of
The Arts Council of Northern Ireland

© Alison Johnson, 1992
All rights reserved

Typeset by Textflow Services Limited

Printed by The Guernsey Press Company Limited

British Library Cataloguing in Publication Data
Johnson, Alison
Wicked Generation
I. Title
823.914 [F]

ISBN 0-85640-398-9

How we enjoyed ourselves in those far-away days – the old as much as the young. I often saw three and sometimes four generations dancing together on the green grass in the golden summer sunset. Men and women of fourscore and more – for they lived long in those days – dancing with boys and girls of five on the green grass. Those were the happy days and the happy nights, and there was neither sin nor sorrow in the world for us. The thought of those young days makes my old heart both glad and sad even at this distance of time. But the clearances came upon us, destroying all, turning our small crofts into big farms for the stranger, and turning our joy into misery, our gladness into bitterness, our blessing into blasphemy, and our Christianity into mockery . . . O dear man, the tears come on my eyes when I think of all we suffered and of the sorrows, hardships, oppressions we came through.

PEGGY MACCORMACK
(from *Carmina Gadelica*, ed. Alexander Carmichael, 1900)

AUTHOR'S NOTE

'Glencalvie people was in the church here May 24 1845
. . . Glencalvie people the wicked generation'

These gaunt statements are scratched on the window pane of a little church in Ross-shire. The people who wrote them were awaiting deportation: Glencalvie had been turned into a sheep run. The words in the old brittle glass outlive a vanished community, a last assertion of its existence. The wicked generation: the tradition-bound, fatalistic generation, bowing to the judgment of God.

This story is not about Glencalvie's people. The islands of Fladday and Rona, indeed all the geography and all the characters in this book, are entirely imaginary. So, too, with events. It is not intended as an accurate account of the historical Scottish clearances. It is less about rights and wrongs than about inevitability; as at Glencalvie, a traditional, static community is overwhelmed by the juggernaut of modern economic growth. It is still happening, every day, to ethnic peoples from Siberia to Sarawak.

HOUSEHOLDS IN BORVE KILMORY BEFORE EVACUATION IN 1846
(AGES IN BRACKETS)

DONALD MACDONALD (31), nicknamed Cam: with wife Mór (24), baby son Donald, sisters Effie (24) and Eilidh (16), great-uncle Dougie (81)

JOHN GILLIES (28), nicknamed Blackie (Iain Dubh): with wife Rachel (25), mother Annag (51), brothers Neil (18) and Alex (14)

CIORSTAG MACLEAN (53), sister of Annag: with father Alasdair the Bard (89), daughters Lexy (23), Kirsty Mary (19) and Sara (15), son Alasdair (17), husband Sailor John often at sea

JOHN MACDONALD (34), nicknamed Blondie, brother of John Blackie's wife Rachel: with wife Seonag (34), mother Catriona (64), daughter Katie (13), sons Shonny (9), Muti (6) and Lala (3)

JOHN MORRISON (44), widower, nicknamed John of the Rock, foster-brother of Donald: with daughter Peggy (17)

HECTOR THE SMITH (Old Hector) (59): with wife Johane (50), sons young Hector (19) and Angus (15), mother Katie Morag (76)

RODERICK MACLEAN (47), brother of Sailor John: with wife Annabel (37), sons Norman (19), Roddy (16), Hughie (11), Ewan (4), daughter Annabel (Baba) (1)

KENNETH MACDONALD (40), widower: with daughters Neiliann (9) and Kennag (7) and sons Doodie (6) and Lachie (5)

RANALD MACDONALD the carpenter (60), uncle of Donald and nephew of Dougie: with sister Barabel (64)

The emigrants are joined by blind Angus and his crippled daughter Flora, and by two stray children, Norrie and Nana, from other villages.

HOUSEHOLDS ON RONA AT ISSIE'S ARRIVAL IN 1862
(AGES IN BRACKETS)

DUNCAN MACLEAY (38), missionary

DONALD MACDONALD (47), now the elder: with Mór (40), sons Donald (16) and Duncan (14), daughters Morag (7) and Chrissann (4), sister Effie (40), aunt Barabel (80)

CIORSTAG (69): with unmarried daughter Lexy (39), Kenneth's son Doodie (22); daughter Kirsty Mary and Doodie's sister Kennag work away but return periodically

JOHN BLACKIE (44): with second wife Marsaili (26), son Neilie (7), daughters Annie (5) and Elsie (3), mother Annag (67)

JOHN BLONDIE (50): with Seonag (50), sons Muti (22) and Lala (19), daughter Rebecca (14), mother Catriona (80)

YOUNG HECTOR (35): with wife Sara (31) (Ciorstag's youngest daughter), daughters Mary (12) and Drina (8), son John Hector (4) and father old Hector (75)

JOHN OF THE ROCK (60): alone, his daughter Peggy having left the island

RODERICK (63), now a widower: with sons Hughie (27), Ewan (20) and Alan (12), and daughters Baba (17) and Florann (10)

BLIND ANGUS (81): with crippled daughter Flora (56), looked after by Nana (22)

NORMAN (35), Roderick's eldest son: with wife Dora (26) (a shepherd's daughter from Fladday), daughter Mamie (4) and son Bobby (1)

RODDY (32), Roderick's second son: with wife Katie (29) (John Blondie's daughter), son Archie (6) and daughter Bell (3)

NORRIE (28): with wife Neiliann (25) (Kenneth's daughter), daughter Murdina (4) and son Kenny (2)

SHONNY (25), John Blondie's son: with wife Dolina (18) (a Boreray girl)

1845

The chieftain's daughter was married in a gown of rich white *Gros de Naples*, the bodice ruched at the shoulders above a flounce of Honiton lace, and trimmed with seed-pearl embroidery. The sleeves were unadorned save for *mancherons* and cuffs of the same lace, bordered with the tiniest pearls. The four lace flounces of the skirt were split *en tablier* and looped back shepherdess-fashion – a dainty touch *à l'ancienne* felt by all to be most appropriate to this 'land of hills and glens, strayed o'er by woolly flocks'. The underskirt thus revealed was embroidered in the same exquisite manner as the bodice. Another romantic recollection of antique fashion was afforded by a sash of the bride's hereditary tartan, wherein the chequered colours, predominantly tints of crimson, mauve and blue, were displayed against a background of white silk, presenting a most tasteful and delicate appearance reminiscent of one of the heroines of Sir Walter Scott. Most charming was the veil, of the same costly lace as the trimming of the gown, unornamented save for a chaste wreath of orange-blossom, which had been conveyed posthaste through the night from the steam-heated conservatory of Lady S—— of Perthshire. The bride's parure, the wedding gift of her father, was of freshwater pearls and amethysts, which though less in worth than diamonds, how right they are to grace a Highland beauty may be judged from the recent favour shown to such ornaments in Royal circles, so that they have now become quite the fashion.

She is *la belle Hélène*, and though her French is not so fluent as it might be, who would notice bêtises from such rosebud lips?

3

The subtenant's daughter was married with prayer and with blessing, with music of pipe and music of fiddle, with singing and with dancing, with abundance of meal and abundance of milk.

'A feast – even in March! Your housekeeping is good, my dear,' said the old women to the bride's mother. There were just about enough potatoes, with what everyone had brought, but the cheese ran out very early. 'It was too good to last, indeed,' they said, consolingly.

'Plenty drams, anyway,' a young man grinned. They'd escaped the exciseman that year.

The grace of goodness, the grace of wisdom, the grace of charity were on the maiden that day.

'She is shelter in the cold, an island in the wild sea, a well in the desert,' an old man sang in a high shaky voice without teeth.

'Och, ye silly old fool,' said his brother amiably.

The blessings of wifehood and conception were wished on her at nightfall. The young girls hammered on the door each time the reel swept them past it.

'Don't sleep late now – remember the cows are needing milked.'

'Make us a wee boy for Christmas.'

'Fire! Help! Everybody out!'

She is the brown swan, the unfledged, the maiden bride. In the morning she will hide her loose brown hair under a wife's white kerchief.

1 8 4 6

CHAPTER 1

'What will the people do, Father?'

Hector George Alexander Macdonald of Drumharg frowned irritably. His tenants' rents were in arrears and there were far too many of them. Besides, his younger daughter's voice grated on his musical ear. She squeaked in timorous agitation and spoke all in a rush. So unlike her sister: a wavering geniality reclaimed the chieftain's brow, and he smiled benignly on his elder child.

Helen, approved and golden in the pooling sunlight of the window bay, smiled back over her embroidery. 'Issie dear, please don't sit on your hands. And try, my sweet, to speak a little softer, won't you, and not so fast?'

'Like your sister, Issie.' Augustus Green bent over his wife Helen's chair, glad of the excuse to touch his lips even to her hair ribbons. He was greatly in love with her: she was so much what he had always desired, to whom desire implied desert.

Issie, not long released from the nursery, hardly ever dared speak at all and finding her efforts thus disdained, she bunched the large red hands which so embarrassed her inside each other on her lap. 'Hands like a kitchen-maid's', she had heard Augustus say to Helen once, and laugh. Recollecting it, her face reddened too, wretchedly. But her question would not go away. She tried again, with choking effort. 'Please, Father . . . '

He was an indulgent parent, but the matter was of no concern to a young lady. There was, therefore, a touch of warning sarcasm in his playful tone.

'Why, my dear, they must go away.'

Green's fraternal kindness – for he must feel kind towards Helen's pets – saved Issie the forward question strangling in her mouth. 'We have made provision for them, Issie, don't be troubled about them. They may go to our lands in Canada if they will do so; your father hopes and fully expects that the best among them will and he has given generously to facilitate their voyages. So you see, even if they are poor, they will not be hindered. All they need have is four bolls of meal apiece, stout clothing and good brave hearts, and a new life is theirs. A new land, and freedom to make what they will of it.'

Hands under his coat tails, with a brisk half-nod indicative of approval, he gazed out across the lawns and leafless beech-stands to the steep slopes of Ben Harg, blue in the clear February afternoon. 'Why, what a capital life for a young fellow. I might almost fancy it myself. What, Helen? If . . . ' He bent to her again, with the brief teasing murmur of a recent husband. She rewarded him with her dimpling smile.

That smile reminded Issie of her own prominent teeth. She closed her lips over them as well as possible. *Issie*, the nursery nickname whispered, *those teeth, those teeth*. 'Couldn't you call me Isobel, now I'm grown up? Or Belle?' she had asked Helen once, feeling a fool for asking. But Helen had laughed her back to the nursery. 'Certainly not! Issie you have always been and Issie you must stay, Issie dear. Why, how *could* you be Belle?' And how could she? For she was very ugly. Besides, their father often called Helen *la belle Hélène* or *ma belle*. It would be confusing, Helen said, and she rather liked her own nickname. Helen's teeth were somewhat stuck out too; not near so bad, only not as perfectly lovely as everything else about her. But she never showed them. She smiled so prettily, and spoke and sang with such a sweet little pout, it quite concealed the defect.

Mr Green raised his handsome smiling profile from Helen's curving cheek. But they do stick out, hers too, thought Issie, with a sparkle of something hateful inside her, and immediately cried to herself – I should be glad she's loved; I *am* glad. But there was a qualification she thrust aside, which broke out as perspiration on her nose.

So pleased was Mr Green with Mrs Green that her father too must hear compliments.

'Sir, you will not take it amiss if I tell Issie more of your excellent arrangements for your people on Fladday?'

'As you wish, my boy – do as you wish.' The chief spoke rather indistinctly, the front teeth which had been the pattern of Issie's having succumbed many years before to a passion for Edinburgh confectionery; which lack, coupled with the somnolence induced by two pints of claret at their early dinner, disinclined him now to conversation.

Helen smiled amiably as the old man's chin nodded on the old-fashioned lace stock which he wore to complement the tartan of his forefathers; though his own father in the portrait above the piano wore, as was the sitter's habit in life, blue worsted breeches.

Green smiled too, though privately he felt some humiliation at old Drumharg's lack of interest in the conversation. He had himself taken great pains over the Fladday matter, and besides, it was time (as Helen too had said) that her father paid more attention to Issie. In looks the child was a perfect fright, but a little encouragement might at least lend her some graces of speech and manners to fit her better for society.

'You see, Issie,' he continued gravely, 'these people are not like the decent souls you see around your father's policies. You imagine, don't you, a pretty village like ours here at Inverharg, with neat white cottages and a church and school? And that the inhabitants are well-doing folk like old Janet the hen-wife?'

'Indeed, Issie is very fond of Janet. She spends more time, I'm sure, with her than with me.' Helen pouted a little, but relented reliably at her adoring sister's vehement denial.

Mr Green had to deny it too, for he could not entertain even an implied slight to his wife. 'Nevertheless, though it is a harmless enough acquaintance, and indeed it does you credit to show a tender indulgence for the poor, I would venture to say that now you are very nearly grown up, it would do you more good to be at home with your sister. There you may learn all womanly graces.' Helen's ribbons absorbed a further kiss. Somewhat agitated by his own ardour, Mr Green paced away from her chair and back again. Recollecting himself, he continued: 'But the wretched inhabitants of Fladday, Issie, you would hardly recognise as Christians if you were to see them issuing from their miserable hovels, all black in the face with soot – for their huts have no chimneys, you know. They live whole families together with their cattle in one smoky, filthy room, so unwholesome that it is a wonder any survive. You might mistake them for Hottentots, and indeed they scarcely have more knowledge of the Word of God than those, for a minister has not been among them these twenty years, save to preach three times a year.'

'Why is that so, Augustus? Have men of God become so scarce?' Helen was capable, sometimes, of a quiet acerbity. It fell womanly innocent on her husband's ears.

'My dear, of course you wouldn't think of it, but even a minister could not be expected to do all for love and nothing for remuneration. When the island throve in kelping days – that was when they made potash from burned seaware, Issie; it's used in the manufacture of soap and glass – yes, then they could afford to keep a minister. But now – oh, you should see how such poor islanders live, although I am glad you cannot, for it would distress you. Besides,' he added, pacing again after another stealthy assault on the ribbons, 'it would scarcely be humane to condemn an educated man to exile in such a place. No. When the people remove to a less inhospitable spot, one may hope that religion will be restored to them and with it all the comforts of industry and honesty which now they lack, for they may truly be said to be in a state of nature, where nature is at her most rude and unyielding. The miserable crops they grow are hardly enough to feed themselves and their beasts, let alone to trade for those simple comforts which our cottagers here regard as necessaries. Can you imagine, Issie, some of the articles which these poor people must do without?'

Issie, startled from her intense contemplation of Mr Green's features and gestures, stammered, 'I do not know', but as he continued to bend a pedagogic eye upon her, she tried hesitantly: 'Sugar? Tea?', thinking of the little packages that so pleased old Janet.

Green shook his head. 'And worse. They lack even sufficient clothing: their children go unclad, and all are unshod. They can scarce pay rent without starving in consequence: they are crowding on land which should support less than half their number. Indeed' – here he paused to pare his next revelation of an indelicacy – 'for some years past your father has been obliged to order that no persons who marry shall remain on the island, except if the predeceasement of a relative shall have left vacant for them a home and a share in the common rights by which a family may be supported. So you see, on all counts it is an infinite improvement for young persons to emigrate.'

Issie, waiting for the unveiling of her father's excellent plans, wondered if she had missed it from other preoccupations, for the impression cast on her pitying mind by Mr Green's description had been vivid and painful, and her study of his lineaments minute. He had turned aside to finger Helen's embroidery.

'Issie, why don't you take up your work?'

'Yes, Helen. But . . . '

Both regarded her tolerantly.

'But . . . what about the old people? Won't they be grieved to leave their homeland and go on a long voyage? Will everyone not feel so? I know I should. Wouldn't you, Helen?'

Mr Green paced again, a little impatient now, for he had employed simplicity without sacrifice of precision to make the lesson easy. He felt his lively little discourse slighted. 'They have none of these advantages to which you are accustomed and so can hardly miss them. Those who are vigorous in mind and body will desire, I imagine, nothing more than help to remove to more hopeful climes. Oh, I dare say there will be some who cannot or will not go, from feebleness or old age, or more likely from stubbornness or defective intellect. Any such may depart to a neighbouring island, which is useless for sheep, but it will be a poor life and only the worst elements of the population will choose it.'

Issie, silenced, took up her sewing. He had thought her stupid and forward. She laboured inwardly for a few moments over a sentence of appreciation that should be quite graceful and proper. 'Thank you, Augustus. I feel my understanding of the matter is much improved.' But looking up to utter it, she saw he was again bent over Helen's chair, whispering and smiling. Issie's eyes stung with the sudden tears of desolate calf-love; struggling to restrain them, she knew that she did not understand at all, and could not see how this should be, for surely Augustus knew all about it and he could explain things so well. She stitched with bowed head, hating the red hands which swelled and blurred under her welling eyes.

'I have to leave early tomorrow, dearest.'

Helen took three knowing stitches over the hint. 'Must you, Augustus?'

'I'll be gone in twelve hours.' His fingers pressed her neck, sliding a little beneath her collar of Valenciennes lace.

'But not for long.' She clasped the fingers cunningly, thus removing his ardent pressure.

'For a week, perhaps.'

A week, she thought, might save matters.

Augustus, having waited due time for a response, raised her hand to his lips. 'Shall you and I walk outside a little?' he asked softly.

'Oh, my dear, there's such a chill, damp wind. You know I am never quite well on such days.' Lady Drumharg and her eldest daughter had died of consumption and Issie had been a near victim in infancy. It could be claimed as a family weakness.

Augustus fingered her delicate wrist and thumb. 'The garden is sheltered and still in sunshine. A little air will only make your cheeks rosy.'

Helen pouted. His attempt to overbear her indicated increasing desperation. She had no wish to be alone with her husband: in such fervid mood the conversation and caresses of a private moment would certainly arouse in him expectations that she had reason not to fulfil at this time. Her aunt, Mrs Livingstone of Charlotte Square, shortly to remarry to an English peer, had promised a London season, which plan, confided on her own honeymoon visit to Edinburgh, had caused her to exercise great prudence. Augustus would never permit it if . . .

She pursed her lips over a smile, striving to conceal her good health and good humour. 'Issie will walk with you, Augustus. She loves to be out of doors, whatever the weather. How strange it is that what strengthens her enfeebles me. I am sorry, dearest, but I think I must rest, I have such a headache. I shall go to my room now. Will you ring for my maid?'

He escorted her upstairs. She leaned on his arm with judicious heaviness, while arching her waist away from him, not wishing to enflame where she could not gratify. But at the door, as she wished him well on his journey to meet the tenant of Fladday, he clasped her suddenly by both shoulders.

'Helen, forgive me, but . . . have I offended you in any way since we became man and wife?'

'Indeed no, my dear, you are the best of husbands.' She slipped an arm free to reach the door knob.

'Helen . . . Helen, I want an heir!'

She kissed his chin with firmly closed lips and cast her eyes down. 'Here is Elsie,' she murmured, and withdrew in a rustle of silk. The maid curtseyed past him and left him staring at the closed door. Except in respect of his wife, he was not a patient man. With an exclamation unfit for her ears, he rushed downstairs and out to the stables to give orders for his early journey and to berate the grooms as lazy Highlanders.

He had his horse led out round the new carriage drive, the better to expatiate upon its lame front foot, its unkempt forelock and the mud of the previous day diminishing the gloss of its buttocks. As the harangue passed the drawing room window, old Drumharg's lolling head jerked into wakefulness. He woke grumbling, 'Damned young . . . ' but broke off. He had good reason to keep to himself his lingering contempt for the son-in-law who had been his servant. Green was what the Drumharg estates needed: a modern man with a head full of figures and theories. 'A modern man,' mumbled old Drumharg, grimacing with a mixture of scorn and admiration. He himself could trace his ancestry back five centuries and was of the aristocratic company of the Society of True Highlanders. Even though he had attended Eton College as a boy and in his prime had known Brighton more intimately than Drumharg, of late he had seldom ventured further south than Edinburgh, and dressed for all occasions in well-cut tartan. The home of one's youth and the customs of one's forefathers, he was fond of saying, are the bulwarks of a gentleman. Though Drumharg House was much different from the dark fortified farmhouse of his parents' day, having been remodelled in the height of Georgian elegance during the lucrative times of cattle and kelp: and might have had to be demolished again, if young Green hadn't proved such an able factor, so able the Duke of Argyll would have wooed him away, if Green hadn't had a fancy for Helen. Drumharg's brow furrowed. It was still a gall that a commoner, a mere Mr Green, the son of a manufacturer of woollen goods, should have married his daughter. But he had taken her without a settlement, which would not have been the way with his neighbour Strathbeg.

14

A fat, cross old widower, Drumharg remembered, chuckling over Helen's words. She had shown no reluctance to have Green. 'A good girl, *ma belle*,' he muttered.

Presently his eye fell on Issie, stooped over her sewing in the opposite window-corner. 'Where is your sister?' he asked, suddenly aware of Helen's absence.

'She is not well, Father. She went to her room to rest.'

'Not well? She ate a good dinner. What's the matter with her?'

'I don't know, Father,' Issie stammered, being aware, without knowing how, that her sister was as fit at that moment as she had been during her hearty consumption of roast duck and boiled mutton.

Drumharg mistook her confusion. An inward smile leant amiability to his somewhat drooping features. 'Not well, hm? We'll see, I suppose.' They had been married five months. Green might be the better choice there: Strathbeg's first wife had had twenty years' trial of him, and no heir.

Drumharg consulted his pocket watch, heaved himself, groaning slightly, from his chair and stumped out of the room, ringing the bell by the door and at the same time shouting impatiently in the corridor for his valet and his dog. It was the hour of his afternoon stroll to Inverharg. Here most of his estate workers lived. He went amongst them in this way each day, 'as a father in the bosom of his family', as he liked to say, on foot and without ceremony, shaking hands, distributing coins to the needy, remonstrating with the idle, stopping often to take a cup of whey or a tot of whisky at a cottage threshold. They usually remembered to gratify him with the old Highland mode of address – Eachann mac Sheorais, Hector son of George. In return, he spoke to them in Gaelic, rather haltingly, but sufficient for the needs of 'How are you?' and 'Put your back into it, my lad!'

In truth he knew them about as well as he knew his own children. There were eighteen families, some one hundred individuals, living in the neat model village built twenty years before

15

to match the refurbishment of the Big House. The village had replaced nineteen straggling settlements of crofters and cottars that had been cleared for reletting as two sheep farms in the 1820s. Of the hundreds of his clan who had wandered from his lands at that time, Macdonald of Drumharg knew as little as he did of those further hundreds whom, in the past five years, Augustus Green had caused to be displaced, removed, or redistributed in the interests of economy, industry and progress.

CHAPTER 2

Therefore the said Defenders ought & should be declared
& ordained by Decree & Sentence of me or my Substitute:

To flit and remove themselves, Bairns, Family, Servants,
Subtenants, Cottars & dependants, Cattle, goods and gear,
forth and from possession of the said Subjects above
described with the pertinents respectively occupied by
them as aforesaid, and to leave the same void, redd and
patent, at the respective Terms of Removal above speci-
fied, that the Pursuer or others in his name may then
enter thereto & peaceably possess, occupy and enjoy the
same in time coming.

Donald Cam, squint-eyed, not squint so much as one-side-blind
from the blow of an oar-end in boyhood, Domhnall mac
Dhomnuill 'ic Iain 'ic Dhomnuill, with difficulty mouthing
unfamiliar vocables, found himself there crucified among the
said defenders, above the sheriff's black signature. 'Donald
Macdonald residing at Borve of Kilmory,' he read slowly, voice
and breath fading in a wondering silence.

His great-uncle Dougie took off his bonnet, bowing a meek
head. The old man was deaf and nearly sightless and his
understanding was clouded, but the hush of the moment had
reached him, as it did at the reading of the Gospel, and so he
made the fitting action. 'Amen,' he said in his high shaky voice.

Donald said nothing, staring at the paper in his hand. His
wife's brother, John, Iain Dubh, also evoked above the sheriff's
signature – 'John Gillies, alias Black' – rapped the paper upward
in Donald's hand.

17

'What is this here?' he demanded. 'We have paid our rents, Donald. Our fathers paid their rents, increasing they've been, too. How can they make us remove? The land is ours, we pay for it and we work it.' He rounded suddenly on his young brother Alex. 'What was with you that you took the papers?'

The eyes of a dozen silent men turned on the boy. He hunched miserably away from them, shivering in the icy rain. When the sheriff's officer had put the papers of ill luck in his hand, he had not entered the house even to get his coat. He had spent the afternoon alternately pacing and frozen in the out-by fields, waiting for the men to come from dyking on the hill, trying not to see the old women, and later the younger ones too, trailing between one home and the next, looking his way but not coming near him.

'Minister's William gave them to me. My mother was telling me take them. She was giving the old man hot sowans with whisky in it, he was near perished crossing the water this morning.'

'Then better he'd stayed on the other side, devil take the old fool.'

The other men shuffled, embarrassed by such disrespect to the sheriff's officer, not for his position, which was a lackey's, but for his age and his kinship to the last minister to serve Fladday, whose nephew he was.

Donald, intent on the writ, looked up with his good eye, his hawk's eye, at John Blackie. 'Better he didn't, then. There's three named here: yourself, myself and Sailor John.' He cast his eye over the knot of men, mutely requesting permission to speak further. He was not much over thirty, but for that intelligent eye they looked to him, as they stood grim and still in the fading sleet-steely light. Still as blocks, blockheads, boneheads, ragged, rawboned men with grimed faces and wild whiskers: so an outsider, a civilised man, would have seen them, but to Donald's eye they brightened with a small new hope, like children. Encouraged, he went on: 'As I see it, the writs should have been given into the hands of us three. Since that was not done, the thing has no force in law. It's as if Minister's William never came here today.'

There was a buzz of approval. John Blondie twitched a grin and replaced old Dougie's bonnet gently. Young Alex snivelled in relief, knuckling his eyes with chapped fists.

John Blackie wasn't so sure. 'Ay, well and true. You'll be right there, Donald, there's books in your head. But what good does that do us? They'll be here at Whitsunday to put us out just the same. Where do we go then?'

Everyone answered at once.

'We won't be going – nowhere to go.'

'We pay good rent. Maybe a wee bit behind.'

'Can't be putting us out if we were never warned.'

'It wouldn't be justice.'

Donald repeated, bright-faced, revering justice. 'It wouldn't be justice. "Lawfully summon, warn and charge the said defenders *personally*" – see? That has to be done first. Then we go to the court to hear it verified. After that they have power to remove us.'

'Where to, remove us where to?'

John Blackie cut in on the protests. 'Ach, it's no use. Minister's William will be here again, soon as court day's past and we haven't appeared. Then more writs – back where it started.'

'Don't you see? It gives us time, time to explain ourselves. It is my belief that Hector Macdonald knows nothing of this, though it is in his name. We paid our rents, we've been here since his father's father's day. Didn't himself visit us, it's not four years, wasn't he playing with the children and saying the place was paradise? Didn't he speak to your mother, Kenneth, what was it he said to your mother?'

Donald's voice grew louder, almost pleading. Grizzled Kenneth (cottar, squatter; a weak-chested widower whose neighbours paid his rent and fed his children) straightened up and said his

19

piece, his one piece of pride, often rehearsed, how the laird, the chief, had spoken so familiarly to his dying mother.

'My mother was at that time in her last sickness, lying in her bed in the wall. And himself, speaking outside our door to myself and my children and my wife, who was then alive, said, "Isn't there another one, or have too many years gone by? I remember a kind old soul who gave me good cheese and bannock once in this lovely spot." Then I knew it was my mother he was meaning, for as you all know she was a most hospitable woman, though she had little to give, my father having died young and me her only son being infirm. And when I said she was within and very weak, there was no stopping him, he must go in and see her. And he went straight and took her hand, just as familiar as that, see, and spoke to her so kindly, and in the Gaelic too. "You gave me good cheese once, Mrs Macdonald," he says. "Now what can I give you to make you comfortable?" And Mother, she cries out, "O Eachainn mac Sheorais 'ic Alasdair" – that's how she called him, for she had the old ways with her – "give me my heart's own wish." "What's that?" he says. "They are saying you will send us away," she says. "They are saying the roofs will be taken off over our heads, they are saying you will send your children away and put sheep in their place. Eachainn mac Sheorais, give me your word, before God and his angels, is there truth in what they are saying?" "No truth at all, my word on it," he says. "Where could I send you, out of this heavenly place?" That was his very words, just exact as he said it. "Where could I send you, out of this heavenly place?" And afterwards he sent us coals – it was April before the peats – and he was noticing the fire was so low, and he sent her something for her rheumatism too.' Kenneth's wheeze caught up with his narrative and he fell to coughing.

'Didn't work, though,' John Blondie mused.

'No,' Kenneth agreed between coughs. 'She died bent double, like a wee gnome.'

The well-worn narrative had lulled the tension. John Blondie began to pack his pipe, and one for old Dougie as well. 'Ach, his lordyship's no bad. Could be you're right, Donald. We'll ask Macdonald Kilmory what's going on. He's the tenant. If this is right, he'll be going too.'

'Macdonald Kilmory went on a journey. Now who did he go to see?' John Blackie asked. His tone was unusually restrained. He aimed his question at Donald, who got his meaning: he would not voice his suspicions of the laird and his tenant-kinsman, from whom they held their land, in front of dying Kenneth, who spat blood and savoured the treasure in his memory. 'A heavenly place – ay', and he sat down suddenly on the wall, grey-faced. He had four stick-legged children: Neiliann, Doodie, Kennag, Lachie, all under ten.

Donald's good eye sparkled. 'He went for the kelp money. You know, you got your share and a good price too this year. They were saying we got more than it was worth, more than it sold for over the water.'

'Ay, ay.' John Blondie sucked Dougie's pipe to a glow and put it to the old man's lips. 'The chief's all right himself, I'm thinking. But there's that factor of his – '

' – son-in-law – ' said someone, ominously.

'Ay.' John Blackie's voice cut in quiet, final. Everyone fell silent, aware of Kenneth's stertorous breathing and half-shut eyes. 'We'll get this sick man home to his bed.'

The two Johns flanked him down the hill, and the rest followed slowly, Donald last. The bitter sleet had turned with dusk to snow, winsome soft, dusting with deadly peace the village wall, the boulders which had used men's strength and the thorn-balls which taxed urchins' wits to keep the cattle in or out; snow now speckling the skinny winter-patched black backs of the beasts, as they hunched in the wall's meagre shelter, with steamy noses longing towards the newly planted potato patches on the other side; snow thickening too on the bare earth, inviting

21

frost, and if frost came they had planted too early, deluded by a soft day when the larks had sung and sun had warmed the south-facing slopes.

A heavenly place it was in the larks' days, and home.

'Minister's William never came here today.' The words forced between his teeth. It was a vow of defiance. Donald Macdonald could read, knew the law and the Bible. He was not a defiant man, only steadfast. His mouth was sour as he trudged down the hill.

Before the drowse of Mór's own sleep had faded, she knew Donald had not slept, though she had put the baby to her breast at the first stuttering cry. He had said nothing as they ate their evening meal, and eaten little. His sisters Effie and Eilidh had divided the bit of salt meat left from Sunday while he crumbed bannock slowly in his fingers; the dog got most of it. Plenty talk later from the women in the ceilidh-house, but all of omens and the vision her Auntie Ciorstag had had a week before of Minister's William stepping from a black boat, so that she had brought the whisky to her sister Annag's, ready for him, though it was very scarce since the excisemen raided the still at Kilmory. Peggy was for putting a curse on, making it up in the old way, and the men were agreeing with her, when they came in from their meeting at the end of the house to finish the whisky. 'Don't talk nonsense,' Donald said. The men looked ashamed then. He had that way with them. He had a different sort of talking, putting all that old uncanny kind of thing away, making it look as if it wasn't a Christian way to do things. Mór's pride in him informed her fingers, touching his arm with her free hand under the heavy blanket.

They both listened before speaking. No sound from Effie and Eilidh in the box-bed opposite, and at the far end of the house Uncle Dougie's wheezy breath whistled in even gusts between his sparse old whiskers, alternating peacefully with the slow champing of his bedmate the cow.

'He's as warm with her as I am here with you, *mo chridhe*, but he'll never have a son of her.'

Donald's hand reached across her breast to touch the baby's head. They laughed together, tangling fingers. They had been married only a year, and had waited seven before that.

'There's three things,' he began, suddenly. 'The law of God, justice, and the law of man. The law of God: "Thou shalt not covet." Now I take that to mean "anything that is thy neighbours'", not just anything that belongs to folk according to the law of the country, like things you might have bought with money, or land you might have – how are they calling it, a *title* to – but what people live on, what they need just to live, to live in the way they always did and their fathers did before them. Like our land here, the land we farm and what our houses are built on, we can't live without that, that is all we have – something like that. Our neighbour isn't to covet it – should not try to take it from us. It would be, see, like David stealing the wife that was as the one ewe lamb, he that had so much. He was sinning against the law of God. Coveting – stealing – what was his neighbours'.'

Mór had been dozing off, lulled by the child's sucking and by the hard toil of the previous day and every day. She forced her eyes open against the thick darkness, to see through his different way of talking to his meaning.

'But he's the laird, not our neighbour.'

'Ay, but we're all equal in the sight of God. All neighbours.'

She had a vague image of King David looking over to the next-door house and seeing a woman undressing or something. Maybe he was a king but they must have lived in the same village? She tried to picture the laird's house, unimaginably far away, 'over the water and days and days through the mountains, so you couldn't see the sea even from the tops of them,' Auntie Ciorstag was always saying, who had been there as a young girl, carrying gifts of cloth and cheese to the chief's wedding. She brought back four wee chickens in her shawl and they were the father and mothers of all the hens on Fladday.

'And justice,' Donald went on. He had withdrawn his hand from hers and she could hear the soft rhythmic thumping of his closed fist on the bolster as he thought out loud. 'Justice is when we live by the law of God. And standing up to those that don't. It's just for the master to treat his servants right, or his tenants, as long as they behave themselves right to him. It's not just for him to say, "You were good servants and did the work, but I'm taking back the pay I gave you." That's what it would be if we were turned out. We cultivated the land, paid our rents. When Eachann mac Sheorais wanted more men for the kelping, we took them into our own homes from over there on Boreray, and from further away, too, helped them to build new houses and settle here – look at all of them over at Dun, that's how they came to Fladday. And weren't our fathers fighting for his brother in Spain? Carried him off the battlefield with the cannons turned straight on them. He can't forget that. My father was often speaking of the letter he sent at that time, the minister read it out to everyone in the church in Kilmory, "Our everlasting gratitude to our men of Fladday".'

There was joy in his tone, even in a half-whisper. She knew it was a beautiful thing to him. He had spoken like that on their wedding night, and when the child was put in his arms. Uneasy, she ventured obliquely, 'Minister's William was saying there will be provision for us. That himself will not leave us destitute.'

'Ay, you heard what provision.'

His voice was grim now. Mór's heart sank, to whom justice was a word and men were men. The hope of his clarity, his different way of seeing, had buoyed her up since the writs were placed in her young brother Alex's unwilling hand. Now it smothered under what she had heard from Minister's William. The baby caught her tension and let out a cry, kneading her breast with futile fists. She hushed him and put him to the other side.

'Rona,' Donald snorted. The sour black island across the Kyles wasn't worth a thought. 'Or Canada. What do we know of that country? Though they say it's a good place for young people, plenty land – '

Her fear and revulsion broke forth. 'Plenty land? What sort of land? It's a desert, a terrible place. Will we leave our homes for that, to die there and be buried among strangers? And to leave the old folk. They aren't to be permitted, did you hear that, Donald? They will be left behind – Grandad, Uncle Dougie . . . ' Her speech strangled in silent tears.

'*Ach Mhór, mo leannan*, now don't cry. You see, that is what I am telling. To turn us from our homes to starve in the wilderness, that's no provision, no justice. A Christian man could not do it, not knowing the facts. Himself could not hold up his head again if he did such a thing. I'm telling you, he has been advised to do this by his factor. I believe the laird himself has never set foot on Rona. How would he know what that grim place is like? And Mr Green has never come across the water to us at all, he was only as far as Boreray. If they knew how it was with us here, they would let us be.'

'He has the right.'

'Ay, the right in law. In men's law – not before God. Laws can be just or unjust. Wasn't it once law that the chief could hang a man without going to court? Laws change, a wee bit more justice here and there. This country's getting civilised. You heard what's happened about the Poor Relief? The landlords have to pay now to support their parish; that's a new law and a good just one, though heaven forbid we will ever need it, we're not rich here but surely we will never be beggars. Well, and even a bad law is just in its way. It's exact. The law was not executed today when Minister's William gave those papers to Alex instead of to us.'

'But he knows . . . everyone knows . . . it's not you three only, it's all the village is being put out. You and my brother and Sailor John's Ciorstag collect the rents, but you don't pay them all. How can it matter who got the papers?'

25

'That's the law. It's exact. That matters.'

'And what good will it do? If there's a mistake has been made, Minister's William will be back again and this time he'll find the right men, and they will be sending us all away – the law will send us away. Didn't it happen, it's three years now, over in Garve and Achmor, on Boreray? They all went – we don't know where they went, God help them, but there is nothing there now but sheep. Old Hector was seeing it. Walls – black with burning. And white sheep.'

'They were not paying their rents, not for years, Mór.'

'It wasn't that. When they got the writs they were offering all they owed and more. But they were turned out. The sheep were pouring out of the boat, into the kailyards and the corn. The people were told to go aboard and they went away in the boat, God alone knows where.'

She closed her eyes on tears and saw white sheep, white sheep swarming and nibbling, devouring the sweet green grass behind the sand dunes, the patches of oats and barley, the potatoes, her mother Annag's little garden of kail and blackcur-. rants, rue, mint and tansy.

'It's time we need,' Donald said. 'We can win time if the writs have to be sent again. We can see Macdonald Kilmory, write to the laird himself at Drumharg, even send someone there, maybe. When he learns how it is, he can't go ahead. He's our chief, he's a Christian gentleman. Not what his father Seorais mac Alasdair 'ic Alasdair was before him, but all the same, I believe the son of such a father is a just man. We will get justice, if it is God's will.'

He was silent a minute. 'Sure the will of the Lord is for justice,' he said in a very low voice. Soon after he was asleep. He had said his say.

The white sheep under Mór's weary eyelids swelled with her tears, great white devouring brutes, swarming further and further up the hill, right up to the summer shielings, and there they dwindled again and were only the few little dun-coated animals of the township, tripping on dainty feet between the slow black cows, and one red cow with turned-down horns, her mother's favourite that she had kept through winter after winter when the other cows were slaughtered, and fifteen summers Mór had milked her, singing into her warm flank at the shieling pastures. Donald was there, nearly every day, and they would lie and kiss in the heather, away from the eyes of other folk. Some of the girls would be out of the bothies all night sometimes, and in the morning they would be singing songs about lying with their sweethearts under one plaid. And Mór sang too, but it wasn't like that with Donald; he wouldn't have it in case the first baby would be a bastard. The other lads laughed at him and said he should try her first or risk a barren bed, but all he'd say was 'I'll risk it', and never angered at them. In the sixth year his father died of the cough, and the seventh, the year of mourning, was hardest of all, coming and going about his house and seeing the bed in the wall where they would lie as man and wife. The rough blanket under her drowsy arm tickled like heather buds and the slow black cows and dun sheep moved through the night in summer brightness. *'Mo ghille dhubh,'* she whispered, or remembered.

She woke suddenly to a chill drool of milk on her breast. The baby was long asleep and the closed door was outlined in pale light. She rose and laid wee Donald in his cradle and pulled the door back as quietly as possible, shooing away the dog who lay curled against it in the shelter of the thick wall. He would wake Donald if he got in, licking his face. She stooped outside under the low lintel to use the piss-tub and to look at the day. The peaks of the island of Boreray were clear across the Sound, the open horizon to the north-east sharp, the drift of snow against the end of the house already puddling. Auntie Ciorstag's white cock was crowing, and thick morning smoke was beginning to seep from her thatch. Mór smiled, not so much in hope as knowing change impossible, and went in to resurrect her own fire, crooning over last night's embers the same blessing as her mother and her aunt and their mother before them had used on every morning of their married lives.

CHAPTER 3

Alasdair mac Iain Sheoladair was the grandson of Alasdair the Bard, and he too could make songs. He had made one for Eilidh but he couldn't utter it there in the green hill meadow while she went to and fro with the other girls, dividing their bundles between the bothies, collecting fresh heather for bedding and bickering over who should cook the supper. The previous day most of the village had been there, feasting and singing till nightfall. Now on the second day they had work to catch up on at home and only he had been left with the girls, to keep the beasts from straying too far on the unfenced summer pasture while they sorted themselves out, and to repair the calf pen. After that the other lads would be back, and old Katie Morag was threatening to stay up there to keep an eye on the young folk, when her rheumatism let her climb the hill. She'd got Hector at the shielings sixty years ago off a boy from Boreray, and never the chance she'd give another girl to go the same way.

There was only this one day to be private in, and Alasdair was tongue-tied. He stared gloomily at his bare feet, pollen-dusted from the buttercups, then again at the sprightly figures below – Eilidh and her sister and his own three sisters, with John of the Rock's Peggy, and a buzz of little children. The girls were down to their shifts, with their skirts hitched up to the knees, all except Eilidh, and she hardly showed an ankle as she picked her way across the burn, rinsing pails and setting-basins ready for the evening milking. She knew he was watching; she twitched her long, light brown plait over her shoulder and let it hang where her cheek could hide behind it.

'Hi! Alasdair! What are you at, boy? Stop gawping and get the cows up from the water. Can't you see they're turning it to mud?'

That was Lexy. She grabbed a pail from Eilidh, held it high, and poured a stream of peaty murk from it. 'Not noticing much today, are you? Where's your eyes, girl?'

There was laughter and exaggerated whispering on the bank from Sara and Peggy. Eilidh hid behind her pigtail, abashed. Alasdair, throbbing with embarrassment, whacked the cows out of the water.

'What about a song, Alasdair?' Peggy's question and his young sister's fit of giggles assured him his secret had been betrayed. He was usually quick with an answer, but could manage nothing now except a shouted imprecation at Barabel's cow, raising her tail to dung contemplatively in the stream. He couldn't even put much colour into insulting the cow, though, because Eilidh's dad had been Barabel's brother.

'Come on, then, there's a good lad!' Peggy's voice had a hint of spite in it. She had been putting herself in his way since he led the boys round the houses at Hogmanay, but she was as dark and sly as Eilidh was fair and guileless and he had no fancy for her. Still, she had a reputation for getting her own back on people who disobliged her. She had fairy blood in her. At least that's what her grandmother's story about John of the Rock was, said she'd found him left by the fairies out on the hill. And maybe that was right enough, because people were saying then she hadn't looked big before she brought the baby home, and she had no milk. But she was showing a big belly with Donald and Effie and Eilidh, after she married old Donald.

To be on the safe side of Peggy, he gave them a song – not the one they were waiting for, though, but by the time they had sung through all the refrains they had forgotten about that and were fussing around, ready for milking, calling the cows up to the calves' pen so that their milk would flow. The hungry calves cried and jostled, while the girls hobbled their charges to prevent them kicking the cogs over, each singing blandishments about silken fetters to her queen of the cows. Fourteen black, five dun, and one brindled red, the twenty queenly cows of the nine households of Borve Kilmory; with Kenneth's two yellow-eyed black nanny goats, and the fifteen petted ewes whose milk made Alasdair the Bard's daughters' cheeses famous all over Fladday, sought after for every wedding and for Christmas and Michaelmas.

The cogs were filled and the hurdle lifted from the calf pen to let the ravenous youngsters have their suck. Eilidh, with no longer a cow to hide behind, was slowly looping and unlooping her hobbling-fetter, not of silk but of green heather stems. When she saw Alasdair looking, she ran off towards the bothies. He groaned. The day was over. His sister Kirsty Mary was busy stoking the fire for evening. The children were already straggling down the hill, two little ones to a bucket or one bucket to a big strong one. The evening milk went home to the village, while the morning's milking was kept at the shieling for rennetting and churning. Everyone's mother and granny would be up next day to make sure they were doing it right. He cursed himself for the long cool shadows, for the evening haze on the distant sea, for his unsung song.

Lexy shouted that Kenneth's children were coughing too much to carry their vessels without spilling. They set them down on the grass and went off snivelling, offended.

'Poor wee things,' said Sara, indignant. Lexy was the eldest and she the youngest, but she had as ready a tongue as her big sister, and a kinder heart. She snatched up one of the lidded tubs and ran off, spilling, reproved and heedless, after Kenneth's wretched four.

Eilidh had emerged from the bothy, with her red shawl round her against the evening chill. She looked up – he thought she looked up his way – then hitched the last tub onto her shoulders by its straw rope and set off down the hill, quickly at first, then slower. By the time Alasdair caught up with her she was only pretending to walk, in her red shawl down the green valley, with the burn singing at her feet.

'I'll take the milk,' he said.

'Och no, Alasdair!' She turned shy grey eyes on him but held the ropes tight across her chest. He held on too, and her face dimpled up with laughter. 'You with a beard now and all! What will they say at home?'

'They can put a petticoat on me if they like, for all I care.'

She gave up her bucket then, blushing and pulling her shawl round to hide it. Neither could think of anything to utter all the way home, except she said, 'You're spilling' twice, about a mile apart, and the first time he mumbled 'Sorry', but the second time, just above the in-by wall, he dumped the load down suddenly, slopping milk everywhere, and caught her arm.

'Eilidh, I'm thinking of going to Canada.'

'*Canada?*' She stared, round-eyed.

'Ay. If a ship calls in. You know they're saying the laird will send a ship and pay the passage money. It would be a good life, plenty land, build your own house. And no bothering with his lordship to . . . I mean I could get married . . . '

She had bent her head so that he could see only red shawl and the tip of her nose.

'Eilidh, if I was going to Canada, would you . . . '

He was going to say, ' . . . would you be sorry?', but a tear dropping off the end of her nose revived the fast talker in him.

' . . . would you come with me?'

She would. The song got sung in the end and the urchin who was sent back to look for the last of the milk would have made a great story later, if graver news hadn't come home with the men who had been cutting peats over on Rona, where Minister's William had found them.

'Whitsunday. When is that?'

'It is the third Sunday after this one coming.'

There were some who thought it might be the one nearer, but they kept quiet out of deference. Alasdair the Bard was almost blind, stiff as a corpse with arthritis, and vague about recent faces and events, but his memory for dates and genealogies, for the customs of holy days and the songs of his forefathers, was hardly dimmed by his ninety years. He crouched in his chair, the one chair in Borve, with his feet propped on a peat-creel, being too bent to lie on a bed. They had brought him out to the door of his daughter Ciorstag's house, which was the ceilidh-house where all the news came for discussion, as it had been back to his great-grandfather's time when Borve was first settled on the proceeds of black cattle.

'Ay, that was the meaning of the saying of Lachlan mac Iain 'ic Alasdair 'ic Lachlain 'ic Alasdair. That was the meaning we never comprehended till this day: "On the white day of the Lord will come the black sorrow of the people." That was the meaning of Lachlan of the Prophecies.' Old Alasdair's voice was still light and sweet. It was said he had never raised it in anger or distress, and he did not now, but gave his sentence precisely, with a nod of satisfaction at the solution of the puzzle handed down from his mantic ancestor. 'Now, Donald, will you make me a pipe?'

Donald was his favourite. His own three sons had died young without issue: one at war for the chief's brother, one drowned cutting kelp, one of typhus when he went south with the cattle. His Ciorstag's John was a wandering sailor, not a Fladday man, and Annag's Neil had been a poor ailing creature all his days; but Donald, who had none of his blood, was more like his kin than any of his grandsons, though old Donald his father had been a very dour fellow, with the Bible always open on his knee, one who wouldn't hear a song because it was vanity. Yet the son was a man clear-headed and slow to anger, who thought of more things than weeds in the potatoes and the diseases of cattle. Old Alasdair had seen weeds and murrains come and go, cattle and herring and kelp come and go, the

33

factors piling on more tenants, and then it was, wouldn't they like to go away on the white-sailed ships? Dearth and plenty and dearth again. But never evictions. 'Never evictions,' he muttered to himself, 'but it could be. Lachlan mac Iain was seeing it.' He sucked on his pipe tranquilly; if it had been foreseen, it would happen. A woman was crying in the house behind him and men's voices were a babble on the grass outside, but for old Alasdair there was not much eviction could do that ninety years hadn't done already.

Next day was a Saturday and, in Ciorstag's view, expressed with some vehemence, for that reason no enterprise begun on it would succeed. Her sister Annag rounded on her for heathen superstition, but nevertheless recalled several events in the past that seemed to prove there was something about Saturday that couldn't be set aside if affairs were to prosper. The bard's daughters were well respected for their wisdom, canny and uncanny, but on this occasion they were overruled. Donald Cam, John Blackie and Sailor John's brother Roderick would go to seek an interview with Macdonald of Kilmory, whose subtenants they were.

It was still very early as the three men walked round the coast from their little hamlet of Borve to the main village of Kilmory. On the east-facing slope above the bay Macdonald's farmhouse stood alone, upright and square-edged, another thing altogether from the windowless and chimneyless homes of the village below, huddled and rounded. The rising sun flashed from its glazed windows.

'That's bonny!' exclaimed Roderick. He was an easy-going, home-loving man, who had hardly strayed from Borve in the forty years since he came there kelping with his wandering older brother. Three times a year he walked to Kilmory to hear the minister, otherwise it was usually, 'Ach, I'll stay here and mind the place.' He had always admired the five large twelve-paned double sashes of Domhnall mac Eachainn's house, two below and three above, set so nice and even under the neat slated roof, but church days weren't the time to mention it.

The others didn't respond. There was something far from bonny shadowing the May morning for them. They were inclined to linger in the village, getting the news. Bad news it was.

'Same here.'

'Don't bother with Macdonald, didn't we tell you that weeks ago?'

'Canada here we come.'

'Not Rona, anyway. Them cliffs! What a place!'

'Domhnall mac Eachainn looks soft, but he's stone. Don't be wasting your time on him.'

They were silent as they trudged up to the door. It was taller than a man and wider than a cow, with a white step up to it and a bell like the bell at the side of the church, with a long chain hanging down. They stopped clear of the whitened step, conscious of dirty feet.

Donald squared his shoulders and put his hand to the bell pull. 'Them in Kilmory, they're not in our position. The half of them are Boreray folk. They'll be going back there and nothing said about it.'

The bell jangled harshly in the quiet morning air. Involuntarily, they all jumped back a pace, staring up at its clangorous arc. Footsteps sounded behind the door. They removed their bonnets.

They knew what they had to say to Macdonald, but did not know at all what to say to the young girl in a print frock, with a face as clean as her apron.

'Good morning to you, Mistress Macdonald,' Roderick managed at last, beaming.

The girl giggled. 'Is it the mistress you wish to see?'

Donald nudged Roderick to silence. 'No, but Mr Macdonald himself. Will you be so good as to let him know his tenants from Borve are waiting to speak with him?'

The girl closed the door. They had never had the door of any house closed in their faces before. Even that very door, grand as it was, stood open on rent day and they would walk right in and shake hands with Domhnall mac Eachainn and give him the money. Now they looked away from the inhospitable barrier and away from each other, embarrassed and uncertain.

'She's bonny,' Roderick ventured hopefully, without effect.

After the interview Macdonald threw open his fine sash window to get rid of the smell of soot and sweat and stood for a while frowning down at Kilmory village. Thirty miserable drystone huts, near sunk in the earth, with smoke curling through their blackened thatch. Their blackened inhabitants, clothed, furred or feathered, clustered enquiringly round the three men from Borve, distinguishable, even at a distance, by the relative cleanness of their shirts. The effort implied in their bleached linen had not been lost on Macdonald. He was not of stone, but he was in debt. They were all in debt, cottars to subtenants, subtenants to him, he to Drumharg. Drumharg himself – well, his daughter's wedding hadn't cost nothing. The whole estate was one stinking, running debt. Macdonald gnawed his forefinger, surveying the squalid black hovels. Insanitary, he thought – his wife thought. Eight deaths from consumption last winter, and one in four babies died before the mother was even up from her bed. No life for them here. Might as well go. He rang for the maid to sweep the telltale black marks from his wife's new French carpet. They wouldn't quite come off.

'Put a drugget over it in case . . . er . . . in case the same thing happens again.'

'In case herself notices,' explained the maid to the groom, unrolling the drugget in the stable loft.

Macdonald Kilmory frowned unseeingly at his ledger, gnawing his forefinger.

'He was saying we should write to himself at Drumharg.'

'He was saying we *could* write if we felt like it.' John Blackie's voice and look were bitter.

'No, but he meant more than that, John,' Donald persisted. 'He was telling us there is a boat out tonight for Boreray to bring his provisions home. The big ship takes the mails from Port Long on Monday and that way a letter can reach him in two, three days.'

'Well, that's wonderful. Them fast horses. It takes near a week to walk, I'm hearing.' Roderick was impressed.

Most of their Kilmory audience sided with John Blackie.

'Ay, you'll write. Will he read it, though?'

'It'll never get there, not with Lachlan the Boat in charge of it. He'll be for the inn at Port Long and that's him for the night.'

'Give it to his wee lad, he'll do it, maybe.'

Donald stuck to his plan. Pen, ink and clean paper were begged from the old woman who had charge of the church. A small store was kept there for the minister, to register marriages and the like.

Donald wrote a good copperplate hand. His father had seen to that, sending him to the minister for schooling, while minister there was, and later labouring with the boy himself, seeing he had the brain for it. The hand was good but rusty, and the ink glutinous with age. He worked slowly and with great care. A mistake would cost him a sheet of paper and a consequent argument with the crone who minded the church.

His companions went off to take refreshments at John Blackie's cousin's house, while the inhabitants of Kilmory too young or too old for work squatted quietly, watching him, a dozen pairs of bright and dimmed eyes. He shut them out; the white paper and its black content became all to him. Forming the letters grew easier as the morning wore on, but he would not hurry, giving himself time to recollect polished turns of phrase in a language not his own, known only from a book of Chalmers's sermons and a few copies of the *Inverness Courier* that his father had kept, for didactic use, at the bottom of the blanket-chest. It was well into the afternoon when he finished, with cramped and shaking fingers:

I and we all the Undersigned do Earnestly Pray and Beseech, Sir, that you will consider our Requests above Set Out: and we make certain to you at all times of our complete Loyalty towards Yourself and all your Family and Dependants, as True Clansmen, only beseeching to you to be treating us with that Justice and Clemency which you and the Illustrious Ancestors to you have hitherto accorded us.

We remain, Sir, your most Obed' Servants,

Donald Macdonald

John Gillies al. Black

Roderick Maclean

Donald signed his name, John Blackie signed in a more wavering hand, Roderick put a cross and Donald wrote his name under it. As an afterthought, he added, 'For and on Behalf of all your Loyal Tenants of Borve Kilmory on Isle Fladday'.

'Come on now, let's get back before the wives eat all our dinner. You're wasting your time, Donald.'

John Blackie's tone betrayed that even he felt better, seeing their three names there in black and white under Donald's incomprehensible copperplate. They set off home in hopeful spirits, leaving Lachlan the Boat's wee lad with the letter and two copper coins borrowed from John Blackie's cousin.

CHAPTER 4

No reply came from Drumharg.

Whitsunday came and went. In Kilmory and Borve, Ardmonach, Kyles, Diriclet, Dun, the townships of Fladday, life carried on as usual. The girls and grannies were up at the shielings with the cattle, while the ungrazed machair below bloomed in heady fragrance and the strips of oats and barley grew up straight and blue-green between the swathes of yellow and white meadow blossom. At home the women were busy pressing cheeses and salting butter against the winter, with sometimes some over to barter for a new pullet, or to tempt the itinerant pedlars who might come later in the year to part with a red shawl like Eilidh's, or a pound or so of sugar-candy for the children. The women also had the peats to turn and stack, and the potatoes to weed, and walking to and fro between tasks they had always a spindle twirling from their fingers, or a stocking growing between twinkling needles. Sometimes they sickled for sand-eels in the shallows and baited and set long lines for flounders. The men sat and watched the lines.

'Och, they're sitting there all day watching the lines and smoking and talking, and hardly a fish they're bringing us. It's the life of kings they're leading!' their wives complained. And they would ask in the evening, winking at each other, what the important business was they were talking about all day that they let all the fish get away.

Their husbands stuck out their chests, except Roderick, who always spoilt it by laughing, and said, 'We have been discussing the flitting.'

They had been discussing it for so long that it had ceased to have any reality. It was summer, the season of milk and honey, of long, long days with no night at all; a bloom of sleek health on the grass, on the coats of the cattle, on the young girls' cheeks; crops promising well, silver salmon nuzzling the coast. What else could ever be? Winter's certain darkness was hard enough to imagine; the uncertain whims of a distant chief's henchmen as flickering as a half-forgotten dream. 'Ay, we'll have to go some day,' they said, when they remembered, or even, 'We'll wait till the tatties are lifted, see what's doing then.' No one came to tell them how they would live, in those unimaginable other worlds of Rona or Canada. There was no word of an emigrant boat: no one in Borve had ever seen a ship big enough to carry the whole population of Fladday, except for old Hector and Donald's uncle, Ranald the carpenter, who had both fought for the laird's brother, and John Blondie, who went with some Boreray men every few years to drive surplus cattle to Inverness market. How Minister's William had delivered the writs, and how at Borve Sailor John's wife Ciorstag had foreseen his coming and laid in the whisky for him; how Donald Cam had written to the chief in as fair a hand as any man's alive, and in good English. These and a dozen similar tales from the other townships had passed into history and become the stuff of the ceilidh-houses, to be rendered by the best storytellers with appropriate embellishments. People from all over the island dropped by on Alasdair the Bard to hear his version, which was distinguished by the authority of his prophetic ancestor. They heard of a tragedy already polished and pleasing, of a black sorrow foreseen and fulfilled.

'Well, the old man's wonderful!' they said to each other, strolling home in the pale summer midnight.

'Your Grandad's doing great with all these visitors, but how am I to get the cheeses laid up, with this one and that one sampling a wee bit here and a wee bit there?' Ciorstag complained to her daughters at the shieling. She got the girls to keep half a dozen of her truckles in their bothy, out of temptation's way, though they didn't like sleeping with the smell of them.

'That'll stop the lads from poking their noses in, anyway,' their mother pointed out with relish. Her foresight let her down there. Young Hector braved both the cheeses and scoldings from Lexy and Kirsty Mary, and in July little Sara came home with a sweetheart.

Eilidh came home with more than that, in spite of her sister Effie's pious warnings and old Katie Morag's vigilance. Mór looked at her sharply. Eilidh tried to rise before her in the mornings, or lay on late in bed with her eyes tight shut, forcing the nausea back. Mór and Donald had held out seven years, and she not seven days.

Alasdair had urged her hard. 'Why should we, Eilidh? What would we be waiting for? If we stay at home we'll not be allowed to marry; if the ship comes we'll go to Canada and be married as soon as we can.'

If the ship would come! For those two alone, perhaps, the ship was a reality: not a certainty, but a hope and a secret excitement. They said nothing of their plans to their families, knowing the opposition they would arouse. Ciorstag would not easily lose her only son, she whose husband had been gone a year already on his latest voyage. The cash he brought home from his wanderings was little enough, a purse to pay the rent and some frippery for his girls. It was the sea life itself that took him away, not the money. His wife distrusted the same adventurous spirit in their son and though she had known from his birth that he would die over the sea, she had told that to no one, not even to her sister who had delivered the child.

Eilidh hoped, but she was afraid too, thinking of the baby being born, maybe on the ship, with the waves breaking over where she lay, and it would be so cold for a baby; or maybe in the new country, with women round her bed she didn't know, instead of kind Annag, who had brought her and her sister and Alasdair and all their friends into the world, and put the three drops of water on their heads. And looking round her family as they sat together eating a summer supper, curds and buttered oatcake, she would feel the homesickness already, and couldn't eat, couldn't sing when they sang their evening hymn together and was afraid, afraid of the Lord, who would punish her and Alasdair for their sin and visit it on the head of the poor baby, so that maybe they would all drown before they reached the new country. Effie was always talking about things like that. They had never worried Eilidh before, but now she had a sin on her head, its secret guilt weighed upon her. She prayed: please, no, forgive – but the fear remained.

Alasdair had no fear, only hope. 'Och, we're as good as married. It's his lordyship stopping us, not God. It'll be great when we get there, Eilidh, and it'll be long before our time. The boat will come by September if it's coming, to get there before winter. The baby will be born in a good house, they make them of wood out there, there's so many trees. Wood's very warm and dry. And we'll take plenty blankets.'

He made a lullaby for the baby that would be born in Canada, lying under the blankets brought from home, who when he grew up would have lands and money and a ship to visit the island of his forefathers. He sang it to Eilidh to cheer her up. She looked preoccupied.

'What's wrong now?'

'How do you know it's a boy? It might be a girl. I'm thinking it's a wee girl.'

He burst out laughing. 'She'll marry a rich farmer, and have six brothers after her. Now stop your worrying, girl!'

'Stop your worrying, girl!'

Mór could not stop worrying. As the nights began to darken at the end of July, the fear came creeping back, like a black bogle squatting by the unseen hearth, so that her mouth dried as she lay in bed staring into the darkness. There was much to worry about: the top-growth on the potatoes was looking sickly and her mother said it was blight; Eilidh was looking sickly, too, and everyone knew why; the baby had worms; the new heifer was poor in milk. She voiced these worries night by night as soon as they lay down, and Donald put them by with kindness and good reasons. But after he slept the big worry, the real one, the unnamed, crouched on the hearth and dared her to speak.

A week or so into the darkening nights, when the Milky Way was showing again, and then not showing for cloud and rain, the potato shaws had turned to leafless slime, and everyone knew there would be no crop, not in Borve or in all of Fladday, and in Kilmory they said they were hearing not in Boreray either. That was a worry pressing enough to keep the whole township up late talking, recalling a grim year of hunger a decade earlier. But in bed, after the girls had stopped whispering, when Mór asked, 'What will happen to us, Donald?' he knew she was thinking of worse than a hungry winter. He was so long answering, she wondered if he was asleep after all. The thought lightened her heart: if he was sleeping, not lying pondering in the dark, then maybe there was not so much to be worried over.

'I don't know,' he said at last. 'It depends on what sort of a man the chief is. And if he knows how it is with us here.'

'But you wrote to him.'

'Ay, if he ever got it. I've been thinking, maybe it would be better to get someone else to speak for us. The minister will be here at the end of the week. I was thinking we could talk to him, if he will see us. Or maybe I'll leave a letter for him with Macdonald Kilmory. He might look on it better in the English.'

'Mr Cochrane? He'll never be on our side. He thinks we're no better than heathens here. He'll be telling us it's the will of the Lord.'

'Mór, if it is the will of the Lord, we must do it.'

'I said he'll be *telling* us that.'

'He's a man of God – '

' – and well paid for it!'

'Och Mór, you should not be talking like that.'

'I'll talk like anything, Donald, before I'll take quietly my family being sent across the sea and my home burned. Did you hear what they are saying in Kilmory?'

'Ay.'

Everyone knew Macdonald Kilmory had had mail from the mainland that morning. There had been a letter from Drumharg and a roll of papers that Lachlan the Boat swore related to the emigrant ship.

'He'll be sending round for us to put our names. Tomorrow, maybe. It's too late – too late for us to do anything.'

'Well, and we don't have to put our names. We are free subjects of the Queen, not slaves. Some will want to go. Not from Borve, but they are saying near everyone in Ardmonach and Dun is talking about it. But we don't have to go. We'll stay and see the consequences.'

'Rona.'

He was silent.

'Oh God help us!'

'God will help us, even if it's to be Rona.'

'That place! It's nothing but rock. We've nothing to take there – no tatties, the oats won't be in . . . '

'There's time yet. When himself hears about the blight on our crop, he'll think again. He'd have to, Mór, even if he's a worse man than I believe. See, if his people are starving he has to send relief. Cheaper to let us stay here than send us meal all year, if that's the way he's thinking. But I do not believe he has so little care for us – for justice and gratitude.'

'Justice and gratitude won't pay his debts. They are saying his daughter's wedding gown cost three hundred pounds.'

The yearly rent for the whole of Fladday was ninety-eight pounds.

The staggering computation caused another silence. Donald reached for her hand.

'Stop your worrying. We are in God's hands, not the laird's.' He stroked her hair till she fell asleep. He did not sleep himself. He was remembering a report in one of his father's old newspapers of clearances in Sutherland, when from a hilltop two hundred and fifty dwellings had been counted burning in a single night.

The list came round next day. No one signed.

'We'll not put our names yet,' said Alasdair to Eilidh, 'not till it's too late for them to make a fuss. Only two weeks to go.'

'Will you take another glass of wine, Mr Cochrane?'

'Thank you, Mr Macdonald, I will. My voyage was a cold and wet one this morning.'

Replenished, Mr Cochrane eased himself comfortably into his host's best armchair, spreading his knees to allow the heat from the fire to bathe his intimate parts.

'Cold and wet, after a breakfastless start. Thank you, Mrs Macdonald, this cake is of an excellent baking, far beyond what I am used to. My housekeeper is a good woman, but her cooking is of the simplest – which indeed is all it need be for a man in my station.' He became momentarily inaudible over a mouthful of Madeira cake, but being a talkative man by nature with little opportunity for civil conversation, he continued almost at once. 'I often remark to others of my cloth, when I travel to the Assembly, that those who dwell in the cities or the more favoured parts of the country can hardly conceive of the life led by those of us who carry the Word to these rude outposts – of the lack of congenial company, of books, of the comforts of life, if comforts matter – though to me, of course, being a bachelor, they do not – but I have never been of that school which says that when comforts are offered they should be abjured. Nay, accept them gratefully. Gratefully, Mrs Macdonald, for God is the giver of all good things. Whatever He gives, we should rejoice at His gift, whether it seem at the time good or bad in our sight.'

Mr Cochrane paused to rejoice at another mouthful of cake. Macdonald smirked slightly behind his hand, till his wife's freezing glance pierced him. Mr Cochrane complimented her upon the new carpet – 'An outward sign of those material good things in which you have been so blessed.' Mrs Macdonald had discovered the black marks that very morning, when the drugget was removed for the minister's visit, which circumstances rendered her smile less grateful than might have been proper. Macdonald stared absently out of the window, till she kicked his ankle. He wished he had not accepted the letter from that poor fool from Borve.

Mr Cochrane pinched his last crumbs of cake into tiny pellets, popping them into his mouth between sentences. 'Yes, my friends! I say that reconciliation to whatever God sends us is one of the signs – nay, the very hallmark – of a true Christian. Contentment with His blessings as the outward and visible signs of His grace freely bestowed upon our souls: meekness before His chastisements, as the measures by which in His just wrath He punishes our sin, and as a loving father spares not the rod to make us worthy children and co-heritors of His kingdom.'

As Mr Cochrane warmed to his homily, he leaned forward in his chair, occasionally tapping the open letter that lay on its arm. His clean-shaven pink face had taken on a look of fixed and majestic authority. In his university days his forceful preaching had won him a bronze medal. Mrs Macdonald knew of this and sat respectfully alert, with hands clasped on her puce silk lap.

'It is said, Hebrews 12.5, "My son, despise not thou the chastening of the Lord, nor faint when thou art rebuked of him." Oh, that God will give me grace today to expound this message – this teaching most needful to our ears, that our hearts may be laid open in meekness to the divine salvation. God grant I may be the instrument today in bringing to their senses those rebellious ones who would flout the command of the chief whom God in His wisdom has set over them; who in their stubborn pride bow not to His chastisements. Is it not written, Peter 2.18:

"Servants, be subject to your masters with all fear."? And again, Titus 3.1: "Put them in mind to be subject to principalities and powers, to obey magistrates." '

Mr Cochrane leaned back in his chair, pink and a little shiny, pulling the skirts of his frock-coat around his overheated knees, the action of the brisk fire upon his metal buttons having made the rearrangement of his legs a delicate operation.

'How truly you speak, Mr Cochrane,' agreed Mrs Macdonald, wondering inwardly if Mary had tried brown paper and a hot iron on the marks yet. Then after the greasiness had been lifted, perhaps soft soap. Macdonald gnawed his finger, and then his thumb.

The folk of Borve left the church as they always did, with decorous pace and bent heads: the men first, hats in hands, and with boots, in the case of those who possessed them, greased with home-made blacking; after them the women, with shawls pulled close round their heads and children firmly under control. At a wedding, a funeral, a communion, or at this the wreck of their hopes, the people left the church so, with composed faces and meek deportment, reconciling themselves to whatever Mr Cochrane told them God had sent them. But on this one day they could not overcome their stubborn hearts. As they turned up the hill out of Kilmory, John Blackie's wife Rachel fainted, being heavily pregnant. Her mother Catriona began to weep and soon other female voices rose, imploring, hysterical or scolding, all tearful. The men stood apart in a cowed silent knot.

'Ay, it's the will of the Lord. Ay, ay,' old Dougie repeated several times. No one else said anything. And though Donald's good eye fell on each of his companions in turn, seeking some understanding, some affirmation of their courage and their faith, no one would look him in the face.

'The will of God! It's the will of man – of greedy, grasping men. What sin had my Rachel done, to fall there in the mud?'

'Ach, nothing, John, nothing.' Old Hector was conciliatory. 'She's a good girl, Rachel. But it's not the sin of particular persons, John, but of the whole lot of us – original sin, like. That's what he was saying, maybe. Was it, Donald? Is that what the minister meant?'

'No. Not original sin. He was talking about the way we've been carrying on here all these years, that we haven't been doing what it tells us in the Bible.'

'Oh ay. That's right.' Hector fell silent, miserable and uneasy. He had a feeling one of the things Mr Cochrane was down on them for was doing business on the Lord's Day, but Donald and John Blackie had frogmarched him out to the end of his own house, and there they stood out of the blowing drizzle with the dog and the hens, talking about how much it would cost to cross to the mainland and how much meal they would need to see them through the journey to Drumharg. It wasn't business like bargaining over a calf or such, but it seemed an unchristian way to carry on on a Sunday, after all the minister said about what was coming to them.

Hector turned for his door. 'We'll talk about it tomorrow, lads – '

'No!' Donald grabbed his arm. 'We'll be leaving in the morning before it's light. Lachlan the Boat will be going over with the tide. Hector, you must come with us. You were fighting there with his brother in Spain, you were helping to carry him off the field. Remember the letter, the letter he sent to all the men of Fladday? John and I, we've done nothing for him, but you . . . he can't deny you, Hector.'

'I don't like it. You heard Mr Cochrane. We're out of grace already. It's going against God. It's a sin you're leading me to.'

John rounded on him. 'If your mother hadn't sinned, you wouldn't be here. Would it be God's will you never to live?'

Hector's face mottled. He clenched and unclenched his fists. He was a big man, fit still for his old trade as a smith. But John was of his township. The moment of fury passed and he said quietly,

'Ay, well, and maybe that's what Mr Cochrane meant. Maybe it's the sins of the past are being visited on us now.' He turned more resolutely to go. Again it was Donald who held him back.

'If it is the Lord's will, it will happen so whatever we do, and when we see that we will not fight against it. But maybe it's the Lord's will that Eachann mac Sheorais should hear from us what is being done in his name, before he commits a great injustice.'

Hector hesitated, and was won. 'You'd have made a minister yourself, Donald,' he said, escaping at last to his own door.

Eilidh was downcast, to the point of tears. Old Uncle Dougie, her brother Donald off on his journey, poor Rachel and her baby, Kenneth's thin children soon to be fatherless: she wept for all of them into the flank of the cow, as she milked her in the evening rain. Alasdair lurked round the cow's back corner, not too obvious to censorious eyes.

'And who else?' he asked, teasing, as her sad recital dwindled into a sniff. He knew more about her by now than her soft brown hair and her shy eyes.

'Oh, Alasdair!' she sobbed into the hairy hide. 'It's ourselves. Effie . . . she was saying all the way home from church, crying and saying it's me that brought it on the family, it's our sin.'

'Och, your sister Effie!' He bounced round the cow and caught her round her breasts. 'Nose in the Bible, face like a slab o' cold porridge. Not much sin coming her way!'

'Alasdair!' She began to laugh between sobs. She couldn't help it, he was tickling her nipples. They danced round the cow, laughing their heads off. Only old Barabel saw them from the far side of her own cow across the field. She was so horrified she couldn't speak a word about it for days, seeing her own niece jigging with a lad on the Sabbath. But later she said, when she saw the daughter of her godly dead brother behaving like that, she knew Mr Cochrane was right, that Borve Kilmory was a very Babylon of sin.

CHAPTER 5

'Oh God save us.'

'It's the devil himself!'

'Get up! Get out quick, in Christ's name!'

The three men leapt to their feet as the *Island Princess* hooted a loud farewell to Port Long. A couple of English gentlemen leaning on the rails laughed outright at their terror. John Blackie and Donald sank back slowly on their bundles, gathering their dignity about them with their scattered possessions. Hector slapped his sides and paced the deck, shouting in his agitation.

'Oh, look at that. Look at the smoke, boys! Oh, the noise of it, it's no like this the ship I was going to Spain on – it's the devil's own, smoking like hell – '

'Shut up, you,' hissed John, 'you're getting us laughed at.'

Hector, abashed, crouched down so as to place his friends between himself and the English gentlemen. 'What are them toffs doing here, anyway?' he muttered.

'They come to shoot the deer. They were staying at the inn. They're building a big new house just so as gentlemen can be staying there and shooting the deer and birds. Oh Christ, their dogs even are grinning at us.'

John bent his head in shame while the gentlemen puffed smoke rings and the silk-haired setters looked down their noses.

'How's our wee dog?' asked Hector, after a bit.

Donald opened the basket. The puppy placed his fat paws on the edge, squeaking lustily. Eilidh's blue hair ribbon was hooked over one of his ears, the black one. The rest of him was sandy brown. The men tried not to smile: the puppy was children's play, a present for the laird's younger daughter, whom Ciorstag thought wouldn't be very old at all. Ciorstag took more interest in the chief's family than anyone else, because of being at his wedding and because of her cousin Janet the hen-wife who gave her the chicks. It was one of Ciorstag's cheeses John carried in his bundle as a gift for the chief's table, and he had a letter for Janet as well.

Donald attempted to stuff the puppy back into the basket before his antics attracted further derision, but he began to howl and scrabble and had to be let out to squirm on their knees.

'Maybe we could take off the ribbon? Just till we reach,' Hector suggested sheepishly.

Donald folded the ribbon away carefully and put it in the purse which held their money.

'Should drown it,' growled John. But when the puppy continued to bite gleefully at his fingers he added lamely, 'Not but it's bonny.'

'Macdonald's terrier got to our bitch,' explained Donald.

A slight embarrassment fell on them, like the time that John had found Donald washing blankets with Effie when Mór was pregnant. Hector filled his pipe and they passed it from one to the other in silence. It was the last of their tobacco; they had voted against buying more in Port Long till they saw if their store of coins would suffice their journey. It did not have its customary soothing effect. Their early start, apprehension about their journey, and the unaccustomed stink and throb of the devil's own vessel combined to make them, one after the other, thoroughly seasick. Even the puppy puked up the titbits the innkeeper's children had fed him and crawled back into his basket. Borve's inhabitants were herdsmen, not seafarers.

After that the many boats and smart white houses of the mainland port passed almost unnoticed; indeed, Hector wouldn't open his eyes till the gangplank went down. They climbed the first stretch of winding road eagerly, but with shaky legs. Dusk was coming on, with rain and low cloud. When it was too dark to see the path they ate the last of their buttered bannocks and huddled down under a rock to sleep. They had to dislodge several sheep from their shelter to find space. The animals ran from their evening prayers and stole back to mill about them all night, with sometimes a stamp of the hoof or a loud bleat of reproach for their dispossession. Hector woke several times, shouting about the devil's hooves and horns.

'It's sheep,' the others told him.

'Terrible lot of sheep. There was never so many sheep before,' he grumbled, subsiding.

Next day the mist was down but they trudged on, confident of Hector's memory, across a desolate moorland pass. There was a metalled road, wider than any they had seen, but hard on the feet and deserted. There were no houses and no travellers, only sheep.

'There was a village, I'm sure, under that crag,' said Hector when the mist swirled up for a moment. 'Maybe I've mistook the way.'

When they reached the green turf under the crag, though, they found the village, a mess of low roofless ruins on either side of a burn, where Hector recalled crofts and hospitality. A group of bulky well-fleeced ewes broke from their shelter as they ducked under a fallen lintel to look inside. The drumming of their hooves faded rapidly into the mist.

'No good,' said John, and not another word was uttered about it. But the palpable history of the place cast a deep gloom on them. The puppy's insistent whining, from his basket on Donald's back, made matters worse. He was unweaned and the bit of meal and water they gave him didn't quiet him. There was no conversation but John's curses, with threats of drowning at every one of the many streams they crossed, countered by Hector's shocked reproofs.

'Not in the army, not among the Papists even, did I hear such language, John. You are crucifying the Son of God again.'

About noon Donald halted on the bank of a river, fingering the strap of the basket.

'Well, maybe we should drown it.'

John and Hector stopped bickering to stare at him. 'Och no!' they both exclaimed at once.

Soon afterwards they met two girls with a cow. The puppy filled his belly with milk and the men got some too. The girls spoke only English and pointed to a solitary grey house on the breast of the mountain as home.

'Dad's a shepherd,' said one, and the other added, 'Mee-ee-eh!' to clarify the matter for the wild Highlanders.

'No village.' Hector shook his head as they walked on. 'But the Good Father of Mercy sent that cow. Thanks be to God!'

It was four hard days of walking, dawn to dusk, to reach their destination. God was generous with cows, or sometimes goats. At least twice a day the puppy had his milk, from a herdboy or at a cottage door, or from untended animals met on the moor. John could milk, they discovered, as well as any woman, though he wouldn't let on where he learned the knack. But for themselves, they had little but the meal in their bundles. They avoided the few towns, where folk would want coin they did not have for every favour, whilst the villages where they had expected to receive hospitality, such as they themselves would give to strangers at home, were hardly to be found. Wherever they went it was the same story. Hector would say, 'I'm remembering wrong. There was a village . . . there were bonny bushes growing here . . . there were croplands in this village.' Everywhere was grassland, moorland, sheep; few people to be seen, except shepherds and once a gamekeeper who poked a gun in their ribs and wanted to see what was in the basket, although when they opened it, he grinned and let them go. They talked less and less as the journey wore on: none of them wished to recognise what the failure of Hector's recollections might mean. He himself spoke least of all; the soldier's swing with which he had left Borve dwindled to an old man's arthritic roll.

On the third afternoon they met two battalions of the Forty-second Regiment, marching from Fort Augustus to Fort William. Hector had been lagging that day, so that the two younger men had been discussing in undertones a diversion to the drovers' inn at Glengarry, to get a proper meal and a night under cover, but the soldiers passing charmed the years away from him and he was full of marching tunes and reminiscences till nightfall.

By the following evening they had reached the upper end of Stratharg. The brown marshland where they stood fell away to a soft green and golden chequer of pasture and harvest fields, lush, lordly. The river flung wide meanders of silver across that flat fertile land and above its plain the hills were forested almost to the summit.

'That's it!' Hector pointed, and beyond the several handsome slated farmhouses of the valley they saw the extensive roofs of Drumharg House, reflecting rosy sunlight among its sheltering woods.

'All that? All one house?' Donald and John saw and wondered.

They squatted there till the sun set, looking and exclaiming. The grandeur of it delighted them – their chieftain's seat, the home of the clan, theirs then, too, so rich and so beautiful. But when the sun had faded from the valley their spirits waned with it. They ached in every bone from the long tramp, and their bellies were famished. Each looked at the others covertly and when John said, 'We're not a bonny sight', Hector groaned aloud.

Donald stood up, pushing his shoulders back. 'If he's got all that for his own, he'll not be wanting Borve Kilmory too.'

They could see the reason in that. They spent the night in a birch copse, with a good fire going and two trout guddled out of the river to grill on the embers. Their hearts were high next morning, putting on the clean shirts they had brought for that day and doing what they could to make their boots presentable. Hector's were pristine: he had carried them all the way slung round his neck. Donald took out Eilidh's ribbon and tied it in a careful bow around the puppy's neck.

'And what will they think of us down yonder, when they see you marchin' into town with a puppy dog sitting on your back?' John asked sarcastically. But he whistled off and on all the way down the valley.

Issie had taken advantage of her sister's lateness in rising to visit the Dorking fowls which an Edinburgh visitor had brought. She found Janet pleased with her new charges, but not so much as she expected.

'Don't you think they're pretty? They're so funny with those extra toes.'

'They're fine birds, right enough.' The hen-wife plumped a pullet down in the lap of her apron and peered at it disapprovingly.

'Can't you see very well today, Janet?'

The old woman suffered from rheumy eyes in cold weather, and it was a breezy morning.

Janet tutted. 'I'm seeing too well, my dear, this morning. Have *you* seen your father's visitors?'

'Our cousins who came here to shoot?'

'No, but these wild black men. I hope they are not letting them in the kitchen up at the Big House. I wouldn't have them over my doorstep. I was watching them out of the place in case they'd be stealing eggs.'

'Romanies?' Issie was interested. Romanies were a rare excitement, with their strange clothes and painted carts and their undetectable poaching exploits. No one would see them at it, but though the keepers patrolled all night, they would still find a pheasant covert empty in the morning, or a rabbit warren netted.

'Not Romanies, but near as bad.' Janet pursed her lips, and picked up the Dorking cockerel for inspection. He burbled and kicked, but no fowl was a match for Janet. She checked him for sour-crop and bumble-foot, catarrh and red mite, and set him down again, chastened, amongst his wives. 'Fladday men, these are. Well, I have cousins there – not first cousins, of course. I met one of them once. She was quite a bonny lassie – not overclean, mind you, and dressed very outlandish. It was your father's wedding, so I suppose it must a' been the best she had. They're a poor sort of folk there.'

'That's the island – ' Issie stopped, not sure how to describe the events about to overtake Fladday. 'A Mr Eagleton has rented it for sheep. He was here last week.'

Janet sniffed. 'Well, that way it might produce something. If these people know what's best for them, they'll go to Canada as your good father has arranged. All this complaining when the laird is so kind. Who would want to live in a place like that, except heathen savages? Not,' she added hastily, 'that I was ever there, or my mother or grandparents. It's a wicked thing, dearie, when your father is so thoughtful for us all. But I know there's always some who will grumble.'

Issie was silent. Her heart beat against her stays, flushing her cheeks. 'Mr Green is of the opinion they will be much better off on Lake Huron,' she said, reassuring herself with his name.

'That wee cousin of mine sent me a letter. Hardly any English. And the writing! Well, my dear, they might as well be Romanies. The keepers had better watch out tonight for the blackcock.'

Issie felt unaccountably depressed as she walked home. She had told Janet that she was glad to hear her opinion, that she had been very troubled for the people of Fladday, but that if they were really in such a dreadful state, then it was right that someone should decide for them what was best. As Mr Green had done – as, at any rate, her father had done. You couldn't expect, she reasoned with herself on the woodland path between Inverharg and home, that poor, desperately poor people, who could not read or write and never met anyone whose conversation would improve them, you could not expect such people to know even what benefits they lacked. If her poor cousin could see Janet in her clean white mutch and apron, sitting outside her comfortable cottage, she would know that Mr Green was right and would be glad to have all that Janet had. Issie had begun to notice, on her walks and rides, the many mossed ruins of past villages, which, Augustus explained, had once been inhabited by just such poor and degraded peasantry as now crowded together on bleak Fladday. It was only because so many had been removed that the land could now be properly managed and the remaining population decently accommodated, with a modicum of respectable employment on the farms.

Issie rehearsed her lesson, setting in imagination her father's meek, well-scrubbed tenantry against the sweep-black Romany-wild savages of Fladday.

'Miss! Hey, miss!'

One of these same savages had stepped unheard from the wood behind her and now barred the path in front of her. Two more gypsy-silent figures appeared from her right and left and positioned themselves behind their comrade, bonnets held to their chests. Home was just visible beyond the next stand of trees but Issie's knees quaked too much to allow of running.

'What do you want?' She spoke between a squeak and a croak, searching the unsmiling faces.

The first man, the one with a strange dead-looking eye, unhitched the basket from his back. 'We have brought a present from Fladday for the daughter of our chief.'

His accent was so peculiar to Issie's frightened ears that his meaning only became clear when he opened the basket.

'For me? Oh! Oh, for *me*? How lovely! How lovely!' Issie gabbled in her delight, laughing aloud as the puppy chewed her gloves and licked her nose. The three grim dark men began to laugh too, then to slap each other's backs and exclaim in Gaelic. They gathered round her, grinning, patting the puppy.

'My sister's ribbon,' said the spokesman. Issie had to ask him to repeat it several times. 'My sister Eilidh was putting the ribbon of her hair thus upon the dog for you.'

'Oh, please thank her. It's a lovely ribbon . . . a lovely puppy. She's the loveliest present I've ever had. It *is* a she, is it?'

This occasioned puzzlement. 'My sister?'

'No, no, the puppy. Is it a . . . a girl puppy?'

They consulted together in embarrassed whispers. 'Madam, we think maybe he is a boy puppy.'

That was enough for the Fladday men. They bowed and withdrew, replacing their bonnets. Issie's profuse thanks followed them down the path.

'Wish we had smoke,' said Hector, rubbing his forehead. 'Och, that went well, anyway. But she's no' very bonny. Them teeth!'

'Of course I shall have to see them, my dear.'

Helen pouted. 'Oh, that really is too bad. It's so tiresome Augustus being away, and you did say you would drive me out to call on Strathbeg's sister and her son.'

'I wasn't aware you had much affection for that family. Though there was a time before the young man went out to India . . . '

'Indeed not. But one has a duty, after all. You know I go every year when Mrs Drysdale visits.'

'Aha, and every year I have to drive you, and then old Strathbeg cadges an invitation to shoot my blackcock. And it'll be two of them this year, with young Drysdale at home. Wait till next week, when your cousins George and Willie have had their chance at them.'

'You cunning old thing.' She rose to kiss his cheek. 'But couldn't you make these wild Highlanders wait till afternoon?'

Drumharg looked somewhat sheepish. 'Ah well, my leg has ceased to pain me now, and as the rain has stopped, I intend to join the guns later. So I must see my tenants this morning, my dear. They cannot be refused. You know it is the right of every man of the clan to shake his chieftain's hand and speak to him freely. That is the secret of our glorious past.'

Sir Hector eased himself out of his chair and strode to the window with as warlike a stride as his gout would allow. 'Free men in a free society, not the chief's vassals but his children. This wonderful prospect says it all: the farmlands, the flocks, my loyal, proud people. As it has always been and always will be. You know, my dear, how I have struggled to keep the estates together, the lands of the clan. In so many, many cases in these sad days the hereditary chiefs are selling their birthright to upstarts, mere upstarts from the Lowlands, or to English lords who buy solely for the sporting. What becomes of the clan, then? I pray God that may never be said of me, Helen.'

'Of course no one could say such a thing, Father. Everyone knows how devoted you are. But I do wish you would drive me out this morning. Couldn't these men wait till Monday? I'm sure they are being well looked after – I gave orders for them myself.'

'Next week.' The answer was a little terse. Some unsettlement of his features had succeeded his explanations. He put his hand to the bell to summon a restorative dram.

Issie burst in, with red face and bonnet awry.

'Issie, what *have* you brought?'

'He's a present. Isn't he lovely, wasn't it sweet of them? They were such kind men. They did look strange at first but when they smiled they were quite different. Oh, Father, do help them.'

'Sit down, dear, and let me take your bonnet. Please, please don't talk so fast – ooh! Keep the creature away, I'm sure it has fleas.'

'Fleas?'

'Yes, I'm sure. Do put him off your gown at once, Issie. At once. Here Farquhar. Farquhar, when you have finished here, take this dog down to . . . oh, to the kennels, I should think, unless perhaps the gardener's children might like it?'

Issie stood speechless while Farquhar poured the whisky. At last she choked out, 'The men from Fladday brought him all this way for me, Helen.'

'Yes, my sweet. I hope you received it civilly, though really I think it was a little impertinent of them. But of course one couldn't expect them to know better, I suppose.'

Farquhar advanced to scoop up the puppy, which was biting Issie's boot-buttons.

'No!' Issie, crimson, scarlet, booming and throbbing with heat and heartbeat, snatched him to her chest.

Drumharg put his glass down slowly, goggling with surprise. Helen had the wisdom to say nothing except 'You may go, Farquhar.'

Drumharg's old pointer padded over to sniff the newcomer's tail.

'Issie, is this rebellion?' Helen asked in a low voice.

Issie's eyes streamed with tears. She could not speak, but she nodded. With a little shriek Helen caught up her skirts and whirled from the room, leaving her father to look after her interests.

For once she had misjudged him, not understanding that enthusiasm for the clan still yearned, even towards its outer reaches.

'You've vexed your sister,' he grunted, shuffling to his feet again.

Issie clutched her wriggling armful tighter, in a paroxysm of despair, as his long toothless face loomed nearer through her tears.

'Hm. They have good terriers in those dear old islands. Fighting dogs for fighting men, eh? He looks promising. Better keep him out of Helen's way, though.'

She heard, but did not see, her father go out of the room. She sat down suddenly, on her bonnet as it happened. The little dog danced and growled on her lap. She drew her brows together, shaking her head as if she had received a blow. What it was, what she had seen through her tears, she could hardly contemplate. She did not love her father. She did not know if she loved her sister. There was no one else she could – should – love. Should. *I should not . . .* she formed, and no more.

'I love *you*,' she whispered to the puppy, kissing his flea-ridden muzzle.

Hector's impassioned speech exhilarated the chief as far as he could understand it. Indeed, so delightful was this rhetoric in the ancient manner to his ears (Nature's gentlemen, he thought to himself) that he was anxious to know all the big fellow's meaning. He turned to the one who spoke English.

'Donald, I fear the old language is somewhat rusty with me. Can you tell me what our friend has been saying?'

Donald spoke slowly, taking pains to render it with elegance, as befitted Hector's panegyric on his chief. 'First of all, Eachainn mac Sheorais, he was praising your noble ancestors, with the courageous deeds that they did against the Macphails of Lochfearn and against the Camerons of Glenhelvie. Then he is . . . he was . . . referring to the richness of this place, that is Drumharg, which is as beautiful as the palace of the queen herself, and he was saying that your two daughters are as lovely as two white swans on the wave of the sea, may they be blessed with wifehood and procreation. And how your tenants are the finest men he has seen and their wives the fairest women, even though he has been as far away as Spain himself and has seen many lands and people. Furthermore, in no place has he found hospitality to be equal to what we have been given here today. The kind words you were speaking of your care towards the children of your clan were going into his heart like the words of a dear father to his only son. Hector is saying next that until this day he knew only the dear man your brother, for whom he was fighting and would have fought to the death if God had so willed it, but from today he is knowing you also, and is ready to die for you, as for the most noble of chieftains whom he is proud to call his. May God's blessing be on you seven times over.'

Hector nodded vigorously, beaming. Drumharg beamed too, and with his own hand replenished the four empty glasses from a crystal decanter.

'Donald, my lad, please assure them that I too am proud to call such stout fellows my followers – my friends – my kinsmen.'

Donald translated, his good eye shining. The three Borve men raised their glasses.

'Slàinte Eachainn mac Sheorais!'

'Slàinte!'

'Slàinte!'

The laird, pink with pride, raised his.

'Slàinte na-Fladdaich!'

After they had made their farewells Drumharg poured himself another dram, and another. 'Ah, nature's gentlemen,' he quavered, watery-eyed, shaking his head at the empty decanter.

'Ay, a health to Fladday folk his words were, boys. That's what we'll be telling them at home tonight. Maybe there's blight in the tatties but by the kind mercy of God we'll be harvesting our corn yet, then it's all snug for the winter.'

'You're glad you listened to us that Sunday night then, Hector?' Donald winked at John. They were all as light-hearted as boys, clambering along the steep hillside to Ardbuie, almost at their journey's end.

'Oh well, it would have been better not on a Sunday, right enough. But maybe it was a work of necessity. That's allowable.'

'It's not allowable snoring in the church on the Lord's Day, Hector, that's for sure.'

'Och, John. I'm penitent, you know that. Them pews were that comfortable – cushions and all – I couldn't help myself. But I'm telling you, I was never so happy as on the Lord's Day at Drumharg, in that fine church full of godly folk, with Eachann mac Sheorais at their head. I was never so happy.'

John dug him in the ribs. 'I thought you was never so happy as when you rolled out of that old sieve down there.'

Hector groaned. 'Oh, thank God for our deliverance! What a tub! And I was thinking the *Island Princess* was bad.'

Rather than wait three days for the steamer, they had haggled for a passage on a fishing smack headed for the Minch. A rough day and a rougher night under her straining patched canvas and fraying hemp had cured Hector for ever of his distrust of steam.

To reduce his detour from the fishing grounds, the skipper had put them ashore on the east of Boreray, where they must climb over the headland to Ardbuie, in the hopes of finding a local boat to ferry them home. Donald was the first to reach the summit. His exclamation brought the others up quickly. A three-masted ship lay two miles across the water in Kilmory Bay, bigger than any vessel they had seen there before, dwarfing the low grey pier and the green undulating fields, and even Macdonald's tall house of squared stone. Smaller craft moved around her, wallowing in the surf.

'The emigrant ship.'

Their hearts sank, remembering all that had happened before the dazzle of Drumharg put it from their minds.

'No one from Borve will be going in her, anyway,' said Donald at last.

CHAPTER 6

Macdonald Kilmory personally supervised the packing of his wife's carpet in hessian and canvas. It was the only item left in the house. Lachlan the Boat had already made three trips with Mrs and Miss Macdonald and the rest of the household effects, loading them into a waiting wagon (a pony trap in the case of the ladies) for conveyance to Port Long, to await the Monday steamer. Lachlan, his son, and the groom had staggered out with the long canvas bundle, and Mr Macdonald locked the front door as his wife had directed him, though since she had not imparted to whom he should entrust the key in a village consigned to desertion, he could only raise his eyebrows and leave it in the lock for Mr Eagleton.

'And good luck to you, sir,' he said softly, with a grin that sent sourness into his throat.

A new enthusiasm in his terriers' voices, wearied with day-long barking, alerted him to the presence of strangers. It was a party from the ship. The captain, a short, paunchy man, accosted him with an unmannerly bellow of 'Hi, you there!' Macdonald waited on his doorstep while the terriers took pains with the visitors. The captain thrust a paper under his nose, accompanied by a waft of spirits.

'Hae ye seen 'is, man?'

'Certainly. I myself wrote most of the names you see there.'

'Hunner-thirteen names, 'at's a'.'

'I dare say.'

'Twa hunner, Ah wiz telt. Twa hunner Ah wiz peyd fur. Ah dinna tak siller wi'oot daen' the wark Ah'm peyd fur.'

'Ah.' Macdonald tucked a terrier under each arm, seeing them in danger of a kick from a heavy boot. They continued to bark.

'An' Ah'm no' gaen back on the sum agreed.'

'One hundred and thirteen for fourteen hundred pounds seems a good bargain for your company.'

'Ah dinna tak' siller wi'oot daen' the wark.'

Macdonald shrugged and made for the gate. The captain followed, louder and more spiritous than before. 'Ah wiz telt youse wiz seein' tae't. Whaurs a' the rest?'

'My good man, the rest are as you see them. They refuse to go. I have advised, threatened, pleaded. I have extended my stay here in order to oversee their preparations for departure. But depart they will not. If you require . . . ah . . . an additional eighty-seven passengers, you must go out into the highways and byways and compel them to come. Certainly they might as well. The burning party will be here on Monday.'

Macdonald pushed his way out with barking elbows and walked quickly down the hill through the knots of excited young and sobbing aged, the boxes and bundles and hen-coops and meal sacks, to Lachlan's waiting boat. He jumped aboard without a backward look, or a nod or a shake of the head to those he passed. 'A man of stone,' some remarked, whose own troubles had not yet overwhelmed them, but Lachlan's wee lad had noticed that Domhnall mac Eachainn was weeping as he stepped aboard.

The captain swayed after him, breathing hard. 'By Jings, Ah'll tak that advice,' he shouted down the hill.

Neil and Alex had come to see their cousin Alasdair off. It had been the best-kept secret there ever was in Borve, where secrets were almost unheard of. The general confusion of the preceding weeks had helped them beyond all expectation. Eilidh's tears and pallor had been put down to her condition, while Alasdair's mother Ciorstag had been much preoccupied in nursing not only his grandfather, bent rigid by the onset of damp autumnal winds, but also Kenneth, who was expected to die at any time.

'You should have told her,' Neil said several times, and Eilidh thought so too, feeling their sins compounded by denying their families the solace of a proper farewell.

But Alasdair had been determined. 'It would make things worse for her. She'd not manage to stop me and she'd take that harder than never getting the chance to try. I'll be sending her a song from Canada before too long.'

So only Annag's younger boys were let into their plan, and helped augment, hide and carry their little store of possessions. Neil, who had earned a bit that year haymaking for a farmer in Boreray, insisted on buying Alasdair's boots and Sunday shirt off him, and Eilidh's red shawl, so they had some money.

'We're still a bit short on meal,' said Alasdair, weighing the bag in both hands, 'but it'll do.' He was seventeen, ravenous and growing, but he never doubted it would do and that if it got short he would give his share to Eilidh, to make the baby grow.

They had had an anxious morning, dodging the other men of their village who had come over to see the ship at close quarters and to wish the emigrants well. But the departure of Macdonald and his servants had set a plan afoot to net the Borve inlet that flow-tide. Mr Eagleton might prove stricter about such matters: it looked like a lean winter ahead, and a barrel of salt salmon would be welcome. So by midday their neighbours had drifted off and Alasdair and Eilidh stood openly by their baggage on the pier, shaking with excitement, wide-eyed and, even Alasdair, ghost-white.

'Let's get it over quick,' muttered Alasdair, casting a longing glance at the second boat-load pulling away from the pier; a third boat was almost full. Neil scuffled the dust, shaking his head miserably. Alex began to sniff, affected by the wailing relatives on the quay. Eilidh burst into outright tears.

Some shouting sailors, one with a paper, lurched up to them. Alasdair recognised the document. 'Our names are there,' he said, pointing eagerly. 'I put them there yesterday.' The men were big and loud, between him and his friends. One gave him a shove towards the waiting boat. He looked round for Eilidh, but there were more sailors jostling between them. One had his bag of meal and another thrust his bundle of blankets at him. 'Eilidh . . . my wife, I must go back for her, please . . . ' The drunk men elbowed inexorably, roaring in a language he didn't understand. Desperately, he recollected the English word. 'Wife – wife – ' he cried, struggling and pointing.

'Wife? She's no your wife, the wee slut!'

Laughing uproariously, the two men grabbed him by the arms and flung him into the boat among the legs and laps, dogs and chickens, with his meal sack after him bursting on his head. Eilidh's screams reached him through the smother of meal and the outcry of voices. He struggled to rise but a crewman forced him back, and when he didn't subside, knocked him behind the ear with the end of an oar.

She had seen what was happening – Alasdair in a heap and the boat drawing away. She plunged into the water, grabbing frantically for ropes that burned her hands, a flashing oar blade, the gunwale lurching towards her as people leaned out to help her. A sailor whacked at her clutching fingers. 'Get aff! Next boat for youse!' She sank, spluttering, scrabbling at merciless planking and slashing oars, got her hands, at last, round the rudder. A towering, bellowing figure, a red hole of a mouth, a devil's mouth with jagged teeth, roared down at her in the language and spittle of hell. 'My sins, my sins, oh forgive,' Eilidh cried, but silently, sliding back, back into the vengeful water, the desert of sinners: her soul would have slid in unprotesting meekness, but the feeble drowning flesh hung on, with broken fingers and battered skull, till two women forced the steersman aside and dragged her limp body aboard.

At first hardly anyone on shore had noticed what was going on, there was such a press of people there, lamenting, embracing, checking their children and baggage. Young Alex's howls had raised a hubbub. Neil and a few others had run into the water but no one there could swim more than a few strokes and the waves beat them back as the boat pulled strongly away. A horrified crowd ran up and down the shore, stretched useless arms from the pier, sobbed entreaties to the sailors. One of the crew, less drunk than the rest, realising that the girl couldn't swim, ran up to the captain, gesticulating and explaining, with Neil and Alex at his heels.

'She'll hae tae droon, then.' The captain was very drunk indeed. 'Shouldnae jump i' the wa'er if yiz cannae swim. Get on wi't, youse!' This last to the crewman who had begged help for Eilidh.

The other two boats, delivered of their first load, had pulled back alongside. Some of the men were leaping into them, imagining the crews' next step would be to rescue Eilidh.

'Bliddy savages,' growled the rolling captain. He braced himself on a bollard and bellowed out his terrible command: 'Ge' on there, boys. Al' aboard – like Ah telt yiz!'

CHAPTER 7

'Alasdair! You knew, girl?'

'Oh, Mother, he never told me, I was only guessing.'

Sara cowered sobbing on the floor. Kenneth's children gasped and coughed, blubbering out their lamentable tale, clawing at Sara, at their inert father, at Ciorstag, usually so sure a source of comfort, now as unresponsive as the dying man on the bed. She sagged, corpse-faced, in the visionary certainty of her loss.

Annag had seen the tearful group hurtling down the hill. They rushed to her as she stepped through the door, howling and clinging, all but the youngest who had crawled into hiding in the dark bed recess beside Kenneth. Annag yanked him down promptly.

'Let your dad be, now – what's all this – Ciorstag!'

'Eilidh's drowned!'

'Alasdair – '

'Christ have mercy! What's happened?'

They brought it out in jerks and gasps: sailors with sticks, with guns, running through the village, the people had to go, beating and knocking them down, Eilidh jumped in the water and they pushed her out of the boat, we were hiding in the sand-hills, sailors running past with big sticks, we hid till the ship sailed, everyone better hide, they were dragging people back, old Calum Cobbler fell, they kicked his head, he's dead, he must be dead.

Ciorstag interrupted the jumbled narrative in a voice of ice. 'They took Alasdair. They took Neil and Alex.'

Other women had come running, hearing the commotion. Mór pushed through to support her mother. No one ever doubted

Ciorstag: the children's corroboration hardly got notice.

'It's a mistake,' said Donald, slowly. 'When the transport puts in at Campbeltown they will be seeing a terrible thing was done and sending the boys back.'

'A mistake?' Mór's voice hissed in her despair at his failure: he had been wrong, and there was no justice, no hope. 'Was it a mistake they killed your sister?'

'Maybe she's . . . alive . . . ay, a mistake. If they knew what they were doing they . . . ' But his head sank on his arms.

Effie began to wail again, rocking to and fro. 'Oh, it was her sin! Her sin! Oh God have mercy!'

Mór rounded on her furiously. 'Shut your mouth! She had no sin, she was the gentlest girl that ever walked. I'll say that before the good God on Judgment Day with my own sins on me.' She turned to Donald. 'What do you believe? What do you believe, man?'

It was a challenge, not a plea. She had believed as he believed, all the years of her love, willing away the inheritance of prophets and wise women to conform to his reason. And he had been wrong; he had come home from the chief's house confident in the justice of man and the mercy of God, but the black sorrow of the people was there before him, as it had been foretold, as it had to be. The years of love and pride rose mocking, mouthing, and scorn burned in her throat like vomit.

He did not answer, though she asked a third time – 'What do you believe?' – but he raised his head. They searched each other's faces, equal in anguish, in the uncertain firelight of the smoky little room. He did not answer: justice, reason could not answer. But because he had no answer, she turned from him, and taking the baby in her shawl, went out to her mother's house to lament her brothers.

Sunday broke grey and blustery, with driving rain flattening the failed potato beds and the unripe corn. People tried, at first, to keep human pain from sullying the Lord's Day. Blessings were said and hymns were sung as usual in every household. An hour or two on in the day, when griefs and fears were beginning to surface in spite of all efforts, a young lad staggered in to the village with his little sister on his back. They were speechless with terror, but someone recognised them as from Ardmonach, the township round the bay from Kilmory. Their story, when it came, was pitiful. They had been sent out to the corn plots on the machair, to keep the wild geese from plundering them, and had been playing hide-and-seek in the sand dunes when the boat came. Their mother and uncle were among those forced aboard. As soon as they dared, they had run to Kilmory to get help from their father, who was giving friends a sendoff, being a noted piper: but Kilmory was empty and the ship was weighing anchor. They hid in a cottage there all night, too frightened to return to their own home. They were sure everyone had been taken, except for four of the men, including their own brother, who were away on the mainland working at the harvest.

The Sunday decencies disintegrated. Men, women and children pushed into the ceilidh-house, questioning, lamenting and embracing the waifs, Norrie and Nana, who were being fed and warmed there. By midday a group from Borve had set out for each of the other villages. Though it was Sunday, Alasdair the Bard argued that to go was a work of mercy; there might be old and sick untended, cows unmilked, tethered beasts perishing. They would have to go, anyway, for they could no longer bear not to know the fate of their friends, but it was the old bard's talent to put a grace and a dignity on whatever he spoke of.

Roderick and his two eldest sons, with Ranald the carpenter, went to Diriclet and Dun, small twin settlements at the south end of the Ardmonach machair. The inhabitants, not Fladday folk in origin but incomers who had settled during the kelp boom, had gone willingly, they knew, having sold cattle and goods. All was deserted but in good order. 'Nothing doing here,' said Roderick,

71

mightily relieved. Ranald collected up a few rusty nails from a doorstep, wondering if anyone would miss them, but in the end he put them back. Young Roddy found a mewing, half-starved kitten, and tucked it into his waistcoat.

John Blondie, his wife Seonag, their daughter Katie and John of the Rock searched Ardmonach. They found unmilked cows and tethered beasts, but no old or sick. Piper's Norrie had been right: everyone who had not been at home when the boat came had been at Kilmory, seeing the emigrants off. They stared for a long time at the scrapes and pits in the mud and shingle. There was blood on a boulder. 'Son of Heaven, help us,' said John Blondie. They unloosed two tied dogs and a cooped broody hen, let the calves out of their enclosure to find their mothers, and after some discussion as to the rights and wrongs of it, drove home the one milk cow that seemed to be calfless.

In Kyles, where old Hector went with his sons and Sara, they found four houses empty where they had expected to meet friends and exchange news. In the fifth lived old blind Angus and his daughter Flora, who could only hirple on a stick, having been left with a short leg by infantile paralysis. They were crouched at the fireside, weeping and praying, not knowing at all why the rest of the villagers who had gone out to see the great ship sitting in Kilmory Bay had not returned. Flora had tried to climb the steep path over to Borve, but fell, hurting the wrist that held the stick, and had to slide back home on her bottom. Sara offered to stay to fend for them – 'But not by myself,' she insisted, clutching young Hector's hand.

Old Hector opened his mouth to forbid his son, but hesitated. 'I'll send Lexy down yet today, maybe,' he contrived.

Donald, John Blackie, Annag and Peggy went to Kilmory. They came first to the house of Annag's brother-in-law. The door stood open, but the fire was out. The hens were scratching in the ashes. A sheep had its head in the meal bin. John rushed at it in a rage of grief.

'Let the creature be,' his mother said. 'This is no hearth or home now, nor ever will be again.'

Between the houses the ground was trampled to mire, and all down to the shore the sward was torn and scuffed by chasing and fleeing feet, scattered with the forlorn possessions of poor people: clay pipes, coloured kerchiefs, a half-unravelled stocking on its knitting pins, a painted wooden doll like the pedlars sold.

Donald stood in the midst of it and stared without seeing. The others went from house to house, looking for those Annag knew to be aged, sick, or in childbed. All were gone, even poor daft Donda who couldn't speak and had fits. They rounded up such milch animals as could not be left. Peggy and John hurled stones to drive away the hopeful dogs that followed them, but Annag wouldn't have it. 'There is enough pain already,' she said.

When all the stories were told in Borve the people knew that they had nothing to look for. Some eyed Donald with a remnant of hope, expecting he might say, 'We'll speak to Mr Eagleton', or 'Word will come from Drumharg', but he was mute, seeming hardly to hear or see. Cowed and silent, they all assembled as usual for Sunday evening worship. Ranald gave out the first psalm, 'O God our help in ages past', and it started well, but no one could keep it up and the music floundered in stifled sobs and whispered lamentation. Ranald passed the great Bible to Donald, who nearly always read, being more fluent than any of the others, but this time he put the Book aside. 'I am unworthy,' he said in a strangled voice, and walked out of the room. The clatter of wind through the door as he opened it surged into a sudden babble of anguish from the congregation. Children howled, women broke into an outcry of open sobbing. Hector rose and began to read from the Book, very loud, though with difficulty and shakily. Most of the men strove for decorum and sat with bowed heads, but the women would hardly stay to hear. Outside they ran from house to house as on any other day, but now with tears instead of friendly banter. Their laments filled the air, reproaching the providence they bowed to. Their husbands cowered in corners, appalled at this unholy escalation from resignation to railing. Children escaped, tired of adult griefs, and played in the rainy dusk on the forbidden day, unreproved, as if no reproof, no small reformation possible to puny flesh and blood could serve to avert the giant wrath thundering down on them. 'Shush, woman,' the husbands urged, and 'Get you inside!' the mothers ordered, between sobs, but there was no conviction in it. The Lord's Day, the holy Sunday of love and affirmation was crushed in the trampled mud of Kilmory, with the self-respect of generations. There was nowhere to go and nothing to be done, since God's face was set against them.

Hardly anyone went to bed, but no one could bear the dark. Fires and rushlights burned unthriftily all night, flickering as the doors opened and closed in the blustery darkness, while people wandered aimlessly from neighbour to neighbour, and waited without hope.

CHAPTER 8

'Mine, Mr Green.'

'I beg your pardon, Mr Eagleton, I must insist that the beasts are sold to pay their owners' passage out.'

The two men stood peering through the rain-smattered sash windows ('Leaking,' Mr Eagleton had observed) at the constables' inadequate attempts to round up the cattle and ponies of Kilmory, rendered skittish by smoke and noise.

'My shepherds will make a better job of gathering them when they come over. The proceeds of the sale can be put towards the accommodation I see I shall have to provide for them. I had understood, Mr Green, that the island was supplied with houses for my workers.'

'As you can see for yourself, there are three cottages of more substantial build than the others, which I have ordered not to be fired.'

'Huts.' Mr Eagleton turned from the window, testing a rotten floorboard critically with the heel of his boot. 'I wouldn't put my sheep in them.'

Green, aware that he was being pushed into squalid wheedling, was becoming flustered.

'To return to the question of the cattle. So far, Sir Hector has paid everything towards his tenants' emigration, at considerable cost to himself. It was his understanding, and mine, that the people's poverty would not allow them both to pay the passage money and have anything left to start a new life abroad. Since, however, in their improvident lethargy they apparently did not bother to sell their stock, I require that it goes to repay Sir Hector.'

'Some of them didn't have much time for selling, I hear,' remarked Mr Eagleton drily.

'They had notice to quit in March. Out of compassion Sir Hector forebore – '

'Ay. I've heard all that. Now, one of my shepherds, looking through his spyglass from over yonder on Boreray, saw some rag-tag driving away six head of cattle yesterday. I want them back, or we can settle a price if not.'

Green reddened, sweating at the other's coolness.

'Impossible. There are no "rag-tag", as you call them, left on this island. You have vacant possession, as stated in your lease. Now as to the cattle – '

'Aha. Not quite vacant, I hear. One bunch of miserable savages is there yet. But that's why you brought the constables here, I dare say?'

It was against Green's principles to tell, or even imply, false-hoods, and to be found out in the telling was intolerable. He paced across the hall, slamming doors, swithering between natural fury and expedient mollification.

'Damn it, it's not my fault. That fool of a tenant should have got rid of them. They'll be removed today. Yes, I admit they have proved somewhat intractable – apparently. Of course I had nothing to do with them personally. They are a degenerate and feeble-minded remnant, I fear, but one sight of the constables with their batons will put them in mind of the law, where neither duty nor self-interest has prevailed. Rest assured, Mr Eagleton, that if further persuasion is needed, I shall not hesitate to call up the military – though I fancy the mere threat of redcoats would suffice. This room should serve you to dine in – a fine sea view, and the mantel is elegant, is it not?'

'It'll do. I'll be supping in the kitchen.'

The burning party consisted of six labourers hired by Green on the mainland, with eight constables from Fort William, who were there not to fire thatches or even to round up cattle but to see that the evicted tenants left peaceably, so that Mr Eagleton might find his lands 'void, redd and patent'. When they learned that not all the houses were abandoned, some of the men grumbled that they hadn't known they were expected to put folk out of their homes. Green promised them an additional fee in consideration of their feelings of humanity, which the flagon of whisky they found in Ardmonach did much to dispel, anyway. By the time they set out for Borve, early in the afternoon, the flames and the liquor had put them in holiday mood.

At the top of the slope above Borve they hesitated, slow to comprehend what they saw through the fog of whisky and excitement. On the green plain behind the white sandy beach the hovels of unworked stone and dark thatch huddled on either side of a muddy track. At the end of this village street the inhabitants stood staring up the hill, women in front and men behind, as they had stood since the first smoke plumed over the hill from Kilmory. When they saw the burning party the women surged forward, shouting and shaking their fists, some picking up stones as they ran.

'Oh Jesus,' groaned the youngest fire-raiser.

The others had more spirit. 'Come on, lads, teach the bitches a lesson.' They plunged away down the hill, led by the constables with batons.

The youngest stayed behind to vomit, then crawled into the bent grass till it was over.

John Blackie's wife Rachel overbalanced at the first blow, surprised and hurt, stretching out her arms to save her eight-months' belly. Picking herself up, she stumbled after the strangers, clutching at the constables' dark coats, supplicating in her few words of English: 'No, sirs, please no, kind sirs!' One fetched her a whack across the knuckles and she fell again, crying bitterly.

Mór lay in a soft cloud of peace. Grey soft clouds raced over and over her head, over the grey sea and green grass. She tried to raise her head but something held it down. It was a pain holding it down. It frightened her. She felt at her breast for the baby and touched another pain that made her cry out, and the baby wasn't there. She heard him squalling at her side. 'Hush now, hush now,' she whispered, feeling for her nipple to give him, and finding wet pain that swallowed her in darkness.

Effie screamed over and over, 'God of life help us! God of life help us!'

Ciorstag stood squarely in front of Kenneth's bed.

'What are you doing here?' the senior constable asked her sternly. Seeing she didn't understand, he repeated it in Gaelic: he knew how to treat such people.

'What are *you* doing here? You curse on the land, you filthy son of the devil, may you rot in hell to all eternity for this day's work!'

The constable was taken aback. He knew some of the language but he was unused to the solemnity of its maledictions. She was making some sort of sign. He felt extremely uncomfortable. Hastily, he called his men in. 'Carry that sick man outside,' he ordered. 'You have quarter of an hour, ma'am,' he said to Ciorstag, quite respectfully. 'After that the house will be set on fire and I cannot be responsible for your safety.'

His firm but polite speech did not have its intended effect. She flew at the men as they approached Kenneth, kicking, punching and cursing, so that there was no option but to use batons, and fairly heavily. Indeed, the senior constable's broke in two as he bludgeoned a way through the press of she-demons rushing to the head witch's aid. Several females were writhing on the ground outside; the men were handling them pretty roughly, but in the circumstances that must be overlooked. The two drunkest of the firing party had lit the first thatch and were now gleefully hurling chunks of blazing turf at the house full of shrieking women. The senior constable was about to overlook that, too, when he remembered the sick man.

'Stop!' he roared.

'Stop!' someone else was shouting, in Gaelic; again and again, and louder.

Donald was shouting out 'Stop!' Mór struggled towards his voice through the dark pain shot with sparks and the soft grey clouds. 'Hush now, hush now,' she whispered to the baby and to Donald, who was shouting out in pain. The pain was her own. It burst out in sparks through the grey clouds. His voice came and went in the whirling of the sparks. 'Be quiet, all of you. Do you not see that the trouble that is on us is the black wrath of God? We are judged and his anger is upon us. This is for our sins and the sins of our fathers, all the sin of the ages has fallen on us because we did not walk in his ways. We must repent and go where the Lord sends us, even to death if that is His will. Take what you can from your houses in the time these men allow us and forgive them as the Holy Saviour forgave – forgive them, forgive!'

Mór forgave nothing. He found her lying in the grass and bent over her, through the clouds of her pain.

'*Mhór, Mhór mo chridhe!*'

She spat in his face. There was blood in her spittle.

In the opinion of the senior constable the one-eyed fellow knew how to deal with overwrought females. After his speech they went about their business as meekly as could be, bundling their household articles out into the street and helping their men to tear down the thatches to retrieve the wooden couples. The senior constable was a little uncertain about this, since the timber was presumably Mr Eagleton's property to keep or burn as he saw fit. But he turned a blind eye to the first three or four and extended the quarter of an hour's grace to half an hour, as a reward for good behaviour.

Flame was put to the thatches. It smouldered in the damp turf, licked along ridge or beam, flared, cracked, burst from the doors, roaring, guzzling, slavering gouts and gobbets of fire. John Blondie's Seonag, distracted, counted her five as four, and threw herself back under her blazing roof, shrieking, 'My children, my children!' John and his mother Catriona dragged her out, with her kerchief charring and glowing in the rain of fire. Effie began to scream again, wordlessly.

The senior constable shooed the people clear of the burning houses. They were like children: there was little harm in them, but they had to be handled firmly. He himself helped to stuff squawking fowls into baskets and screeching cats into sacks, and to hoist infants up on the waiting cart. There was only one, heaped high with chests and stools, querns and pots, looms and spinning wheels. A squat hairy pony stood between the shafts, dwarfed by her load. The people assembled at the cart tail, laden like so many gypsy pedlars, all but the lads who were herding the cattle and sheep down the hill, assisted by a great number of barking dogs, visible intermittently between the streaming smoke and sparks.

The constable remembered something. He bent to speak to the old fellow they had carried out in a chair, who seemed to be some sort of village dignitary. 'Now, my man, there were six cows that didn't belong to you. Which were they, hey?'

The bard regarded him serenely. 'Ay, there was a saying of Lachlan of the Prophecies: "On that day the black cattle shall have upon them the stranger's fetter, and there will be no milk nor buttermilk for the people in the winter of hunger." '

The constable, making little of this cryptic utterance even after he had had Alasdair repeat it twice, shouted to his men, 'Take the best six.' He turned briskly to the cowed villagers, waiting silent in the rain and smoke. 'Now, be off. And be sure you make the crossing tonight. We'll have no mercy on anyone we find here tomorrow. It'll be the county gaol, man or woman, understand? Man or woman.'

They stared, uncomprehendingly. Dark demon figures danced between them and their blazing homes. Roddy led the pony forward. She strained in the shafts, being stiff with age and overladen. Behind the cart John Blondie and old Hector carried Kenneth on the bier of plaited straw they used for funerals: there was little of him left and two could manage him easily. Donald, John Blackie, Roderick and his son Norman came next, with the bard in his chair between them. The rest followed on behind, all, even the children and the limping, staggering women – even Mór – moving slowly under heavy loads. The cattle brought up the rear. The dejected train shuffled off up the ridge separating Borve from Kyles, where the boats lay. Old Alasdair soon began to groan with the pain the jolting caused to his crumbling bones, and then to cry out. John Blackie wept along with him, wrenched by the old man's agony. By the time they reached the top of the rise the whole company was sobbing and stumbling. They paused to look back at their burning homes, at their unreaped corn, at the six of the queenly cows of Borve Kilmory grown small and distant among the strangers.

Annag threw herself on the ground, clutching and kissing the trodden grass. 'Oh, the dear earth, the dear, dear earth of our love! The curse of the stranger is on you now. The flame of hell is on you now. Only the dear God above knows all the evil that is done this day.'

A long wail broke from forty throats, carrying above the lowing of the cattle and the barking of the dogs. The constable shivered, even as he mopped his brow in the heat of the blaze. But he could not afford to let his attention wander, having still another village to burn.

The burners overtook the straggling procession from Borve. By the time the pony had been persuaded down the steep path to the shore at Kyles the thatches of that village, too, were already blazing. Angus and Flora cowered by the boats. Young Hector and the two girls darted in and out of the choking reek, dragging whatever they could save out of the houses and down to the shore, but the constables put a stop to this indiscriminate looting. They clung to each other, helpless, watching the irreplaceable roof timbers, the tables, benches and chests, the precious planking from Archie Boatie's shed, all the treasures of a treeless land, consumed in profligate flame.

Kyles, in its sheltered cove, had been a village of fishermen. There were two good boats, six-oared vessels that could also carry a short mast with a lugsail. The Borve boat, used only for peat-cutting expeditions and for desultory summer fishing, was drawn up alongside them. It was of the same pattern, but old and leaking. The sail had rotted beyond repair; the mast had ended up as legs for a dozen stools and settles. The three boats together would hold the villagers, but not their baggage and animals.

'Make two trips – three trips of it, even.'

'In this?' John Blackie gestured at the foam-capped water, darkening sullenly before a white squall of rain. The wind was from the south and getting up. When the tide turned, as it shortly would, it would be blowing against the racing stream that poured through the strait between Fladday and Rona to the Minch, forcing up high steep waves and treacherous eddies.

Everyone could see what he meant. The unsound Borve boat was loaded quickly to catch the slack water, with Ranald steering and a crew of boys and girls. The four invalids were got aboard, and the spaces were filled with children, sacks of wool and hay – anything that was light. Five cows were roped tail to jaw, the front beast tethered to the stern-post, and the whole panic-struck assembly dragged and driven into the water after the boat.

'Row quickly now – the tide's turning, see.'

'Mind the cattle – keep clear of rocks at the stern, they'll make for them.'

'Keep baling, Hughie.'

'Hang on to Lala, Shonny.'

The parents' exhortations, lost in the uproar of splashing and bellowing, dwindled to 'Oh God help them – Holy Son of God preserve them', then to whimpers and silence, as the inexpert crew flailed out of the still cove into wind and rough water, towards the grim black wall of Rona's cliffs, where no one could live, where no one had ever lived, in all the memory of generations. It could not be: and there, now, their children were headed, white fear-filled faces and red faces split with infant bawling, and then through the spray and scudding rain no faces, only a dark blur tossed high and then vanishing in the turmoil of darker water, and coming up again, then down again, drawn by Rona's darkness. What could not be, was.

There was no time to waste in anxious watching and no will left for it. Speechless, they brought the cart down to the shingle below an overhanging bank and filled it with furniture and cooking pots, hoping it might there escape the attention of Mr Eagleton's men till they could return for it. The cattle and pony were roped, the sheep bundled with tied legs into the bottom of the boats, and people wedged in around mast and rowers, clutching whatever they could least bear to part with. Ciorstag rowed with her white cockerel clamped between her knees, Effie with her father's Bible; Uncle Dougie cradled a clock Macdonald Kilmory had given him for forty years of bringing the peats home, whilst Barabel leaned dangerously over the stern, encouraging her cow with tears and endearments.

There were too many dogs. The old and the strays from other villages were ordered back and ran up and down the shore, barking and whining. Some swam after, scrambling, exhausted, onto the backs of the cattle; but the increasing waves knocked them away, except for a few who made it alongside the boats, with glazing eyes and choking nostrils. These were hauled in. Several people remembered Eilidh.

'O kindly Christ, her soul be on your arm,' Annag whispered.

It was almost dark by the time the last of the exhausted beasts were clear of the surf. They stood streaming from coats and muzzles, some sinking on their knees. The old pony would never get up again and three calves and a cow were already dead.

'Let us render thanks to God who has brought us here in safety,' said Donald.

They bowed their heads while he prayed and sang together the Twenty-third Psalm. Afterwards they turned round slowly where they stood, hushed, afraid, almost, to look at the desolation around them.

1 8 4 7–1 8 4 8

CHAPTER 9

'"The Island of Boreray has two smaller outliers to the south, Fladday and Rona, of approximately 850 and 480 acres respectively. Although similar, doubtless, in geological composition, (as lately surmised by Mr. Robert Thoroughgood), though subject to the same climate, and girt by the same ocean, yet in these twin sisters of the wild Atlantic the curious observer may note a contrast that could scarcely be greater within the confines of their Northern Latitude. The first (whilst admittedly no Tropic isle, being without trees or any tall vegetation) is low and undulating, promising in its fair curves and gentle inclines such pasturage as is afforded by the English downlands; a promise which is not unfulfilled, for the peat soil natural to the cool moist northern clime is sweetened by a continual sifting from the shores of windblown sand, which being calcareous in its composition serves the purpose of lime. A beneficent Providence thus showers on Fladday the riches which in more cultivated parts may only be won by considerable expenditure of ingenuity and toil; and the grassland of this remote jewel of the Hebrides is as fine and wholesome as the best of Sussex or Cotswold – nay, perchance more excellent, for, the oceanic situation all but banishing frost, the isle remains green when more southern pastures are whitened in the icy grip of winter. This peculiar merit, together with an abundance of freshwater springs, shows the isle most favourable to the rearing of sheep; in recognition whereof the enlightened proprietor has recently installed a tenant with a flock of six hundred Cheviots, which should they thrive, as is to be expected, will render the land far more profitable than under the old system of small arable holdings or crofts."'

Mr Green paused for a sip of water. Issie had listened intently; Augustus read so beautifully. Though there had been much in the earlier parts of his discourse that she had not understood thoroughly, dealing as it had with wool yields and market prices, he expressed himself so well in his descriptions of the beauties of nature that she had not felt the reading at all wearisome. Particularly, his account of Fladday delighted her, for ever since the arrival of Dileas she had felt a great interest in his home island and a curiosity about the kind, rough men who had brought him to her. 'Do you hear that, darling?' she breathed into his fur. Augustus frowned at her and she put the dog down hastily, afraid lest he should think her flippant. She was ashamed to notice that her father was asleep: but he had grown pale and old-looking of late, seeming more so in the early spring sunshine of the terrace where they sat.

'Do you feel cold, Father? Shall I fetch a rug?' she ventured rather lamely, in an attempt to wake him before Augustus noticed and was offended.

'Eh?' Drumharg raised a tremulous head, running his tongue over his moustache. 'Ah . . . no, no . . . very interesting, my boy . . . ' His voice tailed off and Issie realised, to her horror, that he was nodding again, with drooping eyelids.

'Do you wish me to continue?' Augustus asked, stiffly.

'Oh, please do!' Issie almost shouted, appalled by the slow sinking of her father's chin upon his neck-cloth. But it shot up sharply at his son-in-law's question.

'Of course . . . really most interesting. Don't you think so, Helen . . . eh?'

Helen smiled wanly. There was a moment's uncomfortable silence. Issie noticed, but did not understand, her father's anxious, almost fearful glance at Augustus, which she had seen before, although only recently. Perhaps Helen's health worried him: she was so listless and fretful. Augustus eyed his wife till she, too – though it seemed unwillingly – gave him her attention, putting aside the book of patterns she had been thumbing.

Mr Green continued: "'How different in aspect and utility is Rona, the sister isle. That oft-humid wind which ever blows from the western ocean and bears to the one plot fertility, in the other hath wrought fearsomely upon frowning heights and awful crags, which being weathered to the bare rock and much fissured by the passage of water, present a gloomy prospect worthy of an Ossian's pen. The entire coast is girded by barren cliffs, in the north attaining a height of some two hundred feet, a grim fortress-wall wherein no living thing, scarcely even a tuft of vegetation, may be thought capable of survival. Yet in due season these storm-beaten walls afford shelter to myriad sea-birds which resort there to rear their young: at which time the strange cries of the fowls fill the air day and night, with a sound so mysterious that the hearer may consider it little wonder that the superstitious of past ages invented tales of mermaids and trolls to account for it. The whole interior is a marshy plain, useless for pasturage, and of aspect more dismal than sublime, since the less pronounced declinations of the inner part lack the majesty of the seaward steeps. There is at present an enterprise afoot to stock the heights with deer, which the coarse grasses of the hilltops might support, for the delectation of Mr Harbottle, tenant of Boreray, and his guests, who might obtain further sport in the shooting of the grey or Atlantic seal, which at breeding time frequents a small cove on the south-west coast of Rona in great herds, lesser numbers being present close inshore at all times of year, either on the rocks or in the water. It may be, thus, that Rona, though lacking in all apparent utility to man, may yet be constrained to profit, or at the very least, to some pleasure. Besides, the few wretched inhabitants of the isle (being the more degenerate part of the former population of Fladday) might by diligent labour make a tolerable livelihood from the abundant fisheries of local waters. It is proposed to further improve their condition by the placement of a missionary of the Free Church among them, to be sent out with assistance from the Society in Scotland for the Propagation of Christian Knowledge, who may – " '

'Eh? What's that?' Sir Hector suddenly sat bolt upright, clutching the arms of his chair.

Mr Green repeated his last sentence, rather more loudly and with a somewhat impatient emphasis which Issie felt was unfair on the old man, though she could understand that Augustus must feel distressed by his audience's straying attention.

' " – who may by his preaching and example bring the light of the Gospel into those all but heathen lives, besides educating the children who are entirely illiterate",' Augustus finished, distinctly.

'Look here, Augustus, this simply won't do. The Free Church . . . their ministers – so-called – they're rebels, breakaways. All seceded from the Church. We can't have that. *Free* Church, they call themselves – nobodies, revolutionaries, some of them. Fanatics! I was reading only last week in the *Inverness Courier* – I'll show it to you – Issie, fetch – '

Issie jumped to her feet but Augustus cut in. 'No need, Issie. I saw the regrettable account you mention, of course, but I fear, sir, that in the absence of suitable ministers of the Established Church, one had better allow the missionary zeal of the other. You will agree, sir, that it is hardly fitting for a chieftain to appear indifferent to his people's spiritual welfare; and that degraded remnant who surely most require it have no one to guide their morals.'

'Mr Cochrane has always seen to them, when time allows. A man of education and taste – '

Augustus swept the weak intercession for Mr Cochrane aside. 'They rarely see him: though I understand from him that their applications for Poor Relief, as for this new Destitution Fund, have been attended with much deceit, leaving no doubt that they require some closer moral surveillance.'

90

Drumharg slumped in his chair, fingering his moustache un-happily. 'Cochrane will take offence,' he muttered. 'A distant cousin of my late wife, Augustus,' he added apologetically.

'My cousin also,' declared Helen, peevishly. 'I do think you might leave well alone, Augustus.'

'I might leave *well* alone, Helen.'

Helen, to Issie's surprise, made no response, but pulled her wraps closer around her shoulders. It was not characteristic of her to sit out of doors so early in the year but she had appeared to wish to oblige Augustus in this respect.

Mr Green continued: 'There is really no question of holding out against the society's appointment. If they are refused, I dare say they know how to blacken names – in either relevant or *irrelevant* matters.'

Helen, who had risen to go inside, subsided again upon her couch.

'Of course,' said Sir Hector, dully.

Issie, pondering Augustus's strange emphasis, was distracted by a sudden flutter of displeasure from her sister.

'Get that dog out of the flower bed, Issie,' she wailed, dabbing her eyes. She had never forgiven Dileas for the manner of his introduction into the household.

Augustus regarded her with something like his old ardour, or at least with an air of pride that had for some time past been absent towards his wife. 'You are not quite yourself, I see. We must take good care of you. Come, I'll take you in to rest.'

Helen protested but he drew her up by the arm and led her inside, adding, to Drumharg, 'While I'm absent, sir, you might care to peruse those plans which I put before you this morning. The workmen are ready to start next week.'

'Yes . . . yes, of course.' Like a chidden schoolboy, the old man picked up the papers that had slipped from his lap, holding them close to his short-sighted eyes.

Issie, seeing his painful blinking, went over to his chair. 'I could read them to you, Father.'

'No, certainly not, girl – ' Drumharg slapped the papers face down, flushing crimson. 'Ah . . . fetch me my spectacles from my study, Issie, there's a good lass.'

Issie ran in, followed by Dileas. The old man peered after her, raising the corner of the top plan cautiously once she was out of sight. The sanitary convenience depicted on the next sheet was hardly fit for tender female eyes. Hearing her returning tread, he rolled the bundle hastily together.

'You're a good girl,' he said, with more affection than usual, settling his pince-nez. 'Bathrooms,' he added, as she stood irresolute. 'Augustus will have . . . er . . . bathrooms. Piped water, hot and cold. Now why not go' – he was at a loss to think where Issie might go, being quite unacquainted with her habits – 'round the gardens. Take your little dog for a walk in the garden, eh? Fresh air's good for young girls.'

Issie, who was used to tramping upwards of ten miles a day, left him somewhat disconsolately. Having discerned the new helplessness in her father, there was nothing she would rather have done than stay to help him: read to him, make him comfortable in some way – anything. Being always one who was not required, not noticed when present, nor missed when absent, she longed more than anything to be of use. In the absence of a human beneficiary she devoted her attention to making Dileas's outing enjoyable, talking to him as she often did. 'You mustn't dig in the roses, darling, it makes Helen cross. It's a pity Father hasn't felt inclined to take you hunting – but then, I don't like you killing poor rabbits, you naughty boy. Look, there's a squirrel!'

Dileas had seen it, anyway, darting between two tall pine trees and up into the branches. He scrabbled at the trunk, rushing at it time and again in an attempt to hurl his stout hairy body skywards, barking joyfully; but finding himself still on the ground, vented his feelings by digging at random between the roots, showering pine-needles, moss and soil behind him. Issie expostulated with him, laughing, but since she was ignored, sank down on the roots of a neighbouring tree, drifting from laughter into vague anxieties. She pushed her big red hands under her knees and made her lips meet over her hateful teeth, a reflex to hostile circumstance that she had practised for so long it had ceased to be conscious. Suddenly she was aware of it. 'How silly,' she said aloud. 'No one to see me but you, Dileas, and you don't care what I look like.'

Dileas didn't care about anything, at that moment, except squirrels. A pine cone driven by his sturdy forelegs caught her on the brow. She swallowed hard, feeling rebuffed in spite of herself. I shall always be ugly, she thought. No matter what Helen says, however careful I am with my clothes. I must just get used to it, I shan't change now. I'm grown up. A woman.

Her consciousness of being a woman brought her to inexpressible realms, and she foundered in a hot tide of shame that washed her from ears to knees. She had been a woman (Helen had said, 'You're a woman now, not a child, you see') only for a year. Elsie came with a laundry bag for the bloodstained linen and whispered and giggled with Helen, but Issie had cried and cried and thought she would never dare leave her room again. 'I'll tell you why it is, if you ever marry, my sweet,' Helen had said with a knowing smile, giving Elsie a little push out of the room.

But she would never marry. She would never know. The desolation of not knowing what she couldn't even bear to guess about filled her eyes with inconsistent tears. She wiped them away impatiently but they kept coming. It was so sad – everything had become so sad. It was Helen. Helen was sad, or at least she never smiled any more and was tired and fractious all day. Nothing was right for her, and it should be, because she was lovely and charming, she always had been, she had always made everyone happy just by being there. When Miss Roberts left them she could hardly bear to go, because of Helen. 'I love you as a dear, dear younger sister,' the governess had wept, embracing her again and again. The scene was so moving that Issie had lain in bed recalling it night after night, till she could imagine how it would feel to be addressed like that. Miss Roberts had begged Helen to write, and she had promised, but then she had made Issie do it and just signed her name under the round nine-year-old hand, and Miss Roberts's letters, which were so beautiful and affectionate, had ceased after a few months. The servants loved her too. She chose pretty girls for the house – 'Because I can't bear frights about me,' she said, which made Issie cringe. She fitted them out with sweet print frocks and called them by their Christian names in the old-fashioned manner, because she thought surnames so cold. The men-servants – all men, every man, must adore Helen. 'From the lowest to the highest,' mouthed Issie, smiling; she had overheard Augustus say that to her when they became engaged. It had been delightful to see them together.

A slight qualm overtook Issie's thoughts, a recollection that she had not always found it unreservedly delightful, but it was quickly swallowed in the unhappiness of the present. Augustus never spoke like that now, never gazed at Helen as he used to do. There was often anger in his eyes and when Helen saw it she looked afraid. She no longer teased him in her old manner. One would hardly think she liked him, or even knew him.

Issie frowned at the fragments of moss and twig on her skirt, arranging and rearranging them, making patterns. Helen teasing Augustus about his journal, which he would not let her see till he had written up a full account of the estates – and now that he was doing so, Helen didn't seem interested. She remembered Strathbeg's nephew, Major Drysdale: 'So Mr Green is exclusively interested in sheep, Mrs Green?' and Helen dimpled. 'Exclusively,' she replied, and they laughed together. It was unfair: Augustus was interested in all improvements, not only in sheep, and Helen should not have let Major Drysdale speak so about Augustus. He had come about Drumharg a great deal in the autumn and winter. He passed silly remarks about sheep often, and if he thought no one was looking, even made a vulgar sign to indicate horns curling out of his head. It made Issie hot with embarrassment. Helen, apparently, found it funny and that was so unworthy of her. Issie thought the young man conceited and flippant and she was sure Augustus disliked him too. But for all that, it would be better if Helen were still in such good humour as she had been at that time. And Father, he was so low in spirits and health, he had even given up his afternoon stroll to the village. The only moment of the day when he looked his old self was when Rory the Piper played him in to dinner.

Issie sighed, brushing the twigs from her lap, with a picture in her mind of Helen at the piano, smiling at Augustus, whose hand was on her shoulder, and Father in his chair, beaming at his cherished daughter, humming the tune. Her pity for their vanished felicity smote her with sudden remorse. She had thought she did not love them, in a childish fit of pique, had grown used to the horrible idea: but surely, surely . . .

The question she could not ask or answer welled up in further tears. 'I want them to be happy.' She whispered into her folded arms. 'I want them to be happy . . . everyone to be happy.' The impossibility of everyone's happiness, her powerlessness to see to it, stilled her sniffling and made her level-headed again. But, she thought, I could help, if they'd tell me. They should let me help.

Dileas thrust his earthy nose against her forehead. He had had enough of squirrels. Issie caught him in her arms but he danced away, barking and wagging so comically that her gloom dispersed somewhat. She rose to follow him. He was heading for Inverharg; the baker's wife always gave him a bun, and Janet gave him a peppermint drop.

Issie was soon cheerful again, following his ridiculous self-important tail to the village. She bought a bun for herself as well, and a white loaf for Janet. The old woman, undeceived by her rheumy eyes, peered at Issie and shook her head. 'Oh well, my dear, you're out of spirits today. What's the trouble?'

Issie felt her worries tumbling in on her again. She swallowed hard. Dileas was yapping for his peppermint and by the time Janet had rummaged in her dresser drawer for it, she was able to speak. 'I'm quite well, thank you, and how are you? I meant to bring some kail for the fowls but I didn't know we were coming today. Dileas decided – oh, be quiet, you bad boy.'

The dog was prancing noisily on the flagged floor, growling at the two broody hens cooped under the dresser. They puffed themselves up indignantly, answering Dileas's taunts with out-raged clucking. Issie got him on her knee at last, turning the chair so that he faced the fire and grew sleepy. The broodies, out of sight and out of mind, settled complaining on their eggs. Janet made tea, polishing her best cups carefully for the occasion, as she always did when the laird's daughter called, though that was every other day. Issie had long given up saying, 'There's no need for the best china', and Janet had long given up other marks of deference. They drank tea companionably, with slices of the white bread spread with treacle.

'Treacle from a factory,' said Janet, dipping her piece in the tea to soften the crust. 'Your Mrs Mackenzie up at the house would scoff if she knew that. Well, I'm that busy with the fowls. I used to be doing jam every year but now I'm having a snooze instead. The wee boys are stealing all my currants. I'm getting too old to bother.'

Janet reminisced comfortably and Issie grew comfortable too, so comfortable that during a pause she said, inconsequentially and to her own surprise, 'It's my father, Janet. He hardly goes out any more. He looks so old and worried all the time. And' – she was going to continue, 'Mr Green seems so disrespectful to him sometimes', but suppressed it – 'I suppose he *is* growing old.'

Janet took her cup away over Dileas's sleeping head. 'Yes, but he's not so old as all that.' She busied herself putting coals on the fire. 'It's the worry, the good name of the family – not that there's anything to worry about. I'm older than Sir Hector is, dearie, and I remember his own father going just the same way, fretting away over his boys sowing their wild oats down in England. Well, it was nothing to worry about. Only high spirits. High spirits and plenty money.' She sat down heavily, clapping her hands on her knees with a chuckle. 'I remember hearing how your father let a hare and a greyhound loose under the table – somewhere, some grand house, I can't recollect where – but the Prince Regent was dining there. The old man – your grandfather, I mean – took to his bed when he heard. But no harm was done. No harm. Young gentlemen will have their fling. Young ladies, too, sometimes.'

Issie's perplexity as to the point of this narrative was dissipated by her pity for the hare. Being unable to make much of Janet's intended comfort, she said, 'My sister seems out of sorts, too. Everyone does at home.'

Janet chuckled again. 'It's her condition, dear, that's all.'

Issie looked puzzled. Janet nodded coyly at the broody hens. Issie continued to look blank till a second and more significant nod enlightened her.

'Oh! Do you mean . . . do you really think so?' She started up in blushing excitement, forgetting Dileas.

'Of course it is. You'll be an auntie, my dear, God willing.'

Issie's whoops of delight and Dileas's yapping started the broodies clucking again. Issie sped home as soon as she could get away, jumping streams and skipping for very joy. It was not until she reached the expansive front steps that she paused with the thought, Then why is Augustus cross with all of us? But finding no possible answer, she forgot there was even a possible question and rushed upstairs to Helen's boudoir.

CHAPTER 10

While the laird of Drumharg studied his lesson on the hygienic advantages of water-closets, the children of Rona were dying of dysentery. The first to succumb was Rachel's baby. She had not survived his birth, and having never had his mother's milk, he had pined and wailed through a miserable half-year of colic and scrofula, to die, wizened and yellow, with the equinoctial gale obliterating his last feeble cries. Mór's newborn was the next. She had not expected even to carry it to term, because of the injuries she had suffered on the day of the burnings. Her right breast was withered and the left long dry, though the child still sucked, big-eyed and languid with starvation. She could not have raised the new baby, who died on the fourth day. It was a girl. 'Nothing but sorrow her life would have been to her,' said the grandmother, but Mór wept silently, with gritted teeth, curled on her bed of heather and rags under the cracking, heaving tarpaulin roof. The third victim was dead Kenneth's youngest, six years old but light as a toddler. Ciorstag washed and laid out the body with practised hands, as well as she could in the stinking hovel that was only a roof of driftwood and divots between two shoreline boulders. She did the job gently, but with indifference, even some relief. The child's father and her own had both died there in the first months, with the living crowded round them for shelter. Every death was a release, and meant a little more food for the survivors.

The storm raged week-long so that the bodies could not be conveyed to the burial ground on Fladday. The relatives buried them uncoffined in the only spot on Rona where the soil was deep enough, above the north-facing beach where they had first landed. Kenneth had been buried there too, in similarly wild weather.

'You'll say nothing about the wee lad's death,' said Ciorstag with command in her voice, as the men turned from filling in the grave. They averted their heads from her, ashamed she should speak so at such a time, when the other women were keening, but no one demurred, knowing what she meant. Kenneth's orphans were on the parish Poor Roll and as such received a small dole of money and meal. Even one half-sized pauper's rations would be something to share out.

It had been agreed that as soon as it was possible to get a boat across, Donald and John Blackie should go to Port Long to ask for more relief. It had been a difficult decision to take: not because of pride, which had been eaten away by a winter of privation, but because the loss of two men for a day effectively meant the loss of a day's fishing for one boat, and the Ardbuie crews said the haddock were due in. Not that the Rona boats ever caught much, having only botched-up or borrowed gear and being dependent on a full complement of oarsmen because of their inexpertise with sails. A turbulent winter had been no time to learn fishing for men who had done little before except drop a line for mackerel on a calm summer evening. Still, they were sure of some sort of catch if a shoal was in and not sure of Poor Relief.

Once away from the graves they fell to arguing over the matter.

'Hopeless!' said John of the Rock, heading straight for the shore to make what pickings he could from the low spring tide before anyone else got there. Collecting shellfish was work for women and children but the men had got used to it, stuffing the first few morsels of tangle stalk or mollusc flesh into their mouths before bowing sheepishly to the task. John, who had been seventeen years a widower, took to it easier than most.

'I'm thinking he's right.' Roderick crouched down on a boulder out of the wind, with his arms over his belly. The dysentery had gone for him badly, too.

'They'll have to be giving us something. I'll go myself.'

'You couldn't go further than I'd throw you, Hector.'

John Blackie's words were true. Recurrent bouts of fever had swelled the smith's joints and wasted his iron muscles.

'I was marching to Drumharg as well as you. And it's myself was fighting in Spain – '

'I might have been too, if I'd had the ill luck to ha' been born in time.'

'We should be sending the women. Minister's William would be feeling sorry for them. He'll no' take to strong men the same.'

'The women! Who'd be watching the cattle then?'

'What cattle? Five bags o' bones.'

'They'll get on to Harbottle's land and that bastard of a keeper will have his spyglass on them. I tell you, he'll have the lot off us.'

The bickering of empty stomachs flared and faded inconsequentially. Donald spoke through it. 'When there was famine in the land, Israel sent his sons to Egypt for corn, not his daughters. That's a sign to us written in God's holy Word. It's not right to send the women.'

The scriptural reference quelled them at once. There was a silence in its honour, till Roderick staggered modestly behind his boulder, groaning and fumbling with his tattered trousers.

'They'll surely give to us,' Hector said quietly. 'Look at us.'

Six gaunt, greying men with worry etched in grime in their faces, and four silent lads, hollow-cheeked and hollow-chested.

'No' bonny,' John Blackie agreed.

'If the Lord wills, they'll give to us,' said Donald.

'It's no good, my lads.' Minister's William spoke through a handkerchief applied to the constant drip at the end of his thin beaky nose. 'I can't do anything more for you.'

'How's that? I'm telling you, we're starving there, William. There's not a handful of meal with us. You know what the weather's been like. We couldn't fish a single day this past fortnight.'

The old man peered at the Register of Poor, cracking his fingers unhappily. 'I put old Angus Morrison from Kyles and his daughter Flora down, look. That's the best I can do.'

'There's Piper's Norrie and wee Nana. Donald told you about them coming from Ardmonach to us. Surely you can give orphans something. What are you here for, man?'

William shook his head. As sheriff's officer, it had been his fate to carry their notices of eviction; as inspector of the poor, he had no option but to deny them pauper status. He was a doleful man of duty to whom duty seemed more imperative the more it went against his inclinations. 'They may be orphans or may be not. But they have an elder brother who has recently got employment in Glasgow.'

'The lad has nothing to spare,' Donald pointed out politely, 'and neither have we on Rona. It weighs on us very hard to support these children when we can scarcely nourish our own.'

'Nourish!' John Blackie turned away bitterly.

'It pleased God to take John's child last week,' explained Donald in apology. 'And mine too,' he added.

'Ah!' William appeared momentarily from behind his handkerchief. 'My condolences. It's been a terrible winter – terrible, everywhere. But there's nothing I can do. I'm stretching the rules for you already, you know, remembering Fladday's kindness to my late uncle the minister, God rest his soul. No, you see the trouble is you shouldn't be on Rona at all. I've kept those that were already registered paupers while they were on Fladday on the roll, but that's the most I can do. You can't be registered as paupers if you're not supposed to be living in the parish any longer.'

John snatched the register from the desk, in sheer agony of frustration. Donald took it from him and replaced it between old William's trembling hands. 'We have been allotted the land we occupy on Rona since November last. We have paid a quarter's rent already.'

'That's where all our bloody cows went.'

William wiped his nose with increasing animation. 'Ah! So you're crofters, not squatters?'

'Yes, as we understand.'

'That's too bad. If you lease or own land you can't be registered for parish relief.'

John and Donald stared in speechless dismay.

'But you said if we *didn't* lease the land – '

'Ah . . . ah, no. Not if you *didn't* lease it: if you don't belong to the parish. If you belong to a parish – let's see, where did they go? – in Canada, mind you, arrangements might be different there – then that other parish has the responsibility.'

John was already at the door by the time the explanation was over.

'Wait, wait!'

They turned to him hopefully.

'These deaths . . . your unfortunate children . . . I don't believe you registered them?' He disappeared, scuffling under his desk among the dusty tomes and bundles of paper for the clean new volume pertinent to his third vocation. By the time he re-emerged, sneezing, they had worked out what he meant. John plunged outside with a stifled oath.

'It's against Her Majesty's laws not to notify deaths these days,' William observed warningly.

Donald stayed to give details. As William closed the register, he said slowly, 'There was a third death', and Kenneth's Lachie was written out of life and out of the Poor Roll.

Mr Cochrane, as parish minister, was entrusted by the new Destitution Board in Glasgow with the task of vetting applicants. Those whom he reckoned deserving were eligible for a pound of meal in return for a day's work on roads or ditches or some such project, with an extra allowance for children. Having little pressure on his time mid-week, he meditated several hours in his study on how to address the waiting candidates from Rona, praising God that their arrival had providentially inspired a sermon that could worthily be adapted for the edification of Port Long on the Sabbath following. He based his admonitions on the text 'Servants, obey your masters': for it was certain that the present trials of these stubborn people were a judgment upon them for their defiance of that earthly chief who had been placed over them by God, both to supply them with the necessities of life proper to their station and to test them for obedience: whose will, therefore, stood in all things lawful, as the revealed will of the Almighty. Mr Cochrane touched upon the parable of the prodigal son, which made plain that those who fell on hard times through their own waywardness could expect no mercy if they asked for bread alone, but only if they begged forgiveness first, with broken and contrite hearts which God would not despise, and that those sinners who would in their pride fill their mouths with dainties, rather than hungering and thirsting after righteousness, would never be hearkened to until they ate the very dust and ashes of repentance. Furthermore, if children as yet incapable of either sin or repentance were suffering, this was none other than the deserved chastisement of their wicked parents, as decreed in the Scriptures: the sins of the fathers shall be visited on the children.

The Rona men heard him out – Donald with hanging head, John with his eyes fixed stonily on the minister's gold watch-chain, which followed every phrase in long rhythmic heaves. As Mr Cochrane sank back in his chair, breathing hard through his nostrils, John's gaze switched to his pink face. Mr Cochrane tensed somewhat and even half rose; he was not used to such a look. But his misguided parishioner's first words were civil enough.

'Mr Cochrane, are you saying that you will not allow anyone from Rona to apply for Destitution work?'

'If I permitted such a thing, I should be flying in the face of God, who in His mercy is pressing you to penitence.'

'Don't you understand?' John slammed both hands down on the minister's chair arms. Mr Cochrane strained backwards, rigid, averting his nose from the sour breath of malnutrition. 'Our children are dying – starving. We have no food – no seed for next year. We had to sell our beasts to pay the rent; the few left are starving like we are, nothing to give them but fishguts and seaweed. If they bite a blade of Harbottle's grass, his keeper's after us – the deer are coming, the deer are coming – drive out the men, bring in the sheep and the deer. Our own chief threw us out of our homes and turned his back on us to bring in the sheep and the deer. Now it's Harbottle, that keeper and Harbottle's men, we've got no houses, we made shelters, poor shelters with clothes and sails over oars, holes in the rocks, that's all – but they wouldn't leave us even with that, they tore them apart three times, three times, Cochrane, you fat swine – my wife died then, in labour in the rain. Will of God, you say Cochrane, God damn you for it, may your fat arse stick to your fancy chair – '

Donald dragged him sobbing to the door. 'I beg you to forgive him, Mr Cochrane. It pleased God to take his child last week.' This time he did not add, 'And mine too.'

Cochrane goggled, speechless, his pink face blanched to the damp pallor of a skate's belly.

John wept and raved half the long tramp to Ardbuie, staggering like one drunk, so that people turned off their path rather than meet them.

They returned to poverty more racking than before. They had already bartered everything not necessary for survival in exchange for meal from Boreray: shoes, clothing, furniture, wedding rings, Ranald's clock, Annag's six china plates, old Angus's turnip watch. The cattle had been bled time and time again to turn a dusting of meal into black pudding; Ciorstag's white cockerel and most of the other poultry had been eaten. The small strip of machair near the graves had been plundered for roots of wild carrot and silverweed before the foliage ever showed. The shoreline around the settlement was scoured all but clean of dulse and shellfish; if they scavenged further round the coast, they could count on a visit from Harbottle's keeper, who lived in Ardbuie with his spyglass trained on Rona. When it was too dark or foggy for him to see, the women and children scrambled over the hills, stuffing their clothes with handfuls of deergrass to eke out the miserable grazing of their stock, but by March the upper slopes were worn to black slime by six months' deadening rain and they could find nothing.

As winter tilted into blustery spring, a new necessity pressed upon them. They must plant crops and hope to harvest them or they faced the prospect of a second winter worse than the first. But there was little seed to be had on Boreray and what there was sold dear in the general dearth following the potato failure. Rona sold its remaining hens, even a broody on hopeful eggs; they sold three young dogs to Eagleton's shepherds and the corpses of four old ones to make dogskin fishing floats; they sold the billy-goat and the great brass-clasped unreadable English Bible which had been the bard's treasure and his father's father's. They got a bushel or so of corn in one place, and more in another, and a hundred or so precious tubers of the blue potatoes said to be most resistant to blight. They began to make their lazy-beds – long ridges of untilled ground heaped with seaweed and dung between drainage ditches, with the sods from the ditches turned earth side up on top of the seaweed. By custom it was women's work but necessity drove the men to help, shamefacedly in ones and twos at first, but later openly, as if they had always done it. Even with the whole community at the task, it was slow and exhausting for people so weakened by hunger and disease. Their ground lay on the dank north-facing slopes above their huts, sunless pockets of peat and gravel between ribs of unforgiving rock, and in the marshy basin of the interior. The first situation was unpromising, the second impossible, but in desperation they tried, clambering up the steep hillside under painful loads of dung scooped up by the children and bladder-wrack collected after dark from Mr Harbottle's coastline, to lighten the oozy black peat.

If the toil was grinding in itself, worse still was the contrast with the old days, when the hopeful planting of the crops had been a time of songs and banter. No one sang the old songs that year: even the old customs of times and dates failed, for though they started as usual on the Friday of the new moon, it had waned long before they finished. Sometimes as they worked in silence, one of the women would begin to weep and within minutes the whole dejected company would be squatting in their half-dug plots, sunk in a lethargic dream of sun-washed Fladday, more kindly and fruitful to their exiled vision than it had ever been in reality.

Annag made a lament for their distress:

> Sorrow is in my heart
> when I think of the peace that is taken from us.
> I see the fair fields under crops,
> I see the fine cows in calf,
> and the girls going to the milking with songs and
>   laughter.
> Sorrow is in my heart,
> all is taken from us,
> the people are gone in the white-sailed ships,
> and the land is given by the hatred of the stranger
> to the devouring jaws of sheep.

It was the only song sung that spring.

CHAPTER 11

FROM MR CHARLES HARBOTTLE
OF 120 TRAFALGAR ROAD, BRADFORD

TO MR GREEN, FACTOR, DRUMHARG ESTATES   30TH APRIL 1847

Sir,

I write to protest in the Strongest Terms against your
Fa.-in-law's so-called tenants on the Island of Rona. As I
understood at the time of leasing this property that I had
sole Rights over it which I never had over the adjacent
tract of Boreray, being there much Annoyed by your
sheep-farms which impede my Sporting, now I find that
by some Sleight you have withheld my interest in the
Lower ground of Rona except sporting. This I take Much
Amiss but if you will have Tenants there which I was not
given to Expect, still I will not Countenance that they
should infringe my Rights. My Keeper gives me to understand in a Communication of 12th Inst. that they continue
to do this, viz. by grazing their Cattle on the high ground
which I aim to put under Deer, and it is feared they may
have the Insolence to burn it off to get a finer growth
which is too late to be done now on account of Nesting
Game Birds, and if I find they have done so I will not
hesitate to take Action against them and your Fa.-in-law.
Furthermore these people are doing all manner of mis-
chief on the shore, removing seaweed and Shellfish
which I much Object to, as I have a Party coming who
wish to get Seals and such activities may disturb this

Game over which I have a Right. Also, Sir, if your Tenants take or disturb the Sea Fowls or their Eggs which are on the Cliffs my Keeper says he will cut their Ropes. I trust your Assurance will be forthcoming that all these Abuses will be stopped Forthwith and especially that the Cattle will be kept penned in the lower ground.

　I remain, Sir,
　　Yrs Faithfully,
　　　Charles Harbottle

Green curled his lip at the gauche ornateness of the signature, then pursed it in annoyance at the lack of ink in the inkwell. It was a commodity the previous occupant of the study had seldom required: as long as the whisky decanter was well filled, the laird had found the room satisfactory for his purposes of reminiscing with friends and whiling away wet mornings. Farquhar was summoned to fetch writing materials immediately from the dark office in the kitchen region, which Green had recently vacated. The reply to Mr Harbottle was terse.

Sir,

I am in receipt of your letter of 30th Ult. Your lease conveys to you sporting rights over the whole Island of Rona and full tenancy over those areas of more than one hundred feet above sea level.

　Should you suspect an encroachment on your rights, your redress is to prove it at a court of law, against those individuals concerned.

　I am, Sir,
　　Yours faithfully,
　　　Augustus Green

Green sealed the letter with some satisfaction. At the time he had arranged Mr Harbottle's subtly worded lease he had retained rights to the coastal strip to allow for the unlikely event of a second kelp boom, or some other new industry yet unforeseen – a market for salt winkles, or the discovery by Mr Robert Thoroughgood of valuable minerals, perhaps. But since it happened that the boggy interior of the island also lay below one hundred feet, it had been convenient to relocate the remnant of Fladday's population there. The intransigence of the people in the matter of emigration could have caused embarrassment, would perhaps even have been taken up by the press as evidence of ill-treatment, had there not been sufficient acreage to resettle them out of the public's eye.

He pondered momentarily, slightly less satisfied than before. The talk at the time of the ship calling in on Fladday had been unpleasant and rather highly coloured. It seemed certain the captain had been disgracefully drunk and that he had over-stepped his duties. Eagleton claimed that he was formerly a slaver, but the man tended to make jokes in doubtful taste, which could almost certainly be discounted. Nevertheless, Green sat for a moment rubbing his jaw before turning his attention to the remaining letters that had accumulated in a week's absence. All were addressed to Sir Hector, but since the old man showed little interest in business and certainly no aptitude for it, his son-in-law had recently given orders that he should not be troubled with mails. The top document bore the stamp of the Society in Scotland for the Propagation of Christian Knowledge. 'Rona again!' exclaimed Green, with some irritation.

Dear Sir,

Having been called by the Grace of God to guide your people on the isle of Rona unto the path of salvation, I repaired there some three weeks past to test their faith and view their condition, in order to know what I should need to bring to them. I give thanks to God that their spiritual state is no worse than it is, for I found several well versed in the Scriptures, though illiterate; and while not by any means free of Popish superstition, they are eager for instruction, so that in my two days with them I gave four sermons which were eagerly listened to. Their material condition, however, is so wretched that the memory of it kept me from study for a week after my return, the while I earnestly prayed God to alleviate their many miseries. Sir, I beheld these people, who look to you as their kinsman and benefactor, living among the rocks of the seashore, with no roof but rags and drift-wood, forced together without regard for sex or age, which is the greater harm as many, particularly of the younger sort, have scarcely sufficient clothing to cover their nakedness. Furthermore, they are much weakened by starvation and sickness, having suffered extremely in this past winter, more so than any I have seen, and six have died. Yet they are meek in their sufferings, and make no outcry against God, and when I chid one for selling the Good Book to buy meal, he appeared very penitent, only complaining against Mr Cochrane, who is the Minister supposed to attend to their welfare, because he would not allow them relief through the offices of the Destitution Board.

Since my return thence, I have written to Mr Cochrane, addressing him as a co-worker in Christ, but to date received no reply. Also I have appealed to the Trustees of the Destitution Fund in Glasgow, and they assure me, Sir, that once the people are accounted my flock (though I am not yet ordained), I may judge whether or no they be worthy of relief, only it is required that their Proprietor vouch for me to them, and also that he advise of some labour which may be done in return for said relief, that the poor 'eat not the bread of idleness'. I beg, Sir, that you will see fit to satisfy these conditions with all haste.

I remain, Sir, your obedient servant, and brother in the love of Christ.

Duncan Macleay

Green, having begun his homeward journey before dawn, yawned several times during his perusal of this missive, but conceded inwardly that while Mr Macleay's prose lacked mellifluous touches his sentiments were entirely worthy, particularly pertaining to the unwisdom of charity given to the idle. Such appointments as his must necessarily lead to the improvement of the people, while reflecting credit on the landlords who supported them.

Mr Cochrane, by contrast, hardly got a reading. His denunciations, by turns fawning and venomous, of his patron, his patron's tenants, the Antichrist, humanity, English factors and the modern age, filled Green with distaste. It was exactly the kind of touchy Highland pride, though here in clerical garb, that had formed the chief obstacle to progress in every enterprise on the Drumharg estates: a devotion to outmoded and even harmful tradition, whether to be seen in a pack of dirty islanders idling all day with their hands in their pockets while their miserable womenfolk went laden like donkeys, or in the laird's ridiculous perambulations through Inverharg, addressing his farm labourers as if they were the fighting men of a century before.

More sympathetically received was the letter on behalf of the Trustees of the Destitution Fund in Glasgow requesting that some work of public utility be made available to the indigent population of Rona. Green penned a cordial reply, pausing only over the precise nature of the work. Public utility on Rona was an elusive quality. A road could benefit no one but Mr Harbottle, yet the building of the people's own houses, or drainage of their own land, in return for wages, would have just that undesirable consequence which the scheme should avoid, dispensing in such cases double charity for nothing. He pondered over the

111

natural resources of Rona, which consisted of stone. A jetty was set aside for the same reason as cottages, a mission house for Mr Macleay on the grounds that the Free Church had ample funds for such a purpose. The remaining stony possibility was a wall, which he considered. 'Ha!' he uttered aloud, presently. Having completed the reply to the trustees, he tore up his letter to Mr Harbottle and rewrote it with an additional final paragraph:

> In consideration of your request, however, I have given
> orders for the construction of a drystone wall of sufficient
> height at the one-hundred-foot contour around the basin
> which forms the common land of the small tenants. By
> this means their stock may be retained within, and the
> deer without.

Green sat back, well satisfied, before closing it. The plan had the merit of being to no one's direct advantage, yet it would certainly produce a greater orderliness in the small tenants' conduct. As for Mr Harbottle – Green's satisfaction grew to a smile in imagination of his fury that a quarter of the available cottongrass and deergrass was to be barred from his deer, as a result of his own demands. Green sealed the letter with slower precision than usual, enjoying the gracious opulence of the laird's marble-banded desk, set upon ebonised and gilded sphinxes. It seemed fitting, when bounds had been passed, to make the culprit the engineer of his own discomfiture.

A previous occasion when the punishment had been made to fit the crime obtruded itself, being never far from his thoughts. The warmth of his satisfaction over his adroit dealing with Harbottle faded, ashen, in the searing memory of that other letter, the intercepted, the destroyer. Words, in her hand, to another: meaning either the unimaginable, or very little. He had chosen, and still chose, to believe the latter: 'Then, my dear, since I have seen it written in your own hand that you desire a *true* marriage, that is what we must strive for.' The circumstances of that speech of mastery sent a hot pulse through his veins. She had not resisted. But the unimaginable lurked, still.

He paced to the window, flicking up his coat tails, and around the room, surveying with compressed lips the policies and possessions that the decision for a true marriage, rather than the less magnanimous one, had made certainly his. A passing agitation stopped him in his dreary perambulation before one of Sir Hector's paintings, of a scantily clad young female attending lambs and kids. It must be removed. Though the subject was pastoral, there was that in the pose and expression of the figure which made it scarcely decent for even the maid-servants to see, and he had always considered it unfit for the daughters of the house. Such laxity had doubtless contributed its effect. The chill of private grief that had sent him pacing round the room seized upon him, but being habituated to regard it as unworthy, he seated himself again in the imposing lion-legged chair to deal with the last letter, a bill from Messrs A. & J. Mackenzie, Builders, of Inverness. There were several items not to his liking: lead piping one hundred feet in excess of specification, four ball valves where only three had been installed, and carpentry much overpriced. He scribbled: 'Amend as per your quotation of 15th March', and set off to give orders for the immediate removal of Sir Hector's nymph. As he turned at the door for a quick appraisal of the room, his eye was caught by the shining black rotundity of the sphinxes' bosoms. He considered whether it might not be wiser to have them draped to accord with modern taste, but on examining the classical sobriety of their features, decided it was unnecessary. A blacking out of certain unbecoming spots of gilding would be sufficient.

' "The Cheviots rose before me in frowning majesty; not indeed with the sublime variety of rock and cliff which characterise mountains of the primary class, but huge, round-headed, and clothed with a dark robe of russet, gaining, by their extent and desolate appearance, an influence upon the imagination which possessed a character of its own." '

Issie broke off, searching for some sign of enthusiasm in her sister. 'I do love Sir Walter Scott's novels. The description is so fine, isn't it Helen?'

Helen shifted among her cushions. 'The light is bothering me. Please draw the curtain, Issie.'

Issie obeyed, but could not bring herself to shut out all of the bright May noon.

'Completely,' Helen demanded.

Issie's hand faltered. The sunlight sparkling on the new beech leaves filled her with something near desperation. Helen's cluttered boudoir was close and perfumed. As if sensing her reluctance, Dileas groaned outside the tyrant's door, in exaggerated martyrdom.

'Oh, Helen, it's such a beautiful day! Wouldn't you like to wrap up an come out with me?'

'You sound just like Augustus. You can go yourself if you don't wish to stay with me.' She had already begun to sniff and dab her eyes. Tears were always near the surface, filling Issie with instant dismay: Helen of old had been customarily serene. Issie ran to embrace her, contrite. There was a bitter tang of laudanum on her sister's lips.

'Of course I'll stay, of course I will. Please don't cry, Helen dear. You used to say, don't you remember, you always told me not to cry so much, it would spoil my looks?'

Helen leaned away from her into the cushions. 'Don't gabble, child.'

'I – oh – ' Issie's own tears rose in her throat. She forced them back, for there was something she had decided to say, that she must say, or stifle. 'I don't want to upset you, but don't you see – don't you think – I know you feel unwell because – of your condition – but it seems so wrong to lie in here moping when everything's lovely outside. It's ungrateful.'

'Ungrateful!' Helen sat up with suddenly wild eyes, but relapsed fretfully on her pillows. 'What have I to be grateful for?'

Issie, appalled, stood speechless. At last she managed, in a small squeaky voice, 'Aren't you pleased about the baby?'

There was no answer. Helen's back was turned, showing the light curls on her nape, unexpressive of the turmoil within. Issie stared, with pounding heart, as if she could make those silk-fine wisps yield up the truth, the burden that was crushing her family.

'Augustus is, isn't he?' she asked, knowing clearly and with pain that she was turning the knife in the wound.

Helen faced her with such a look in her eyes as to make Issie stammer 'I'm sorry', almost before her question was finished.

'Oh, even *you* know something. No, you don't know. You don't know what marriage is. Girls dream of a handsome lover – I did, I know – '

An outbreak of tears brought Issie to her side again. This time it was Helen who threw her arms about her sister's neck.

'Oh, Issie, Issie, it isn't like that at all – maybe at first. Don't marry, Issie.' She mopped her eyes and sat back rather more composed, patting her hair into place. 'Of course you won't, you haven't the looks, but you can't conceive how it is.' She pulled distractedly at the tassels of her cushions. 'It is – you cannot be yourself again, or have friends, letters . . . nothing is private, you have no secrets, all are known.' Her fingers twisted so violently that a tassel fell to pieces, scattering gold threads across her lap. 'All known, even – even the most degrading . . . ' her voice faded in a whimper and she hid her face among the cushions.

Issie trembled, hot and cold, thinking against her will of the degrading thing, Elsie with the linen bag. No, it couldn't be that. She forced it from her mind, with the truth she searched for hovering near, but her resolution was insufficient to grasp it. She turned instead to the well-understood ritual of comforting her sister, with cologne on a handkerchief and a small glass of sherry wine. Augustus's tread in the corridor, usually so welcome to her, made her quail as if from Bluebeard. She rose to her feet with a terrified glance at her sister, but Helen merely pouted, clicking her tongue, and shook her skirts out over the couch, leaving Issie baffled.

Augustus seemed in good spirits. He kissed Helen, declaring she looked flushed and must have some air, and threw the window up; but when Helen complained peevishly of the draught, he shut it with an apology. For Issie he had news.

'I have today had a letter from Mr Macleay, who has been appointed missionary to Rona, where the natives of Fladday removed. He seems a sound and worthy fellow, who will doubtless do much to encourage the population in sober and industrious ways, as well as teaching them the Scriptures. At his instigation I have arranged for labouring work at which they may honestly earn their daily bread, if they apply themselves, for at present they are both indolent and indigent. I know you will be pleased to hear of this, Issie, for you take a particular interest in the land of your little dog's birth.'

Issie was, indeed, very pleased. She often wished she knew which of the men from Fladday had gone to Canada and which to Rona. Augustus cut through her exclamations. 'The said little dog is pining outside the door. You have sufficient time, I think, to take him for a walk before dinner.'

Issie jumped up readily, but as Augustus ushered her out, there was something about the rigid stillness of Helen's head against the pillows that made her hesitate in the corridor. Dileas, though, was already prancing on the Turkey carpet, chasing his tail with absurd glee. Downstairs in the hall he barked defiance at Sir Hector's nymph, propped against the wall on her way to the attic. Bending to pull him away, Issie was caught by the girl's eyes. She dropped on her knees to look at the picture. It had been a favourite when she was little, because of the baby animals, but later disregarded. Now, as her gaze wandered over the curves of plump flesh, sunset-cloud-pink and luxuriant, it

was as if she had never seen it before. Her arms folded uncon-
sciously over her own flat chest. The nipples stung with sudden
pain. She dropped her arms quickly, feeling her hands brush her
skinny muscular thighs through five layers of clothing. With a hot
blush beating round her ears, she ran outside after Dileas.

When they were private in the wood, she began to talk to
him. 'I'll never marry, Dileas. I shan't have the chance, but even
if I did . . . ' Her unheeded voice dried up. It had sprung to her
mind that if Helen had married Major Drysdale, Augustus might
still have done well for himself by marrying the laird's other
daughter.

'Oh!' she shouted, outraged, appalled, pushing at her hair and
clothes as if at a shirt of flame.

CHAPTER 12

Secret as foxes', seven pairs of eyes watched silently from the shattered boulders of Mr Harbottle's deer forest. The gentlemen went up and down between the funny-looking spyglass things, talking in loud voices to the ones who were doing the work – whatever sort of work it was – hammering bits of wood into the ground. The hammer blows echoed tap-tap-tap across the valley and back again, taptaptaptaptap. Maybe the hammering men were gentlemen too; they were wearing clean shirts and one had a watch-chain glinting in the morning sun across his waistcoat. But the others were gents for sure: they wore coats with long skirts like Macdonald Kilmory used to in church. Very hot they looked in the dancing June sunshine, wiping their faces with handkerchiefs in all lovely bright colours. 'Lovely,' mouthed Neiliann, wistfully. It was a red one with blue checks.

One of the gentlemen got so hot he tossed his top-hat over his shoulder. 'Oh, see that,' squeaked Lala; he had thought it was the toff's head was that shape. The other children shushed him and froze animal still, their skinny limbs contouring to the bumps and crevices of the stones. But the hatless gentleman's next action was too much for them. Whistling cheerfully, he flipped out his unmentionable thing and peed a sparkling arc in the air.

The children boiled among the rocks.

'Ooh, he's not turning his back.'

'Mammy walloped me for that.'

'Don't look, Kennag. You're looking too, Nana.'

'Sh! *Ssh!* They'll hear us. Shut up, Muti – Ewan, shut up!'

It was too late. The immodest young man was leaping up the hillside even as he twitched his buttons back. The wretched spies rose as one and fled, but little Lala stumbled on the sharp scree and fell screaming. The terrible No-Hat Man caught him up, laughing loudly. Lala went stiff with fright. The other children faltered, started back, ran on, stopped, catching at each other and pointing. The No-Hat Man was shouting something at them and the other two gentlemen were sauntering up the slope. Ewan and Nana began to wail too. The others tried to shove Shonny in Lala's direction.

'Go on, he's your wee brother.'

'You'd better. They might take him away.'

'Go on, we'll tell your mam.'

But in the end it was rickety-coughing Neiliann who trotted back across the scree and stood with clasped hands before the strangers. They were all talking in loud voices – in English it must be – and laughing, but Lala's face looked terrible. His eyes were squeezed tight shut and his teeth gripped as if he was dying, and he had shat himself. One of the toffs was holding his nose about it. Neiliann bowed her head in shame and stood mutely suppliant.

The gentlemen went through their pockets, and one found acid drops, and another humbugs. Neiliann stared. She remembered long ago, they had these to suck in church; Mammy took them to stop them coughing. The No-Hat Man took her hand, opened it, and put one of each kind of sweet in it. 'For you,' he said, in Gaelic or something like it.

Neiliann, in mid-cough, stuffed them both in her mouth – a great ecstatic burst of tingling, crackling sweetness – and darted back to her wary friends, shouting, coughing and munching at once.

'Oho, that'll bring them running!' The No-Hat Man let his smelly captive subside on the ground, waving an acid drop under his less objectionable end.

He was right. The ragged flock streamed back across the scree and stood before the clean and well-fed strangers, looking up.

'Good God!'

'Little Arabs.'

'They don't know how to beg, though.'

Without clamour or outstretched hands: seven pairs of famished grime-ringed eyes, seven bundles of stinking rags made formless by filth and age. A boy had a man's waistcoat down to his knees, which would have held four of their stick-thin bodies together, a girl with half her face eczematously scabbed wore nothing but a tattered shawl, tied with rope about the waist. They crammed the sweets dealt out to them in handfuls, spluttering and slavering with haste. The biggest boy spat his back into his hand, shouting at the rest. Some regurgitated, others gulped, all bowed their heads and closed their eyes, even the smallest.

'A grace! Would you believe it?'

'They're not heathens, then.'

Fervent munching resumed, interspersed with stares and whispers. The hatless surveyor shouted down to the men at work below.

'Hi! Bring up the hamper.' The hamper held fabulous treasure: bread, cheese, mutton, eggs disappeared into ravenous mouths and folds of unspeakable clothing. Some of the children, filled, rose to scuttle home with their booty.

'Baccy for the dads?' suggested someone.

Searching of pockets produced an ample amount. It was tucked away with the chunks of mutton and half-eaten bannocks.

'What about their mammas?'

'We'd find them too strong for our taste, I think.' But the No-hat Man pulled out his beautiful blue-checked red handkerchief. Neiliann's jaws stopped moving in wonder.

'Here – *gu do mhamaidh.*'

She shook her head, sadly, darting glances at the unorphaned who might be the lucky recipients. '*Cha'neil mamaidh agam.*'

'Oh – bad luck, little girl. For you, then. *Dh'thusa ma tha.*' He tucked it up her sleeve. After she had run off he wiped his hands on a tuft of heather.

'Oh, what dirty little animals. What deplorable gypsies, savages, leavings and scrapings of humanity. I've seen organ-grinder's monkeys better-dressed – and better-mannered.'

'And better fed,' one of his colleagues remarked, shaking his head.

'Better fed, certainly. That goes without saying. The organ-grinder makes his living by the monkey, he'll feed it in recognition. But the laird, now. The laird can't turn a penny from the likes of these dancing in the market-place. Believe me, if he could he would – *ergo*, they can't dance. They're good Presbyterians, after all – dance today, hellfire tomorrow. Better starve here and wait for pie in the sky.'

The young man threw himself full-length in the heather, thumbing his nose at the empty blue.

'You go too far, Mr Gibb. Their condition is pitiable, but – '

'But what? Come now, pray enlighten me.'

'But your flippancy should be confined to human error.'

'Mustn't mock the divine plan, eh, Thomson?'

'That's what I mean, I suppose.'

Gibb kicked his heels at the June heavens.

'Divine plan? Divine fiasco if you ask me – or even if you don't. That factor now, he's spending a small fortune to get this damned wall in the right place, just so that he can crow over a neighbour. Spending enough to feed and clothe these people for the next ten years, I'll bet – *and* house them. Oh Lord, we haven't seen the houses yet. Never mind, we can guess about them. Well, what do you say, Thomson? Kemp? Is there anything divine in that plan?'

His companions looked embarrassed. Thomson coughed and Kemp shrugged.

'It's criminal, vile. The work we're doing here is immoral. It's lining my old man's coffers, but it's immoral all the same. We're seeing the same thing all over the north and west: starving people, or none at all where the job's been done properly, and lairds and baa-lambs getting fat. One of these days I'm going to investigate it – see what's been happening in the Highlands in the last forty years. I'll have to wait till the old man croaks, mind you, he's even surer of the divine plan than you are, Thomson. It's done all right for him, of course – and for all of us here today. Three cheers for the divine plan!'

Thomson and Kemp found it expedient to ignore young Mr Gibb's prattling. One day the firm would be Gibb and Son. Gibb found himself alone with the empty hamper, but cheered anyway.

The children, all of them, were sick after their unaccustomed banquet. Nevertheless, it was the beginning of what counted on Rona as better times. The surveyors worked for two weeks, lodging in Calum the Merchant's house at Gnipadale in Boreray and conveying a hamper of provisions from that rich source every day.

'All charged to the Daddy-o!' young Gibb took delight in pointing out. 'He knows I have a hearty appetite.'

There were other things, too. The young girls got some combs and a mirror, and took again to grooming and braiding each other's hair in the long summer evenings as they watched the cows. The older men denounced this as vanity, having longer and bleaker memories, but the clay pipes and tobacco were not vanity, nor the flagon of whisky delivered when Roderick's son Ewan told the No-Hat Man he had a new wee brother. The women complained that the early celebration was tempting fairies and providence, but the baby lived. 'Maybe the wee drop whisky was doing him good,' they said then.

Their gratitude to God for this bounty ascended morning and evening in prayers and hymns, but the givers they held in contempt. They were the instruments of the hated factor; their habits were outlandish, their levity shocking; they were no kin of any Macdonalds, they were not even Highlanders. Only the little children treated them, after a while, as friends. Yet such was the customary Highland civility, even among such scrapings and leavings, that young Mr Gibb left Rona assured of his own popularity and swearing one day to fight a fight for such as these.

Gibb's explanation of the purpose of their work, politely received to his face, was generally disbelieved, though it raised sufficient hopes to cause an anxious preoccupation with the idea.

'Bloody nonsense. You heard Cochrane. We're to starve till we repent. No Destitution work coming here.'

'Maybe he's changed his mind. Maybe Eachann mac Sheorais was telling him he had to. He paid for Gibb and them to come here; the wall will be his notion.'

'Green's notion, more like. Keep us from a blade of his tenant's grass.'

'Keep the deer out of ours too, though. If Harbottle puts deer here they'll eat the lot – such as it is.'

'Keep deer out? Deer will jump anything we can build.'

Only Donald had much hope of the plan. 'It's a providence, a double providence. We will be getting the food we need, and the land will be ours. We could drain it. We could have our crops growing where there is only bog now, if God blesses the work to us.'

They listened to him respectfully. Since the removal Donald talked less of justice and more of God's will. No one took that lightly: they were proud of his piety, as they had once been of his father's before him. His steadfast faith was something saved from their ruined past, something by which the world and God might see that the men of Rona were worth something after all. Nevertheless, there was an understanding that on practical matters Donald was no longer always the best person to consult, now that his mind was so taken up with religion. The general opinion was that his prognostication about the wall would never happen and that if it did, it must be to their disadvantage.

There was much else to do during the long daylight of midsummer: weeding crops, turning and stacking peat, and building houses to replace the desperate shelters of the previous winter. For a short while, in the anodyne June sunshine, life was tolerable, and food, if not plentiful, at least sufficient. The cows, all but Peggy's, were in milk again, there were sea-trout to be had in the glimmering midnight when the keeper couldn't see, and the coins and keepsakes left by the surveyors could be traded for meal at the merchant's in Gnipadale. But in July an early rain set in, day after wet grey day. The scarce turf around the settlement grew lush and green but the boggy hinterland was perilous for the cattle and lay many days entirely under water. Soon only two cows and Neiliann's nanny goat had much milk to spare. The herring shoals did not arrive that year and the chilling of the water delayed the mackerel. Blight reappeared in the potatoes, as the older and wiser had predicted; even more of a disappointment was the grain crop, which promised poorly after so much effort, with short stems and thin ears sparsely pricking from waterlogged black ground. By late August, the men had begun to gather again sometimes by the surveyors' two rows of white-painted posts, which led from the saddle above the settlement, through rusty bog-grasses and grey pools, to the straight line of boulder beach on the south shore of the island. Beyond that lay the steep green hump of Out End, green even in the drifting rain and mist – but that was Harbottle's, whose sheep grew fat and fleecy on the rich herbage of its basalt slopes.

Its greenness was compelling. Everyone gazed at it, wordlessly, before the foot-shuffling and throat-clearing preparatory to discussion began. Its precluded richness added extra bitterness to the forlorn columns of fading white stumps straggling through the bog.

'Never came to anything. Like everything else.'

'Them bloody deer will be fattening on our land soon as he gets them over here.'

'Maybe they've just forgotten. Maybe it's Cochrane holding things up.'

'Maybe they think we're gettin' on with it? We should've been working at it, maybe?'

They did not remember that they had called it a crazy scheme. With winter looming it had become their only hope. Day after day they talked of going to ask Mr Cochrane if relief was coming.

'We'll have to go. Nothing else for it.'

'Ay, soon. We'll have to.'

But no one felt like being of the party to confront the minister. In the end it was Donald alone who walked to Port Long to ask what was happening. Mr Cochrane was too much occupied to give a hearing that day, but on receiving Donald's enquiry through the housekeeper, he returned an answer to the effect that Destitution Board funds were only available where an honest day's work could be seen to be done, and that since there was no one resident on Rona of sufficient probity to vouch for the labour, the project could not go ahead until such a person could be found.

The message was sourly received on Rona. Donald was more distressed by his friends' complaints than by the fears he shared with them.

'We must be patient with what the Lord is sending us. He didn't say we'd not be given work, only that we need an overseer. One will come in God's own time.'

Any mention of the Deity was enough to produce decent resignation, but people were saying later, behind his back, that Donald was touched in the head.

Mór knew what they were saying and came straight out with it to John Blondie's wife Seonag. 'How will you criticise him? There's none of the other menfolk would even walk to Port Long with him to see the minister. I don't know what was at them. Was it laziness, now, or was it they hadn't a good courage for it? They'd be needing more of the Top-Hats' whisky first, maybe.'

She left them with her head high, but tears stung her eyes. Her own brother had once given the minister what he deserved, but not her husband. He had stood before him meek and mild, while the children died. The shame he had put on her, the shame of his misjudgements, in which everyone had believed, had never left her since the terrible day of the ship. His different way of seeing things, which she had once loved, was now a worm in her soul. She told it to no one, not even to her mother. She would have had Donald see it, but not by laying it before him; and he, blinded by righteousness, saw nothing nearer home than Adam's fall in silences or spiteful words, and humbled by righteousness, never made the reproaches that would have drawn the truth from her. And this humility and pride were growing to the same thing, for it no longer mattered to him what other people thought, if he was right with himself, with God.

So when Mór said that evening, 'I hear you're counselling patience, Donald', he replied only 'Yes', though they were the first words she had spoken to him since his return from Port Long.

'You used to be talking more of *justice*.' She put an emphasis on the word.

'I didn't understand well. We must wait on the Lord, for mercy, not justice.'

'For a roof over our heads, maybe.' They were crouched, the two of them, with wee Donald on Effie's knee, and oblivious old Uncle Dougie, in the shelter of the drystone walls that would become a tolerable home once thatched.

Donald looked preoccupied. 'I was meaning to see about the roof tomorrow, Mór.'

She waited.

'I'm thinking the Lord has put other work in my way.'

'And what's that?'

'The wall is there to be done. Maybe for no recompense, yet, but that will be in God's hands. He has made it a sign for us, when we had no hope of anything, and maybe a test, too. I'm thinking we should get on with the work God has set for us. So I'll be at that tomorrow, as a sort of token.'

'My brother John might help us to a roof, then.'

'Maybe so. I'd rather he would be persuaded by me to do in faith the work God sent us. I'll talk of it to everyone.'

Mór took the boy from Effie, parting his hair for lice till her fingers stopped shaking. 'Donald, do you know they are saying you're crazy?'

Donald sighed. 'Ay, I know. I wish they would not. "Whosoever shall say Thou fool, shall be in danger of hell fire." Effie, pass me the Book for the psalm.'

He chose the first: 'Blessed is the man that walketh not in the counsel of the ungodly.'

Next day, alone, he worked on the wall, and every day after that, when there was no fishing, nicking a tally of the days on one of the markers. He had got to his fifth, labouring in the rain to pack the foundation trench with rock before it filled with water, when Ciorstag came to Mór where she was cutting divots for her roof.

'Donald was right. I've seen the missionary coming. He'll give account of the work. We'll get our dole.'

'How so? The mission house isn't built yet, even.'

Ciorstag, not used to having her visions doubted, bridled, but saw, perhaps, that Donald's wife did not want him to be right. She said, smiling, 'The others will be helping him now and wishing they'd got out there when he told them.'

Next morning every man on Rona turned out for work, and some of the women too. Mr Macleay arrived that evening on an Ardbuie fishing boat, unclerically attired in a shepherd's rough plaid and trousers, with stout boots on his feet and a canvas-wrapped pack on his back. He found the entire population, made as neat and clean as possible for the occasion, lined up to meet him. He was a fit young man, but they seized his pack from his back and carried him ashore, and his baggage after him. There was not much of it: a second canvas-wrapped bundle and a wooden trunk. Mr Macleay stood on the trunk to lead worship and then to make his speech. He used Gaelic, but not of the dialect native to his flock. By speaking slowly and by opening his bundles, he made himself understood at last. He had heard the Destitution work was delayed for want of an overseer, and had come forthwith. He had brought with him, in one bundle, a tent of the sort used by soldiers (for was not he a soldier in the service of Christ?) which would accommodate him till the mission house was built. The other bundle contained meal and other provisions, sufficient that he would not burden them with his wants, but not overmuch (for were they not all instructed to ask for bread day by day?). In the wooden chest, he explained, jumping down to unlock it and raise the lid, were Bibles and catechisms, one for every soul on Rona.

'And let it not surprise you that a minute hence I stood so with the Word of God beneath my feet. No! For on what other base can we place ourselves, what other rock can we sinners climb upon to reach up to God who in His mercy is ever reaching down to us? In the beginning was the Word – the Word which in Christ is our one foundation.'

The young man's round clean face was bright with zeal. The grey or swarthy, haggard and pinched faces before him caught his fire, kindling in his care for them. 'Amen,' rippled round the half-circle, and the eldest and the gravest came up to wring his hand. But Mr Macleay would not stop till he had greeted every one of his new congregation, and heard their names, down to the babes in arms. Hector, the old warhorse, supervised the erection of the tent with more briskness than he had shown about anything for months. But it was for appearance only, since Donald's family had vacated their clean new house, where a fire was already glowing, to welcome the man of God. Here, in the fading dusk, he ate the porridge Annag cooked for him with great thankfulness, and wrote in his journal:

Rona, at last, by the grace of God. Light is fading but I must write. My impression on arrival of these poor people, men on the one hand and women with all modesty on the other, 'neath the rough wild cliffs, will never be forgot. I had thought to come to them unaware, both not to burden them with special welcome, as they can afford nothing, and perchance to catch them in misdemeanours which though slight might better be reproved before they hid them from me, but it appeared they knew of my coming, from what source I cannot ascertain, and were prepared. They are sober people and eagerly disposed to hear the Word, and their poverty, though extreme, I count a virtue, for 'hath not God chosen the poor of this world, rich in faith, and heirs of the Kingdom which He hath promised to them that love Him?' Amen. I pray I may serve God well in serving them.

CHAPTER 13

'Don't leave me, Issie! Issie, don't leave me!'

Issie stayed. In spite of the midwives' clucking, in spite of the doctor's 'I insist!', she stayed through it all, clinging to the bedpost against dislodgement and to Helen's writhing shoulders as an earnest of sympathy. It was more dreadful than anything she had imagined, to see such pain and terror. At first she wept quietly through Helen's moans, whispering comfort, but when it got worse, with the smell of blood and Helen's mouth a rigid foam-flecked gape of agony, Issie screamed with every terrible howl, shrieking, 'No, no, no!' for Helen, who had lost all words, had lost herself entirely in raw red animal pain.

'Oh, it's dead, dead,' Issie cried in ultimate desolation, seeing the dull crimson, compressed, glistening thing in the midwife's hands.

'Not a bit of it!' The big aproned woman swung it by the heels and slapped its back, and the squashed anguished face cracked in a thin wail of fear and loss.

'Don't, oh don't,' Issie pleaded, running to save the ugly tormented creature. But the women elbowed her aside, laughing, and one bathed the convulsed infant while the other made with her steaming bowl for the torn and listless mother.

'Now, miss, it's high time you left. Your sister must rest in a little while.'

Issie began to protest, but the doctor's firm grip under her elbow suddenly reduced her limbs to jelly.

'But is she all right?' she quavered.

'Yes, she has come through it very well. That was nothing. You'll learn, young lady. Now, you must convey the happy news to the father.'

The door was half shut on her before she remembered. 'Oh! Is it a boy?'

The doctor's face at the crack in the door quirked curiously. 'Yes. Quite certainly.'

'Augustus will be so pleased! It's a boy,' she told Dileas in the corridor. 'It's a boy!' She cried over her shoulder to Elsie, hovering in the doorway of Helen's sitting room, and 'It's a boy!' she shouted, bursting into the study, where Augustus and her father sat, one on either side of the desk with the decanter between them.

There was an outcry of delight: shaking of hands and whisky tossed off, the old pointer's deep woof, Dileas yapping. No one scolded Issie for whooping, or running, or bringing in her dog. Augustus made her drink some whisky too, with sugar and hot water, to repair her nerves, 'For you shouldn't have been there, Issie, but the news you bring is so welcome I can't reprove you.' And he kissed her. Servants pressed at the door with eager congratulations. Nothing had been so lovely for many, many months. Issie grew tearful with happiness and whisky, and her father took her on his lap, though she was taller than he was, saying over and over, 'Thank God. Thank God.'

With Helen there was no delight. Issie crept into her room very early in the morning to be there when she awoke, but the joy she hoped to see did not wake with her. Tears trickled from her lids before they were well open. She was too weak, she said, to hold the baby, and she turned her head aside when Issie lifted him up for her to see. She slept most of the time, or feigned sleep. Issie watched over her, stricken, while the September rain battered the window-panes and the day grew bright, then dull again.

Dr Ross called and pronounced the patient well. 'A little more fortitude, hm?' he suggested, pinching Helen's cheek. 'The day after you were born I found your mother embroidering your small clothes.'

Helen would not even give him good-day.

'Don't worry, miss,' the nurse said to Issie, 'it often makes them like that. She'll be in proper spirits again soon.'

But she was not. She languished in bed long after the doctor deemed her fit to rise, reluctant to dress, without appetite or animation. She would not have the baby in her room because his crying disturbed her; she would not visit him in the nursery at the top of the house because the stairs fatigued her. Issie did her best to entertain her, with books and drawings and gossip gleaned on her brief and hurried outings with Dileas, but nothing roused more than a passing interest. She would hold Issie captive a whole day, then tell her fretfully to be off, that her chatter tired her. Towards other visitors she was apathetic, to her husband positively hostile. 'I don't want to see Augustus. Tell him I have a headache,' she would command her sister.

The lie was in itself painful to Issie, but that it should be so between these two was an added sadness. Mournfully, she recalled their engagement, their wedding day, the evenings at the pianoforte. The old rebellious sting of jealousy was numbed to insignificance in her throbbing pity for her sister. Even, sometimes, as she watched Helen's sleeping face, worn of all its lovely curves and colour, she felt resentment of Augustus rising in her. He had done this, somehow. He had pleasure in his son, and Helen only had pain. Issie would press her hands to her eyes to take away the horrible images: Helen's contorted face, her shuddering limbs, the hideous slime of gore defiling her white skin, the dreadful exposure of secret things to others' eyes. 'All known – even the most degrading,' Helen had said, and Issie pushed with her knuckles till her eyeballs hurt, hot with shame for Helen, exposed to the man. In *that* way: like when she had seen a bull with cows. That was what happened. She remembered how Helen, sometimes, had seemed to fear Augustus. 'Now I understand,' she whispered, kissing her sister's thin fingers in a passion of love, and grief that for a time she had felt no love.

She would avoid Augustus, afraid to look at him, afraid her imaginings would leap out between them, stark. But she could not avoid the nursery. Whenever Helen dismissed her she would have to run upstairs to see the baby, and often, surprisingly often, Augustus was there, standing silently by the crib, smiling into it as he used to smile at Helen, even singing softly. He would look embarrassed to see Issie and leave with some excuse about an appointment with a tenant, or some other business. She had not known before that Augustus could feel silly; that knowledge, and his love for the baby, disarmed her.

She adored George Augustus Hector Green. She loved him as much as she loved Dileas, but she supposed she should not love a dog, a brute with no soul, as much as her own nephew. Yet Dileas's lack of a soul and a heaven caused her tears and sleepless nights. Then surely it was disloyal to love any other little creature as much as Dileas, who was her own. So she loved them both. Seeing the dog at first growl and sulk at the rival in the crib, she took the baby down to him and let him sniff and lick till he understood. She would sit with both in her lap, interpreting each aloud to the other, and Georgie's first smile was not for his father, nurse or aunt, but for that hairy face with its one black ear.

She related this to Helen, hoping it might amuse her, but instead it caused tears. 'His first smile should have been for his mother.'

'But Helen – ' Issie didn't know how to continue. 'You don't care about him', 'You scarcely see him' were truths too appalling. She chose her words carefully. 'You have been so tired and unwell, you have not been with him very much.'

'The stairs defeat me. Nurse should bring him down to me.'

'I'm sure she would, if only you would tell her.'

'Not here. I don't want him in here. I can't bear that. It reminds me of that terrible night.'

'Helen darling, if you saw how sweet he is . . . ' She was about to say, 'You would forget that night.' There was something she had come upon in her New Testament: 'A woman when she is in travail, hath sorrow, because her time is come; but as soon as she is delivered of the child, she remembereth no more the anguish, for joy that a man is born into the world.' She whispered it sometimes to Georgie. It should be so beautifully true. But not for Helen: the anguish had broken her. Issie tried again. 'If – when – you come to know him better, there will be other things to be reminded of, won't there? Soon he'll sit up, and say words. When he says "Mama", just think of that! Why don't I tell Nurse to bring him to the drawing room in the afternoon and you can come down too? Father would be so pleased, Helen, if only you would.'

'Oh, some day, but not today.' Helen yawned, and began to flick through a copy of *Blackwood's*.

Issie, more bruised by her indifference than by her previous ill-temper, crept off to the nursery. She found not Augustus, but her father peering into the crib, waving and grinning.

'Ha! See that, Issie? He's smiling – smiling at his grandpapa. That's it, my boy. Good boy.'

Georgie was indeed smiling, with the crossing eyes and forearms of intense infant concentration. Issie saw suddenly the likeness between her father's bushy grey whiskers and Dileas's hairy muzzle, and burst out laughing, although she had learned of late not to burst into words, and kept Georgie's previous excursion in smiling to herself.

'So he is, Father. I'm so glad he smiled at you.'

'Wait till I tell Augustus.' The old man straightened shakily, grunting and hitching up the once well-fitting tartan trews that his wasting muscles no longer filled. 'Very like his father. Don't you think, Issie?'

'I fancy him more like Helen, Father.'

'No, no. That chin. Not a Macdonald chin, that. There, don't you see?'

'He does have a pronounced chin for such a young baby.'

'Yes – very like Augustus. No mistaking who's Papa. I told him so. He's very taken with his boy, is he not, Issie?'

'Oh yes! I wish . . . '

'Eh?' Her father swayed to and fro where he stood, peering at her thoughtfully. 'Helen,' he said at last, with unusual perspicacity. He sighed. 'Does she ever see the baby, Issie?'

'Not often, Father.'

'It's time she got better, came down, took an interest in things again. You mother wasn't like that. Ross says she's physically quite healthy.'

'Yes, but she is so dejected. That makes her feel ill.'

'Shouldn't be. Nothing to be dejected about, now. That's all past. All that nonsense about . . . Well, at any rate, Augustus is delighted. He's not – ah – pushing her, is he?'

'Oh no, not at all. She often won't see him for whole days together. I have to make him go away – oh, I hate doing so, Father. He is very patient about it, but I think he looks sad.'

'Yes, bound to be. Getting impatient. She's a silly girl. I should tell her myself.' Sir Hector pulled his moustache, eyeing Issie hopefully. 'Or you could tell her.'

'Oh, I do, in every way I can. It's very difficult, Father.'

'Yes – yes.' He unscrewed his silver-mounted snuff-horn and applied a pinch, slowly. 'Keep trying, there's a good girl,' he enjoined, sneezing his way to the stairs.

Issie kept trying, but without success. Then, at the beginning of December, something happened that she knew at once must make things better. A large package arrived by carrier, which when unwrapped proved to be a ball gown for the Christmas festivities, sent by Aunt Livingstone in London to her favourite niece and goddaughter. Issie snatched it up in its swathings of muslin and tissue paper, calling Elsie to catch the skirts against dragging on the floor, and together, chattering with delight and excitement, they bundled it upstairs to Helen.

'Look, look – that beautiful shot of green through blue. And the lace.'

'Every one of these satin roses is sewn with little pearls, ma'am, like dewdrops.'

'The flounced shoulders – oh, you'll look lovely, darling!'

Helen had jumped up from the couch, exclaiming at the first sight of the wonderful garment: palest starling's egg-blue satin overlaid with tier upon tier of delicate Brussels lace, trimmed with the tiny pink dew-pearled roses. But she relapsed among her cushions, running her palms over her cheeks. 'Oh, what's the use? I shall look a fright. I've grown so thin. It will hang on me.'

'You'll alter it, won't you, Elsie?'

'Certainly, ma'am, as well as I can.'

'I'm sure such work is too skilled for you. You might as well put it away.'

'Oh, Helen!'

She tossed her head fretfully. 'And when should I wear it here, anyway? What balls am I to attend in the depths of the Highlands?'

'George and Willie will be here.'

'What beaux!'

'Strathbeg will hold a rout as usual.'

'Oh yes, with all the gentlemen over sixty.'

Elsie smiled. 'I heard from their housekeeper, ma'am, that they are expecting a younger party. His youngest niece is lately married, and will bring her husband and friends, as well as her mother and brother.'

'That's Cecilia Drysdale. You always said she was a sweet girl, Helen. So it won't be so dull. Now, won't you let us dress you up, so that Elsie can take in where need be?'

Helen said nothing, but she rose and allowed herself to be undressed, redressed, admired and measured without further peevishness.

'I think this really will help her to get better, don't you, Elsie?'

136

Issie asked, having gone to see the progress on the alterations that evening.

'I think so, miss.' Elsie smiled, smoothing the billowing satin that covered her lap and the table in front of them.

So it seemed. The following morning Helen instructed Elsie to send snippets from the gown to her shoemaker in Inverness so that he could match slippers to it, and she herself wrote to her aunt with profuse thanks, and a request for more of the roses to dress her hair. In the afternoon she let Issie persuade her down to the drawing room to take tea with the family, and the day after, at the same hour, permitted the nurse to be summoned with Georgie. Augustus himself took the baby from Nurse and placed him in Helen's arms.

'Now, my dear, see what you have been missing all these dismal weeks.' He kissed the parting in her light brown hair, quite in his old manner, leaning over the back of her chair. Helen barely smiled, but sat placidly enough. Issie glowed with pleasure, unable to stop herself from jumping up and running to kiss mother and child.

'Isn't he lovely? Don't you see now what I meant, Helen?'

'He looks much like any other baby, I suppose.'

'Not for long.' Augustus took her hand. 'When you are quite yourself again, he will be everything to you.'

She withdrew her hand, but he caught it again. 'I think we can be happy, Helen,' he said in an undertone that Issie should not have tried to hear.

Sir Hector was listening too, with strained features and his ears actually tilted towards the couple. His satisfaction at Augustus's projection of marital harmony was outright. 'Yes, yes! You have everything to be happy for. Look to the future, eh?'

Augustus smiled. Helen at least did not weep.

George Augustus Hector was baptised on the Sunday before Christmas, with Issie as godmother and cousin George as godfather, and all the tenants of Inverharg turned out in their best clothes to see him. Augustus had a photographer come from Edinburgh to take portraits and the family sat stiff and serious in the frosty park while George Augustus Hector was immortalised, a small enigmatic face among clouds of white drapery.

Strathbeg's rout was arranged for Boxing Day. In the afternoon, when Issie went to Helen's sitting room for final instructions on what she should wear, she found Augustus with her. He rose from his wife's couch as the door opened, his hand lingering on her neck. They had, she was sure, been laughing together. Helen looked almost her old self.

'You may have Elsie to dress you later, Issie. I shan't be going tonight.'

Issie stared in disbelief. 'Oh – but how? Not going? But the gown.'

Helen smiled. 'I feel a little unwell. Not very, but it would tire me. I have sent Elsie over to present my apologies.'

'Oh!' Issie sat down, almost in tears. She had longed for the evening – for Helen's sake, for the wonderful entry in that fairy gown. But for herself there would only be trodden toes, or no partners, and the fashionable young ladies from Edinburgh whispering about her behind their fans. She gulped hard. 'I'll stay with you then, for company.'

'Indeed you shall not! You must go, or it will seem offensive.'

'It would give me the greatest pleasure to remain at home with you, as you know,' said Augustus, his eyes dwelling on her tenderly.

'No, they are neighbours. We must be wise about it.'

They spoke quietly, only to each other. Issie, sniffing back tears, rose to leave.

'And you must squire Issie,' Helen cried, darting glances from one to the other. Jumping up, she caught Augustus's arm and propelled him towards Issie to prove her point. 'Now, don't be in the dumps, my sweet. Put witch-hazel on your eyes, and you may have any of my jewellery you want. I'll make sure you look pretty and then you will enjoy yourself.'

Issie did not enjoy herself. She danced with three gentlemen over sixty, who complimented her on her nice red cheeks, the strength of her arm in the reel, and on being a big girl now. She danced with one of the gentlemen under twenty, who paid no compliments at all. She drank lemonade with old Strathbeg's sister, who enquired after Georgie, but plunged into a monologue on her own grandchildren without waiting for a reply. The room was so hot, and the proud grandmamma exuded such a strong odour of orris and bad breath, that Issie began to feel sick, and seized the chance when her companion's attention was distracted by a passing tray of ices to creep by the darkest corners out to the hall. It was pleasantly quiet and empty. Even the footmen were absent, doubtless taking advantage of festive licence.

Issie, slipping from the hall to the welcome chill of the vestibule, realised to her embarrassment that she was not alone after all: Major Drysdale was stamping his feet into boots and shrugging on a beaver cape. But he had his back to her and went out without noticing her. As he opened the door, Issie saw the moonlight gleaming invitingly on the frosty lawn. She ran upstairs to retrieve her own cloak from the surprised maid and let herself out as quietly as possible. Her heart jolted at the groaning reverberations of the great door, for if she were seen, how could she explain herself? No other young lady would think of leaving a party to wander alone in the moonlight. But no one jumped protesting from the shadows. Major Drysdale, walking fast, had reached the double gates at the end of the beech avenue. Issie thought better of him than she used to do, since he too had found moonlight more enticing than a noisy ballroom. She spent the next half-hour very happily on the white lawns lacy with many-branched shadows of leafless trees, so that the evening was mercifully shortened. Augustus danced with her when he had done his duty by all the old ladies, and she thought she had never seen him look so merry.

On New Year's Eve there was a supper party at Drumharg. The doctor and his wife, the chief tenant farmers, and old Strathbeg and his sister were there, but Major Drysdale had returned to his regiment, conveying the younger set with him. Issie was not sorry: they were relentlessly glittering, much too grand for the country. It was more comfortable with just old friends; Helen wore her new gown and was as lovely and gracious a hostess as she had ever been, though pale and very slender, and inclined to lean on her husband's arm.

'Quite recovered,' said Dr Ross, beaming.

'Not quite,' said Mrs Ross, firmly. 'She needs a change of scene. Mr Green must take her away.'

Helen was of the same mind. She had spoken of it to Issie earlier in the week. 'If only I could breathe a warmer air, I should be perfectly well, soon.'

During the evening of the party Helen and Mrs Ross were in confidential conversation for a time, after which Mrs Ross tapped the doctor with her fan to call his attention to something. By the end of the evening Dr Ross had persuaded Augustus that he should take his wife abroad for the rest of the winter, if he wished to see her health fully restored.

There was a fortnight of upheaval. Trunks and valises lay half packed in Helen's apartments, carriers called daily with shoes and linen, muffs and gloves, bonnets and pelisses. Helen was vivid with anticipation, Augustus indulgent. Old Drumharg lamented his coming loss of a daughter and a factor, but no one listened to him. Issie, between the delights and surprises of Helen's parcels, moped for Georgie, to be bereft of his parents for quarter of a year or more. She was sad on her own behalf too; home would be dull and quiet without them, and the duller for imagining their excitements – travelling by steam-ship to Aberdeen, and after that by the railway to Edinburgh, then London, and Paris, and Nice, and perhaps Florence and Rome.

They left in a misty winter dawn, with the horses' breath steaming in the chill air. Issie wept as they said their goodbyes.

'It's not for long,' Augustus protested, smiling.

Helen, at her loveliest under a new bonnet of plum-coloured velvet, did not smile, in spite of the pleasures ahead. It seemed she felt the parting.

Her father handed her into the carriage. 'Come back restored, my dear. Come back soon.'

Helen's gloved hands went to her mouth, then. She did not wave or call goodbye as the conveyance rumbled and clattered away from the steps and down the curving driveway, exhaling morning mist between the night-dark rhododendrons.

CHAPTER 14

Drumharg without them was even quieter and duller than Issie had expected. Helen's recovered good spirits had filled it so completely that her recent languishment was hardly remembered; and even during that dismal period Issie had been so much her satellite that she found she had forgotten how to be alone. The trinkets and clothing Helen had scattered in her many changes of mind over packing made her apartments seem all the more forlorn.

Since Elsie had gone with the travellers, it fell to Issie to put things to rights. She filled several mornings with the task, as there was not much else to do: sleety rain scoured down on the park from Ben Harg, so that even Dileas was unenthusiastic about walks. Georgie slept much of the day and so, more and more, did her father. The time passed pleasantly enough, mending trimmings Helen had torn in her haste, untangling ribbons, folding silk stockings and wraps away in tissue paper. Some of the things she tried on. Helen always invited her to try this or that, but usually she would not, being too conscious of the contrast her sister would see with her own pretty reflection; but being alone, she took courage and perched before the dressing mirror, trying caps and bonnets, parures and collars, adjusting her sleeves to reveal a little more shoulder, pushing up her stays to produce a little more bosom. The weather was dull, and if she widened her eyes, as if to focus on something distant, she could make a blurred image in the glass that might almost be Helen; *la belle Hélène*, with her heart-shaped face, arched brows, and forward-pouting, kiss-enticing smile. She lost herself in a pleasant haze of being Helen, being lovely, admired, Augustus coming up behind her, smiling, with confident lips above his firm round chin, putting his hand on a white shoulder – Issie's own hand, beguiled, rose to meet it. Its redness, even dull and blurred, brought her eyes back to focus and her brain back to sense. She jumped up from the mirror with burning ears and smarting eyes, pulling off earrings and necklet and shrugging her dress to rights. She knelt on the floor amid the litter of finery, missing Augustus as much as – more than – she missed Helen: his swift heavy tread and confident voice, carrying from the hall all up and down the house, with a smell of clean leather and lavender shaving soap. Helen's strained face, when she heard that tread: 'I don't want to see Augustus. Tell him . . . '

'But you're so fortunate,' whispered Issie, aloud, alone, 'so fortunate.' Her imagination overwhelmed her. She shook her head fiercely and began to fold and tidy with unseeing haste. She finished what she had to do quickly and afterwards went out in the rain, intending a long brisk walk, but got no further than the ice-house, under the yew trees behind the chapel. She stood there shivering for a long time; entombing, locking and sealing, while the rain pattered from the dark trees down her dark gaberdine.

There were to be no more daydreams. Issie resolved to devote herself to the care of her nephew and did so with such fervour that the nurse threatened to find other employment.

'With the young lady and that dog of hers there, I can't get on with my work,' she complained to the housekeeper. 'She's fretting the baby and keeping him awake too much.'

Mrs Mackenzie passed this on discreetly to Issie, who was indignant.

'No indeed, she would have him asleep all the time. You see, although he's little, he needs things to interest him, or he cries. I can't bear to hear him cry.'

Mrs Mackenzie looked stony. Though a short squat woman, the uprightness of her carriage gave her an appearance of height.

'It would be difficult, miss, to find another nurse as capable, prepared to live in such an out-of-the-way place. There are plenty who would have her in Inverness. Mr Green enquired most particularly into her credentials.'

Issie, reduced to size, agreed to behave better. She tried her theory of child-rearing timidly on Nurse, but with no better effect than a sniff. After that she was condemned to crouch on the stairs, wringing her hands, if Georgie cried between feeding times, not being able to trust herself in the room with him. But for most of the afternoon Georgie was accustomed to lie awake, not crying but kicking and gurgling, resistant to all rocking, singing and tucking in.

'It's because the young lady has been spoiling him,' the chagrined nurse confided to Mrs Mackenzie. But having no means of dealing with such unruliness other than whisky in his pap, which Mr Green had specifically forbidden, she was glad enough to turn him over at that time of day to his aunt.

Issie and Dileas bore him off around the park if it was dry, or through the many empty rooms if it was not. Issie chattered constantly, about the trees, the birds, Great-grandmamma's portrait, Uncle Alexander's sword and spurs. She recited rhymes, or sang them, loudly and tunelessly, freed from an inhibition about bursting into song by tuneful Helen's absence. Dileas barked and chased his tail around her ankles. Georgie crowed and gurgled and panted, with popping eyes and flailing limbs. The triangular conversation afforded all of them great satisfaction. In the late afternoon, tired with his sightseeing, Georgie lay on a rug in the drawing room before his admiring grandfather, while Issie recounted the triumphs of his day.

'He knows colours now, Father. He reaches out to the curtains in the blue room, but won't look at yellow', or 'He was so excited when he saw himself in the looking glass', or 'I took him to see the horses. Captain blew at him and made him cry.'

All of which the laird received with proper pride. The old man was increasingly frail, often not rising from his bed till noon, and shuffling around for most of the day in a dressing gown and heel-less slippers. Now he walked always with a stick, and seldom further than the terrace, and was frequently absent for meals, so that Issie ate in the company of eleven empty chairs at the long oval-ended table, her human feet lonely in the forest of brass-clawed pedestals. But always as the time for the afternoon interview with his grandson drew near, her father would appear, dressed in his old dapper manner, with lace stock frothing over amethyst buttons, and swollen feet painfully crammed into silver-buckled polished black shoes. Though Issie had learned to tell from his complexion whether or not the whisky had gone down too freely earlier in the day, for these afternoon interludes he was invariably sober. For his sake as much as Georgie's she extended the daily escapes from the nursery as long as possible, till the baby was indeed fretting, blinking and thrusting his fist in his mouth. At first Issie would take him back upstairs herself, to see him fed and settled, but found on her return her father's chair always empty. It was sad to her to see its cushions still rumpled where he had been sitting and the great graceful room empty, and to imagine his recent creaking, grunting progress upstairs, back to bed and whisky. She took to ringing for Nurse to bear Georgie away, but then found herself tongue-tied before the sorry figure of her father. His eyes went dull when the baby left the room – not so much unhappy as lifeless, like a torpid lizard's. The hand that had gripped his silver-topped cane tightly to disguise its tremor would shake uncontrolled, his sleeve on the chair arm scuffing to and fro with a small dry sound like a dead leaf, and he would rise, running his tongue over his sagging underlip with a mumbled 'Goodnight, Issie', and make for the door, with at his heels old Luath, whose hanging head and filmy eyes seemed to Issie to indicate loyalty, but also despair.

So she felt herself: powerless to halt the deterioration in her father's body and mind. He was not much over sixty, but as frail and forgetful as a man twenty years older. He would not seek Dr

Ross's advice, but Issie, sweating at her own trepidation, had done so on his behalf, and the doctor ruefully gave it as his opinion that the whole cause of his symptoms – gout, short wind, loss of memory, loss of balance – was to be found in the decanter.

'There were certain domestic problems which doubtless contributed, but now these are resolved so happily, Miss Issie, this too free a hand with spirits must be amended, or . . . ' He shook his head. 'He is shortening his own life. That is a hard thing to say to you, my dear, but only you can help him while your sister is absent.'

Issie, weighed down by this responsibility, schemed by day and prayed by night to be equal to it. She had never been used to conversing with her father. Helen, with her ready music and small-talk, her winning smiles and endearments, had always been the focus of his attention. Issie began to spend the mornings rehearsing. She practised long and earnestly on the pianoforte, which she had always been glad to skimp before; she taught Dileas amusing tricks, catching sugar lumps off his nose and dying for his country; she took up sewing she would rather have neglected, in order to comment on it in the manner of her sister, or as near as possible.

'Look, Father, I'm embroidering this for Georgie. Do you think he will like it? I've put a dog in the pattern where there should be a bird, because he'll think it's Dileas. I haven't got it to look very like a dog, but I shall tell him it is one.'

At first it seemed absurd and impertinent to employ such monologues to him and she blurted them out with a red face and shaking hands, expecting a frown or a reprimand for her ill-modulated voice, but to her astonishment her uneasy attempts at frivolity had the desired effect. As soon as Georgie was removed she would run to the piano, or put Dileas through his paces, or embark on her prepared speech, and her father would remain in his chair, at least for an hour or so. If letters came from Helen

146

and Augustus, she learned to keep them for that time of the day. Augustus described very elegantly the scenes, customs and economies of the various regions where they passed, which sent Sir Hector to sleep where he sat, without recourse to whisky, but Helen's rush of people and parties, fashions and promenades, brought smiles and animation.

'Helen was belle of the ball, I've no doubt . . . Your sister can hold her own anywhere – anywhere at all . . . Met the Crown Prince . . . I can imagine her! Well, Green's a lucky man, when all is said and done.'

With all of which Issie could wholeheartedly agree, but the drift her father's comments sometimes took afterwards pleased her less.

'A lucky man. I hope he deserves her. Of course, she has been foolish, but – he has gained a great deal by the marriage. Well, it's true he has been very valuable to me. But he's a pompous ass, hm? Don't you think, Issie?'

Issie, unused to being consulted and incapable of denigrating Augustus, stammered, 'Oh no, I like Augustus very well.'

Her father grunted and withdrew shortly to bed.

On the next occasion, Augustus having been designated a modern man, incapable of feeling, Issie knew to steel herself to treachery. 'I do think, Father, it was unnecessary for him to occupy your study and to talk as if it were his. I often think, when you are sitting in your bedroom, wouldn't you rather be there, with your books and papers?'

'Hm? Books and papers. Not these days, child. That fellow – what's his name, Green's assistant – '

'Mr Seaton.'

'Seaton – I dare say he's doing the work. Too late now, anyway. The damage is done.'

Issie, unsure what to say, at first said nothing, but seeing him about to rise, asked hastily, 'What do you mean, Father?'

'Progress, improvement. That's what Augustus has been after.

He's done it, too. But the clan – where is the clan now? That's the modern age for you. There's no loyalty any more, everything has a price in money. In the old days the price was men's lives – live and die for the chief. And the chief for the clan. Your great-grandfather died on Culloden field, with his men around him. Means nothing to Augustus. How much does it cost? That's all progress is concerned with. Progress is profit. We've turned into shopkeepers.'

His tremor increased with his agitation. He tapped with his stick to control it. 'Well, well, nothing you can understand, child.' He heaved himself shakily to his feet, with the dead lizard-look coming in his eyes.

'Oh, don't go, Father. I could understand if you would explain more.'

'No, no. That's enough.' He made for the door, with a whistling sigh of old man's self-pity. 'Damage is done, and in my name.'

'In my name, God help me . . . ' she heard through the closed door.

Throughout the first half of March it snowed bitterly and persistently, over an iron frost. In spite of Drumharg's steam-heating and roaring fires, Issie suffered from chilblains. She was ashamed to notice them, looking out into the park where the bullocks ran to meet the lad who brought their hay, which in the dusk hungry deer broke in to steal, helped over the walls by drifted snow and desperation. The great cedar bowed under the weight of snow, making caves between its trunks and branches, where birds and small animals sheltered, glazed with cold: once a fox and two rabbits together, too numb for pursuit or flight. Out on the hill the sheep bunched at the fences of the conifer shelter belts, their fleeces dingy against merciless white. Issie pitied the wretched animals and pitied her father's poor people who had gone to Canada, even colder, with forests wilder and mountains more rocky, home of wolf and bear instead of fox and rabbit. She wondered how it was with the girl who had given Dileas her ribbon. Once when her father, garrulous at the fireside, lamented the lands Augustus had too precipitately purchased on Lake Huron, she asked if he had heard how the people did who had gone out there.

'Which people?' he asked, with shifting eyes.

'Those from Fladday.'

'Ah, those.' His stick beat a tremulous tattoo on the fender. 'Those and many more – many more. Where is the clan, now? Scattered – gone for ever.'

She did not hear how they did, and it occurred to her that he did not know. Augustus dealt with all estate business. It was repugnant to her that he had not cared to find out, that his laments for his diminished people were for his own loss, not for theirs. But her anger died in pity, seeing the shaking head with its pouched and sagging features, to which the mellow firelight no longer lent either health or good cheer.

'When Augustus comes we must find out about them,' she said earnestly. She half expected a rebuke for meddling in masculine affairs but her father made no reply.

The thaw came, with mud and snowdrops and a roar of unseen waterfalls from the coverts of Ben Harg. Georgie cut his first tooth. The cook evaded Mrs Mackenzie to hand Issie Saint Bridget's bannock, the good-luck rusk. She showed the tooth off to Grandpapa in the afternoon, and Georgie played with the bannock until it broke. They each kept a piece for good fortune. Issie tidied up the crumbs before Nurse came to fetch him, she being very strict against superstition. There was a letter from Augustus that day, too. Once Georgie had gone, Issie knelt by her father's chair to read it.

'It's very short,' she exclaimed, disappointed. Then 'Oh – '

Sir Hector, who had settled back comfortably in his chair, sat up at the strangled sound in his daughter's throat. 'What's the matter? Helen is not ill, is she?'

'Oh – oh, she's dead! She's dead! Helen's dead!'

Later, in the dreary months of her father's final decline, Issie tormented herself with remorse for that outburst. The letter had been addressed to her personally, which she had scarcely noticed at the time. Augustus had so addressed it so that she could break the terrible news, as he put it, when she herself was in a collected frame of mind, furnished with the proofs of domestic affection and religion. Instead, beside herself with grief, she had broken his heart and his reason. After the first few days, when Dr Ross pronounced him out of immediate physical danger, she carried Georgie in to him, but the sight of the child was insupportable pain. He wept desolately for his daughter, as if he had only ever had one; and Issie, knowing that was how it had always seemed to him, crept away with a doubled burden of woe.

Augustus arrived two weeks after his letter. Issie had made it her comfort, her lifeline, that they would mourn together, that he would raise Helen for her out of the numbness that smothered her own remembering: *dead, dead, dead,* it thumped with her heart at night in the darkness, and *dead* when firelight fell on the pianoforte, and *dead* outside the closed door of Helen's boudoir. But Augustus would not speak of her.

'You know all there is to be said, Issie, from my letter. The fever was sudden and she was buried in the English cemetery in Rome, with the offices of a Protestant pastor.'

Issie wept and pleaded, begging for the crumbs of her sister's last hours, last words, to feed her love and grief.

'To know more would only cause you worse pain,' he said, and went immediately to his study.

She saw little of him and learned nothing of what she longed to know. There were no keepsakes, not even a lock of hair: Helen's effects had been abandoned, he explained, because of the risk of contagion in a hot and insanitary foreign country.

Elsie, who might have comforted her, had left for new employment after her mistress's death. Issie asked for her address, ostensibly in order to send on her possessions from Drumharg, but really hungering to write to her about Helen. Even this Augustus would not permit. Elsie was travelling with a German lady, he said, and he himself arranged for the disposal of her belongings to the other servants. Other than on such practical matters, Augustus was relentless in his silence about his wife. That he was grief-stricken himself there could be no doubt; his handsome, once well-fleshed face was fined, skull-like, the skin tanned by Mediterranean sun now yellow as parchment and tightened over cheeks and jaws, by what ratchet of suffering Issie could only guess. There was a sort of fury in his eyes; not the quick impatience or confident command of the old Augustus, but something altogether new. At first she thought she had called it forth by her tactless questioning, but soon she saw it was always there, even when he sat at table, or bent over Georgie.

He was, if anything, more preoccupied than before with his son. He would quiz Issie and the nurse, unsmiling, on every detail of his progress. Nothing to do with Georgie was too trivial for him: each day he gave orders for the child's feeding, clothing and amusement with a precision more appropriate to a general's tent than to a nursery. No longer might Issie toss him chuckling above her head, or feed him sponge-cake dipped in warm tea. She and Nurse at last found themselves allies in the shadow of Augustus's displeasure.

Yet though he spent time every day in regulating for his son, he was not much with him, and hardly ever so alone. The man Issie had surprised, singing by the crib, would never be found again. Issie wept over Georgie, feeling him an orphan even from birth, his mother dead without ever having learned to love him, and his father, it seemed, having forgotten how to.

For a time Augustus was assiduous in visiting Sir Hector in his room. Issie could not understand why, since she knew her father was incapable of any business. In May a lawyer came from Inverness and was closeted with father and son-in-law all morning. Augustus explained at dinner the reason for his visit.

'As you know, Issie, your father regards my son as his heir, and while it has always been the case that he could dispose of his personal possessions as he wished, there was no possibility of inheritance of the title through the female line. A baronetcy may only pass from male to male, as you are aware. In order to regularise the position, your father has today formally adopted Georgie, who will now be styled Macdonald, not Green. This is, I think, according to your father's wishes. The position was made as clear as is possible to him in his present state and he has given his assent and signature to the necessary documentation.'

Issie was astonished. Her hands dropped from her knife and fork.

'Are you not pleased? I thought you had the child's interests at heart.'

'Yes, I . . . '

The glitter in Augustus's eyes turned full on her.

'I scarcely know what to think. I – forgive me, Augustus, but it seems to me as if – as if you are giving away your son.'

'To his future good. I cannot let personal sentiment stand in his way. I intend to be much out of this country, Issie. I must ensure his inheritance now, before I leave.'

Issie stared at her plate, her throat thick with pent-up sadnesses.

'Where will you go?' she asked at last.

'To Canada. The estate lands there are intrinsically profitable; no one knows how profitable, as yet. They have been neglected hitherto but I shall put them to work.'

'Oh, then – ' Augustus looked at her enquiringly – 'then you will see the poor settlers who have gone there. You will be able to improve their condition?'

He pushed his chair back. Issie waited with a glimmer of hope in her deprived soul for his dissertation on progress.

'I shall improve profitability. That may or may not improve what you term their *condition*. As for human nature, that is always and everywhere unimprovable.'

Issie stared. There was no more forthcoming. They finished the meal in silence.

Augustus went to Canada at the end of June. Issie, with streaming eyes, held Georgie up to see him go. Georgie kicked and gurgled, insouciant, intent on the ground and Dileas.

'You don't understand, you poor little thing,' Issie cried.

On fine days they carried Sir Hector out to the terrace. He rambled about his daughter, his children, *mo chlann*. If he caught sight of Georgie he wept unrestrainedly, like a child himself. Issie seldom evoked recognition. She felt his blank stare as the punishment of her failure. Her heart contracted round the child and the dog, making there a pitiful oasis in a lonely waste of grief.

1 8 4 8–1 8 5 2

CHAPTER 15

By the grace of God a full year is now passed since I was brought to Rona. I thank the Lord for His blessings of good health and the sufficiencies of daily life which He has given me in that time, which I see as a sign that He is pleased to continue me in this work, and if I am spared for it from year to year, I resolve annually on this date to set down herein such progress and backslidings as I observe in my flock and in my care of them. I ought to do this more often (even daily) and so intended on my first arrival, but have not kept my journal as I would wish, omitting sometimes to write several days together, through weariness, lack of light, ink, or etc., and other times only a few words, and those often on worldly matters, as observing on poor weather, shortage of meal, etc. Oh God, for this my want of diligence I humbly beg forgiveness. Thou God seest all, and wouldest that I see myself as Thou seest me.

I will make in these pages a report to my Lord and Master, that I may the better in my prayers give thanks for His blessings and ask for what is needful to strengthen me (and them) in His faith and fear, to His glory and our salvation. In particular I pray I may study diligently in all that is needful towards Ordination, which by clear signs I have been shown to be His will.

The mission house is now complete and I have removed there, there is three rooms for my use, all with chimneys, which people here reckon a wonder, yet they do not consider this convenience at all healthful. I have managed well enough without and I fear lest my new accommodations are superfluous; nevertheless, I thank God for such bodily comfort and pray I may use it to His glory in increased study, etc.

There is a room also where the people are to meet for worship, and on this Sabbath day next coming we shall use it for the first time, which will be a joyous occasion. Also behind it is a schoolroom, there is much to teach and I cannot do all, in time God may send me a helpmeet to this task. Most of the younger men and women can now read their letters, and some can make out words in English. The children are quicker to learn, four read pretty well. None had seen the Shorter Catechism before I came, now all possess one, but I fear vain repetition, which God forbid! For an example of this: I asked a young lad the question, 'What is the chief end of man?' To which he replied readily, 'Man's chief end is to glorify God and to enjoy Him for ever.' But on being required to express this in his native tongue, he did so in a manner denoting, 'Our chieftain is very rich and always enjoys himself.'

There have been other like instances which are a great trouble to me, for is not the catechism a clear and reasoned profession of our Protestant faith, and is not such corruption of it (which to some might seem laughable) a proof that the Adversary as a roaring lion stalks ever up and down, seeking whom he may devour even among simple children? Even in this poor remote isle, cut off from the pomp and pride of the world, Satan will find a way into the fold!

I am vigilant and was for some time constantly exhorting the people to vigilance in this matter, but find, though it grieves me greatly to say it, that I was myself

made the instrument of Satan to lead them into sin. For
having preached four sermons on that text 'The Devil as
a roaring lion, etc.' and being pleased to see the impres-
sions of fear and sober watchfulness on my hearers'
faces (many wept, they looked over their shoulders, etc.
It was pride in me to note this as if to my credit. Oh
Lord! The glory is Thine and Thine alone) later I found
many making '*caim*', that is, compassing, which is going
round in a circle as a pagan relief against witchcraft or
devilry: and were very loath to see that by devils they
could not cast out devils. There have been other usages,
spells against the evil eye, and I have seen Peggy
Morrison put the plant Hypericum under her left arm as
a prophylactic. I have remonstrated against all such
abominations, but I fear some (particularly the women)
continue them secretly.

Also I have observed many relics of Popery, taking the
name of God in vain, prayers to the persons of the
Trinity, to the angels and the apostles, which were
offered customarily night and morning, though I shrink to
call that prayer which resteth not in the will of God, but
is uttered as a charm to protect households, cattle, etc.,
being then more loathsome in His sight than the invoca-
tions of the heathen to his idols. I never cease to warn of
the wrath of God to fall on superstitious sinners, and I
believe all households now use instead psalms, with
humble and spontaneous prayer, and will add to that a
daily reading from the Word when more can read.

I found the people very poor on my arrival, now all are
housed and sufficiently fed, there is less sickness, I think.
Therefore I must now use all my zeal to teach that man
does not live by bread alone, but by every word that
issues from the mouth of the Father. Feed the souls, oh
Lord, as Thou hast fed the bodies in time of want. Grant

that faith in Thy redeeming love which alone leadeth to salvation.

The superstitions trouble me greatly. I have heard Peggy Morrison laughing when I speak against them, may be this is but a mark of youthful thoughtlessness. There is only one household in which I am confident, which is Donald Macdonald's.

Preserve me, oh God, for in Thee do I put my trust!

'Only water and his name.' Mór raised herself on her elbow. 'And no singing. Donald said.' She sank back, heavy-limbed after giving birth.

Her mother and aunt stared. Ciorstag's preparatory croon, deep inside her like a cat's purr of delight, growled into uneasy exclamation. 'What!' The baptismal drops from her upraised hand sparkled to the floor in the firelight. 'What's this nonsense? Do you want the fairies to have him?'

'A psalm, if you like. But not the *Beannachd*.'

Her eyes were closed. Annag glanced at her and said nothing, but took the wailing baby from Ciorstag and held it close.

'Psalm 127.' Effie had her book open already. 'There's no such thing as fairies. Mr Macleay says they're a heathenish fancy.'

'Oh indeed, my girl.' Ciorstag stared at her hard. 'Where did your own foster-brother come from then? Was he a heathenish fancy? Or are you miscalling your mother?'

Annag put in hastily, 'No need to miscall anyone. The holy psalm is as good as the *Beannachd*, I'm sure, and the gracious God in heaven will know our meaning well enough. Sing the psalm, Ciorstag.'

'The psalm? Whoever heard of a psalm at such a time?'

'And he's to be called Duncan.'

'Duncan!' Annag, astonished, turned to her daughter. 'No, och no, he's Neil after your father, Mór, Neil is this one's name.'

'Duncan.' Tears squeezed beneath Mór's closed lids.

Ciorstag lamented loudly for dead Neil and his spurned widow, and for the unfortunate wife of an implacable husband, but Annag said no more. The child was named Duncan in honour of Mr Macleay, and Effie sang Psalm 127.

26 AUGUST 1849

I have only this evening returned from my yearly visit to Glasgow, where I ordered necessary provisions and books and had the great solace of conversation with my loved ones. God preserve them! My mother I found very low, in poor health and fearing to lose my sister who was contemplating marriage, but by the grace of God I arrived in time to dissuade her, pointing out her duty to our mother, for which by the end of my visit she was grateful, so that we thanked God together for it (the most blessed moment of my three weeks). My mother questioned me about my studies etc.; she is as eager as ever to see me made a minister and begged me to continue in that course.

I must set aside these personal matters. It is late and there is much to write on this anniversary, besides I must be up early to go fishing. This year crops and flocks do better, I have now a cow in calf and twenty sheep, besides poultry. My neighbours thrive too and we expect to harvest well both of corn and potatoes. Thanks be to God for this sufficiency.

The Destitution wall continues in its second year, if the fishing improves it will be discontinued. Mr Harbottle placed deer upon the island last year, but few survive, there is a parasite in the wet ground which attacks the liver, as also with sheep.

I pray constantly to be resolved in a question which troubles me about my way of life. If as my neighbours do I farm and fish (as I have done), I have less time for teaching and study than might be fit. Paul says, if they do not work, let them not eat, yet is spiritual labour not more work to me than digging, rowing, etc.? I have pondered this prayerfully in my absence, may it not be that God is trying me? Before I left we were making hay, and I am ashamed to say that in two weeks I entered nothing in my journal and was lax in reading the Word of God at my private devotions. I am almost sure I chose shorter chapters than is my wont. Therefore I pray God to enlighten me about His will in this.

In this year I have officiated at four funerals, which are now conducted with due fear and reverence, without the superstitious rhymes and chants of former times. Tomorrow there is to be a wedding, and for that reason I am resolved to be up early to work, as an example of sobriety, for I found that on such occasions (as at certain Popish feasts such as Christmas, St Michael's, etc.,) the people were used to follow licentious customs, to sing 'hymns' pleasing to no ear but Satan's, and even to dance. I have spoken strongly against such vanities, I think to good effect. There was one (John Maclean) who when first he found himself with more money than required to feed his family, straightway purchased a fiddle, but my rebuke so stung him that with tears of contrition he broke it asunder and threw it in the fire. Whereupon I led the family in prayers of thanksgiving for this blessed deliverance from the wiles of the Enemy.

Tomorrow it is my intention to speak not solely of the duties or joys of matrimony. I shall endeavour to turn all minds from passing earthly joys to that Eternal Joy which is in Christ Jesus: from the delusory pleasures of life to the one certain end of death, for which we are all bound, and after which we must render account to that great Judge above. 'The heart of the wise is in the house of

162

mourning, but the heart of fools is in the house of mirth.' Amen.

I have witnessed no unchastity among my neighbours. Nevertheless, unseemly mirth is a strong temptation to such, and I desire heartily to banish it.

There are certain indelicacies in the women's conduct which are perhaps unavoidable where the care of flocks and herds is entrusted to their sex. Also immodesties in dress which might be amended now they are not so poor. I noticed this during the hot weather of haymaking, when some were very lightly clad. I took the occasion to re-prove Peggy Morrison for this, but she is stubborn, I fear.

I am almost resolved that from now on my work should be all teaching and preaching, with outdoor labours only sufficient to keep my body in health, or when there is a shortage of hands towards work in common.

I think I am so resolved from remembering that as a boy I made hay upon my uncle's fields during a holiday from school and thought it great sport, and no labour.

I pray that I have examined my conscience well. 'For everyone shall give account of himself to God.'

' "My son, forget not my law; but let thine heart keep my commandments",' Hector read slowly, pointing the place with his finger for Sara. Obediently, seated side by side on the edge of the clean bed in the new damp hut, they read the chapter of Proverbs Mr Macleay had recommended as suitable before retiring for their nuptial night.

' "The curse of the Lord is in the house of the wicked: but he blesseth the habitation of the just." ' Hector's finger and voice had begun to shake. He was aware of perturbation in his lower regions. ' "The wise shall inherit glory but shame shall be the promotion of fools",' he finished, thickly and rather fast.

'You missed a verse,' Sara pointed out, not looking at him, looking away into the shadows. Her new waist-plaid was clasped roundly to her hips, threaded with bright clear red and blue in the little pool of white light cast by the splint of bog-fir.

'Och well, I didn't do bad.' His hand reached for her chequered hips, rippled round with pinched and pleated colours.

'A wee dance would have been nice,' she said wistfully, 'and you could have had a dram.'

'Och, Sara.' He got both his arms round her, pushing in ineffectual haste at the folds and pleats and pins. 'I'm no' needing a dram tonight!'

She knew she should blow the light out, but she didn't.

26 AUGUST 1850

Once again by the grace of God I am restored to Rona
after my yearly absence. The voyage was very stormy and
there was great terror amongst the passengers. I spent the
whole time steadfast in prayer, not for deliverance, but
that the Lord's will be done, holding in my mind's eye the
example of the Apostle, who tho' shipwrecked thrice was
preserved by God to do His work of salvation.

That God was pleased so to preserve me in yesterday's
tempest, I see as a sign that my work here is pleasing in
His sight. This gives me great comfort. Indeed, if I were
no so persuaded, I could not continue, the island being
so dark, wild and desolate and the people so rude and
poor, in comparison with those lively scenes of industry
and commerce I have lately witnessed, and with the like-
minded conversation of friends and colleagues in the city.
I have been refused entry to the College, the reasons I
find obscure. Nevertheless, I may continue here, as none
can be found to take so small a charge in so remote a
place. I expressed to my mother my conviction that I
cannot be spared from God's work on Rona at this time,

but her disappointment is great. I am anxious for my dear ones, my mother told me Agnes has not severed connection with the young man who spoke to her of marriage, as I bade her. I remonstrated with her, pointing out to her that as I am called to God's work on Rona, a place impossible for our dear mother to inhabit, on her must fall the whole duty of care and obedient companionship which is expressed in the Fourth Commandment. I found her answers unsatisfactory, she would not give me the assurance I sought. I pray earnestly for a resolution. I am so far removed from them. Nevertheless, not my will but Thine be done, O Lord.

This is my third anniversary, which I remember prayerfully, but there is little to set down, as I have executed last year's resolve to spend less time in labouring with my hands (which to a young fit man is but pleasure) and more in teaching and studying, so that in consequence this journal has been pretty well kept up. I do not think I have missed remarking on either progress or stumbling. All the children between six and fourteen years of age can now read in the Gaelic Bible, and study the Catechism in English. Some of their elders are very fluent, others cannot so much as make out the letters; nevertheless, now in every household at least one member (though not always the head, as would be most fitting) can read from the Book, to the edification of all. Thanks be to God, on the Sabbath and at morning and eventide I now hear the Word read in every home, where before was idle chatter, or (worse) vain songs and verses conjuring saints and angels in the manner of Papists. Donald Macdonald is my assistant in this, having ears ever open for such idolatrous practices, and lovingly exhorting those that follow them to turn to the one truth.

There is still much teaching to be done.

If I were to enter into matrimony, I believe I should
find such work more readily accomplished; for instance,
among the younger females, with whom I am naturally
loath to make myself too familiar. Also, in case of sickness, a woman's hand is desirable. When the women are
sick, I cannot enquire after their symptoms without injury
to modesty, yet it may be the stock of medicines I keep
could be more used. Peggy Morrison had a fever recently
and nearly died. Also, three newborn infants died this
year, and Roderick's wife died in childbed.

Agnes twitted me for expressing a desire to find a wife,
likening my case to hers, but they are quite unlike. Is it
not clearly my duty to wed, if God should send me a
helpmeet? I have just now again read Proverbs 31, on
which I have pondered much of late. 'A woman that
feareth the Lord, she shall be praised.' Lord, if it be Thy
will, may I find one so, to Thy greater Glory!

'Your dad didn't stay long from sea this time.'

'Huh!' Kirsty Mary snorted, tugging the Spanish tortoise-shell
comb he had brought her fiercely through her hair. 'The way
things are here, I'll not be staying long myself. Here, try this coral
necklace, Peggy. It'll suit you, with your dark skin. Let's have
another light so we can see the beauties we are.'

She lit a second rushlight from the first and placed them
carefully on either side of Peggy's mirror. It was damp-spotted in
one corner, but the best and biggest on Rona: that summer she
had traded half her Destitution meal back to the merchant's wife
to buy it – and some of her father's too, people said, certainly he
was lean enough. He never crossed Peggy: on that very afternoon, though it was Sunday and raining, a nudge from her had
been enough to get him out of the house. 'I'll be off to hear my
brother Donald read the Good Book, then,' he said without a
visible smile. So they had the place to themselves. It was the last

house in the village, tucked well into the steep hillside, over-looking the sea, and overlooked by no one. They had pinned a sack over the narrow window and put a chest against the door just in case, while they tried on the exotic finery Sailor John had brought home.

'Sara's wedding was a *dis-grace*.' Kirsty Mary emphasised the word with two stamps, forcing her broad bare feet into high-heeled slippers of red morocco, tooled with gold.

'Oh?' Peggy's covetous hand reached for the delicious things. Her own feet were narrow as a deer's.

Kirsty Mary frowned enviously. 'Och, I'll never get into them. I wish I had your wee feet. When I go into service I'm going to get button boots and a proper corset. I'll get myself into shape somehow. And then' – she tossed the slipper to Peggy to try – '*then* I'm going to get a young man, a handsome fellow with a smile on his face and a jingle in his pocket. Och, Peggy, I'm sick to death of long faces and long prayers. I'm going to dance and sing, and see the city streets with lights and shops, and travel in a coach. And in the railway trains. And go to a theatre. All the things you read in the newspaper.'

'You'd be denounced if they knew that's what you're reading.' Peggy stroked from the toe of the red slipper up to her knee with a long 'Mmm' of satisfaction. 'That's not why he taught you your letters.'

'He taught *you* your letters. You taught me.'

Peggy stroked the other leg. Kirsty Mary stood in front of her, hands on hips, seething with suppressed youth. 'Don't *you* want to get out of here?'

'I don't know.' She drew her skirts up to her thighs, stretching and admiring her long slim legs, and the slippers.

'Oh-oh! What's doing, then?' Kirsty Mary bounced up and down on the settle, eager for confidences. 'He really fancies you, doesn't he? Would you marry him? Will you be a minister's wife some day, Peggy?'

'He hasn't asked me.' Peggy squinted demurely at her knees, making her mouth small.

Both girls burst into peals of laughter.

'Marry him?' Peggy stopped laughing abruptly. 'The wee man of God. No-oo-o.' She pulled her skirt down close round her ankles, withdrawing her feet from the slippers. Her dark eyes gleamed with malice.

'Let's make a bet, though,' she said, snatching the coveted objects playfully back from their owner's hands.

'What's that?'

'I'll have the shoes, if . . . '

'If what? What'll you do?'

'If . . . '

'If, if! Come on, tell me!' Kirsty Mary thumped gleefully on her friend's shoulders.

'Oh no, I can't tell you.'

'Whisper! If . . . '

'If . . . ' trilled Peggy, and leaned to the other's ear to whisper a man's downfall.

Kirsty Mary whooped with delight.

'You might as well let me have them now,' said Peggy, smiling with narrowed eyes.

26 AUGUST 1851

Anniversary. Four years.

I write this in Oban, where I have lodged overnight to await the steamer. The room is well furnished, with wall-paper, a china basin and ewer upon the wash-stand, a carpet upon the floor, etc. All comforts which I must soon leave. How pleasant the hand of a woman makes a house.

My mother's last words to me on leaving this morning: Write to your sister. Remind her of her duty. I can do no more, I spoke first kindly to her, then more sternly. I put before her Scripture proofs, as Deuteronomy 21.

This year I had thought to return to Rona in the knowledge that I would not be long there single. Miss Beresford, whom I considered a worthy choice, did not accept my offer of marriage, therefore I must continue alone.

Certain events which at the time I did not note in this journal (they being of a personal nature) convinced me that I was called to matrimony.

At the time of their occurrence, I had in mind a certain young person of my congregation, who, though of no education, was yet (I thought) young and simple enough to be tutored by me in her position, if she should become my wife.

This young person has now left the island.

I know not now whether the call to matrimony (as I so regarded it) was of God or of the Adversary. Yet Saint Paul says, It is better to marry than to burn.

'He is like a refiner's fire.' Malachi 3.2.

'But he himself shall be saved; yet so as by fire.' I Corinthians 3.15.

Miss Beresford gave as her reason for not accepting, that she did not think she could live in a place so dismal and remote as that where I am bound. I put to her my expectation of a charge (eventually) in some better parish but she treated this lightly.

This year was the last of the Destitution relief. The wall is not yet completed, but the people are now sufficiently well off. Two crews now fish regularly and there is some labouring work from time to time on Boreray, where the new road is a-building. Two of the young females have gone into service on the mainland, and a young lad to Port Long.

I have let it be known that if another can be found to take my place here, I am ready to leave.

All day, six days in the week, long days in summer and short days in winter, Donald laboured at or inside the wall. Even after the parish relief was stopped, he never went out with the fishing crews or crossed to Boreray to join the road gangs there. He drained his plot of land within the wall and set wee Donald to drive the sheep out of it when they strayed in from the gap at the far end. He would labour till there was no gap, till all the great brown marshy basin was as green and neat as the plots he had tilled and drained, and drained again, straight rows of potatoes, a grey-green oblong of oats hinting at gold and ripeness, a small sweet lawn of grass where Ciarag and her calf might be tethered. This was the work God had given him, to bring the barren island into bearing, so that people would never starve again. Often he thought to himself, heaving single-handed at the great slabs that tied the wall, Except the Lord build the house, they labour in vain that build it, and the wonderful strength that flooded his limbs at those times was an assurance. In the back end of the year the rainbow arched over the grey hillside and shimmered in his little plot of green, a token of blessing. Sometimes as he straightened his back in the dusk, aching and with the sweat of labour already turning to chill, deep peace fell on him, deeper than any of hearth or bed: well done, thou good and faithful servant.

His crops were good, but he earned no money. His family were the poorest on Rona and held their heads the highest. He was Donald the Elder, the only one of them all judged worthy to partake of the Lord's Supper in the new Free Church at Port Long. Sometimes the other men came to where he worked and put in an hour with him, even those who had never sown a seed in their own plots. They came because of the man he was, upright and sober, one who had no secrets – for what secrets would avail before God? They were proud of him: they boasted of him when they went over the water to other villages, how Donald the Elder had done them out of a dead pauper's rations when they were starving, because he was too honest to cover up; how he had reported his wife's mother to the preacher for bowing to the new moon, though he loved the old woman like his own kin; how he wouldn't have his children blessed against the fairies.

When Donald pointed out the land between the two walls and said, 'If it is His will, the Lord will make the desert bloom for us, one day', they listened respectfully and almost believed it. The neat chequer-work of his potatoes and corn between the straight gleaming ditches made it seem possible.

But if you stood a stone's throw away from Donald's Eden, there was only on either side a long thin ribbon of grey dividing brown from grey and brown: windswept, rain-rotten desolation, under a weeping sky.

26 AUGUST 1852

Thanks be to God, I have now been five years engaged in His work of salvation in Rona. To His name be glory and praise!

Thank the Lord, I am now far otherwise from what I was a year, nay a month, ago. I was prey to worldly ambitions, but the scales have fallen from my eyes. Miserable sinner that I was, and still am! Yet hath He vouchsafed to shine upon my soul that knowledge of salvation through Christ Jesus which is faith. By election I am His for ever: let me never doubt again, or put my feeble desires before His heavenly will!

O God, I thank Thee that Thou didst make trial of me, that Thou didst refine me in Thy fire. Thou hast visited me with grief and despondency. For my wilfulness and hardness of heart He has visited me, as a father who loves his son chastiseth him betimes.

I found myself convicted of sin. I would have turned my hand from the plough, leaving the task which God has appointed me. Then the example of the Apostle appeared before me, 'Persecuted, but not forsaken; cast down but not destroyed.'

It is the Lord's will that I should remain here in my present humble capacity. For 'there are diversities of gifts, but the same Spirit'. My grief for my dear mother's death is turned to joy in the workings of providence, which by her departure from this vale of tears has rendered me free of all worldly responsibilities and aspirations, so that I may continue here (although my sister proved defective in her duty).

That no other was found to take my place, which in my obduracy caused me nearly to despair, I see now was providential.

In the matter of marriage, that which I took as a sign of calling to that estate was but a temptation. I fell, I repented, I am forgiven. My scarlet sin is washed whiter than snow in the blood of Jesus Christ!

Everywhere, I see falling away from that perfection which is Christ Jesus, but I do not despair. Rather I rejoice in the race which is set before me.

Tomorrow is the Lord's Day, which we have been deficient in keeping holy. Ever I look for guidance in God's sacred Scriptures. Today, letting the Book fall open, I found: 'Keep the Sabbath day to sanctify it as the Lord thy God hath commanded thee', and again; 'But even unto this day when Moses is read, the vail is upon their heart', and again, 'Doth God take care for oxen?'

How plainly it appeared to me then, O Lord, by the light of Thy Holy Word, how many of those works we have called 'necessary', as tending and milking the cattle, sheep etc., are not so, and must be left aside during the Sabbath day to sanctify it.

Also it came to me from the Lord that those who leave off the service of God on pretext of sickness, age, extreme youth, etc., are wrong. What sickness of body is to be compared to the sickness of sin which besets our souls, for which our only hope and heal is the Word of God? From tomorrow, I am resolved that all who can walk must attend.

'For I am jealous over you with godly jealousy: for I have espoused you to one husband, that I may present you as a chaste virgin to Christ.' II Corinthians 11.2. I am charged with these people before God.

After the warning meted out at the morning service, not a soul was absent in the evening. Babies did not dare to cry or the aged to mumble, consumptives turned pale on stifled coughs, the queasy closed their eyes and crouched by the door. Mr Macleay preached on the text of Numbers 16, verses 32 to 36, of the man who gathered sticks on the Sabbath and was stoned to death. In the fold outside, Cruinneag, Ciarag, Muirneag lowed in gentle wonderment, painfully unmilked. Their voices bewildered people, so that they didn't take in much about the man with the sticks, except for Donald, who gave the preacher's pale excited face his rapt attention.

'Bride protect you, my bonny dearies,' whispered Annag, bowing her head before the will of the Lord.

Later she used the same blessing to her daughter, too weak after puerperal fever to rise from her bed, for all her husband's urging. The baby, another boy, had died five days before.

'He talked about Job. He didn't shed a tear.'

'Oh well, well,' Annag whispered, shaking her head, but with an anxious glance at Donald, where he sat by the door pointing in the Bible for his two little boys. Mór hadn't lowered her voice out of his hearing, though it was weak enough maybe not to be heard.

'Mother, he was asking if you coming to see me on the Sabbath was a necessity, now I'm over the fever.'

'Indeed it is, dear. But the menfolk don't know much about these matters, that's all, that's all there is to it.'

'Mother, what did I marry? Is he a man?'

Her shaky voice rose to a ring of anguish. Donald's deep confident tones never faltered, as he sat reading the Book in his blue Sunday coat.

Annag whispered her benediction and left, bowing to the elder.

1 8 6 2–1 8 6 3

CHAPTER 16

'Oh dear me, what *does* he think of us?' Issie murmured into Dileas's fur. A plain middle-aged lady with a fat old lapdog, in such a place. She smiled as confidently as possible at the black-clad bewhiskered figure standing squarely, with legs apart, atop the jetty. Mr Macleay inclined his head, unsmiling. Issie, quailing before such monumental gravity, cushioned Dileas to her chest against the slamming surges, with a salt taste of loneliness in her mouth.

The steersman turned sharply inshore, so that the black cliff wall raced up on Issie's startled eyes. The sail flew out, cracking and flapping, and fell with a clatter, swathing her in its dripping folds. Dileas yapped and struggled, lunging for the bare ankles of the lad who ran along the gunwale behind them to leap ashore and stave off the bows. Issie cried out, clutching at the terrier's hindquarters just in time, as the boat lurched downwards on her side. The steersman eyed her with mild surprise over his pipe.

'My dog . . . I'm afraid he'll drown,' she explained. Remembering, she repeated it in halting Gaelic, but the steersman was unsmiling too.

Biting her lip, she tucked Dileas under her arm, hitching up her skirt with the same hand in an accustomed movement, and stepped as steadily as possible across the rocking boat to Mr Macleay's proferred arm. The great stone blocks of the jetty loomed chest-high between them. Issie regarded the insurmountable wall with rising panic. She could not let go of frail old Dileas, therefore she could not climb it: she must follow local custom so as not to appear offensive, but she had no idea, in this instance, what it might be. Her eyes fell on male boots and male bare toes, gnarled and hairy, but no woman was present to advise her. In mute appeal she looked up at Mr Macleay, who still held out his arm, above her head. Suddenly, the steersman behind her thrust his shoulder against her thighs and hoisted her, with hoops billowing, on to the pier. Issie, shrieking, clutched Dileas, yapping. Upright again, she stammered, red and breathless. 'Oh – thank you – how kind – Good-day, Mr Macleay. I am Miss Macdonald – oh, but obviously you know that.' Nervous laughter rose in her at her own awkwardness, but she gasped it back. Mr Macleay's pale features were stern, the grey-bearded man behind him stood unmoving. The boat crew had already thrown her trunk and bags up beside her and were pushing off. Issie half turned, her heart contracting as the water widened between boat and jetty, leaving her among strangers – such strangers! The spray of good-luck white heather tucked into the strap of her trunk reproached her for hoping. The older man's sombre gaze was upon it. She withered inwardly.

'Miss Macdonald, may I introduce Mr Donald Macdonald the Elder, who is a namesake of yours, as you will find many are here.'

As he turned to her, Issie noticed that he had something wrong with one eye. She shook hands very warily, twitching Dileas sideways. His temper in old age was uncertain; he might bite strangers. Don't now, please don't, Dileas, she prayed, reddening again with dread at the possibility.

'Welcome and thrice welcome. May God's blessing be upon you,' the elder said, with such unexpected sincerity in voice and hand that Issie's mouth opened in an involuntary 'Oh' of pleasure. Suddenly, disarmed, with loneliness and apprehension draining from her like water from the sail, she saw that his good eye was clear and innocent in his harsh lined face, and direct as a child's; and that Mr Macleay was anxious, his lowland English rusty from his long exile, his whiskers carefully arranged to lend dignity to a face that was a little weak, and still quite young, at least not much older than her own – but she felt quite old herself, older than he seemed, because of all that had happened.

'I hope I shall manage to do everything that is expected of me,' she said, this time not suppressing her smile.

'With God's help, you will.' Mr Macleay smiled too, at last, but briefly, a fleeting gleam of natural kindliness across a rock face of sobriety.

Removing his hat and clearing his throat, he thanked God rather lengthily for Issie's safe arrival. Then, with a wave of his arm, he conjured four lads from the recesses of the rocks, shock-headed urchins too shy to look at her, who seized her bags and scuttled away with them over the boulders, goat-nimble. Dileas barked furiously. Issie clasped his muzzle to silence him and picked her way more slowly up the steep rocky path.

Mr Macleay cleared his throat again. 'These lads will be among your pupils,' he said, looking at the ground and keeping his hands behind his back but presumably intending friendship in initiating conversation.

Issie could have done with his arm to help her up the slippery rock, but she was more used than most ladies to managing without. She hitched her skirt higher, then seeing Mr Macleay's downturned gaze follow her hem, dropped it again, confused and beginning to feel angry. She reminded herself, negotiating a flow of scree running with water, that she must bear with local custom, that she must not expect gallantry in a place where she had been told the women dug the fields and bore the burdens, and served their menfolk before they ate themselves. Mr Macleay waited ahead of her, with black-clad shoulders slightly hunched to meet his down-bending black hat. Mr Macdonald kept behind.

'And how many children shall I teach?' she asked hastily, to steady the recurring shakiness in her throat.

'Eleven are of an age for lessons. And over there is your classroom, Miss Macdonald. You have the seaward end of the building. There is a room next the schoolroom, which has been partitioned off from my own quarters. This is the best we could contrive in the circumstances.'

They had reached the ridge above the village. 'It looks quite . . . quite . . . sufficient,' quavered Issie, not managing 'delightful' or even 'agreeable', though she wished to.

It's raining, she told herself, it's early March. It won't always look like this. Her frightened gaze touched on one hurt after another: the ugly grey oblong of the mission house, scowling down on the scatter of mean hovels, low and round as molehills; stinking middens at the doors, a skinny calf patched pink with ringworm, a mangy dog hopping on three legs with one forefoot hooked up through a rope collar to prevent its escape. Behind was a steep slope of black rock and livid green mosses, dripping from many overhangs; before, a restless grey sea and mist covering the land she had come from, cutting her off.

She had learned from long experience that it was better to speak before tears got the mastery.

'Where are all the people?'

'The men are at sea. The women, I am certain, will be there to welcome you.'

Issie, heartsunk, thought this a polite nothing. As they threaded a way through the puddles and rubbish, she was aware here of a pair of eyes behind a peat-stack, of a door drawing stealthily shut there, with a mother shushing a child behind it. Thin dogs circled and sidled, throwing Dileas into a frenzy. Dripping hens pressed against the doors, too dispirited even to squawk. They will never by my friends, thought Issie. An impulse to flee brought her almost to a halt, half sobbing, but the boat had gone. All had gone. Chewing on her lip, she followed Mr Macleay's authoritative black back through a smudged and dingy murk of browns and greys.

As they rounded the last house beneath the mission, suddenly there were colours and people: women in white mutches and bright plaids, with children peeping behind their skirts, and pretty pink-cheeked girls with loose hair. More were running up, silent on bare feet, from behind the houses – from behind Issie. They had followed noiselessly along the street from the doors she had thought shut and hostile, and now divided round her and grouped before her, curtseying and each taking her hands in both their own, grimy, field-roughened hands and big red washer-women's hands and clean white dairymaid's hands. The shy girls hid behind their shawls, the matrons voiced dignified greetings: 'May God's goodness be yours, and well and seven times well may you spend your life.'

Issie replied as best she could in Gaelic; this at last brought smiles and one of the older women patted her cheek and kissed her, to Dileas's fury. Some of the little children began to laugh and point at the parti-coloured hairy face poking comically from the crook of her arm.

Mr Macleay cleared his throat again, significantly. At once heads were bowed while he rendered more fulsome thanks, this time in Gaelic, for Miss Macdonald's safe arrival on Rona. Issie did not understand much of the archaic language used in prayer. Privately, she thought it seemed a very long-winded way of saying very little, but reflected that she was by now extremely cold, wet and hungry, and therefore immune to the propriety and beauty of phrase, particularly since Dileas wriggled and growled abominably, to her great embarrassment. Still, she was very touched by the good intention of all around her and the more so when, on entering her new home, she found a bright fire burning in the grate and her bags laid neatly on the floor. Three pairs of woollen stockings and a folded plaid were hung over one of the two wooden chairs.

'We thought you might be cold, my dearie,' said the old woman who had kissed her, holding up the stockings with a beaming smile.

'Oh, how kind – how kind you are.' Issie took them gratefully: her feet were freezing inside her soaked boots.

Mr Macleay averted his eyes from the articles of female dress and withdrew with a request that she should take tea with him in due course.

Mr Macleay's parlour was as Spartan as the room she had just left, uncurtained and unpapered. Two upright chairs and a deal table stood upon bare boards. A shelved alcove held books, a rough plank settle of the sort found in the meanest cottage faced the scanty fire. The afternoon was dull, closing into dusk, but there was no lamp or candle. The only homely touches were a rag rug at the fireside and a framed photograph of an elderly lady in mourning garb on the mantel. Issie had time to observe and be curious, since Annag had ushered her round from the school-house while Mr Macleay was out of the room.

He entered carrying a sooty kettle in one hand and a tin tea-caddy in the other.

'I would be greatly honoured if you would make the tea, Miss Macdonald. We have little of such luxuries here. I have no skill at it.' His voice conveyed an uneasy mixture of wishing to please, and desiring her to know the vanity of such operations.

Issie tried to hide her surprise: she had supposed Annag to be his housekeeper. Mr Macleay went out twice more, for cups and a plate of oatcakes. Issie, in his absence, sniffed the tea doubt-fully. It was very musty.

'May I have the teapot, Mr Macleay?'

Failing an answer, she glanced up and caught a ripple of consternation on his firelit features.

'Usually I make it in the kettle, when I require to make it at all,' he said stiffly.

From which she deduced that he had no teapot. To restore amiability, she admired the china cups, whilst doing her best with the smoky kettle and stale tea. Immediately she had spoken, she supposed she should have said nothing, for china, too, was doubtless a frivolous luxury, but Mr Macleay responded with animation, rocking on the heels of his heavy black boots.

'Ah! They were a gift from my dear mother. She never sent me back here without some such present, some little comfort, which I treasure not for its own sake, but for hers.'

Issie, seeing none but the cups and the rug, wondered about the rest. She expressed regret for Mrs Macleay's passing.

' "The Lord giveth and the Lord taketh away",' remarked her son in a tone of reproof.

There followed a long grace while the tea cooled, then silence while they ate and drank. The butter on the oatcakes tasted rancid and very salty to Issie but she was famished, having eaten nothing since dawn. Mr Macleay seemed equally hungry. Soon only one piece remained on the plate. They both glanced at it. Mr Macleay, after a moment's hesitation, offered it to Issie, who declined. He eyed it, she thought, longingly, but left it there. Issie began to smile at his momentary guileless look of boyish greed but it was hidden quickly by his large hand shading his eyes, while he returned thanks for the meal.

Issie, her hunger within bounds, was feeling increasingly ill at ease. She had something that she must lay before her host but she could not bring herself to do so, to talk of her own intimate affairs to a stranger. She could have spoken to the greedy boy, or to the son of the fond mother, but not to the man of the patriarchal beard, with its few crumbs quivering incongruously in the blast of godly circumlocution. 'Wipe your mouth' floated into her mind, from Georgie's days. She was so tired she was not certain, for a second, that she had not said it aloud. At Mr Macleay's 'Amen' she half rose, desperate to leave before any irredeemable indiscretion escaped her lips, but he signed her to be seated.

'Miss Macdonald, while I understand you must be fatigued after your journey, there are certain matters to be discussed. It is for that rather than social reasons I requested you to take tea with me.'

Issie sat down again on the rickety chair.

'You know that I requested someone to assist me in teaching and medical matters. The population has grown since I came here, fifteen years ago. I am much occupied in preaching the Word to my flock. I hold two services on Sunday, of three hours each: then there is a prayer meeting on Wednesdays, and also on alternate Fridays. I visit each home almost daily, to pray, to exhort, to reprove in the love of Christ. For fifteen years I have taught the people, young and old, to the best of my ability, both in English and in their native tongue, in the Word of God and in the catechism. I have begged over and over again for an assistant, but my requests have been ignored. Ignored!'

Mr Macleay, rising during this speech, rocked on his heels in increasing agitation, speaking faster and louder. At its conclusion he looked at Issie, apparently somewhat at a loss.

'I understood no one could be found willing to come to such a remote spot,' she said gently, 'but I don't think your request was ignored.'

He blinked, almost hopefully. 'Don't you?'

'No. The population here is too poor to support a schoolmaster, is it not? So my offer of assistance was accepted, since I do not require payment.'

'But you are not of our persuasion.'

'I am not of a fixed persuasion, Mr Macleay. I shall attend all your services with' – Issie bit off 'pleasure' just in time – 'due devotion. I can teach children, I like children very well, and I know something of nursing.'

Mr Macleay frowned at the floor, rocking again. 'I had expected a man,' he said sulkily.

Issie could manage no more. A child, and the nursing of him, ran in her mind and swamped her voice. The chair she sat on creaked its lame leg in protest at her inattentive posture. Wearily, she arched her back from it.

Mr Macleay peered into her face. 'Would you be more comfortable on the settle, Miss Macdonald? Nearer the fire? Are you cold?'

'I am a little cold.'

'And tired. I know you are tired.'

'Yes.'

He loomed over her, bulky and clumsy, and so close she could smell the ammoniac tang of his homespun woollen waistcoat. She shifted uncomfortably, but though his presence oppressed her, his concern was worth something. She blurted out what she had rehearsed to say before his resumption of dignity should make her change her mind.

'I have something to tell you about myself, Mr Macleay, which I pray you will treat with the utmost discretion. I tell it to you only as an earnest of my good intentions; for you not to know it would be deceit on my part, I think. I should feel it so, in any case. But there is no need for it to go further. Indeed, I should be very sorry if it did. I am the daughter of the late Sir Hector Macdonald of Drumharg, who was proprietor when you were first appointed and who died shortly afterwards. As you must know from the recent sale of these islands, a sale which my father could never have countenanced, the family has fallen on hard times. All the estates are sold off and the title, which was to pass to my sister's son, has gone to a cousin, the child having died a minor. Family fortunes – no matter. I merely wish to express . . . '

Issie passed her hands over her eyes. In the pain of memory and weariness she could scarcely recollect what she had wished to express, what she could express of the pity, the anguish, the joy of the little boy's infancy, the long-drawn-out suffering of his death. What could she express to this awkward, boorish stranger, whose God was as stony as his home?

He did not help her with any sign of sympathy or surprise. If he had, she would have burst into tears, but the smart of his unfeelingness stung her pride: she was a chief's daughter.

'I have no reason to tell you this, except to explain my motive in coming to Rona rather than elsewhere, and also, that my application to assist was treated kindly because of my connection with the place. You may remember that my father permitted your placement here when many other landlords were hostile to all but the Established Church. And . . . ' The rest she found difficult to explain, even to herself. 'The lands are not my family's now, of course, although I hope I made all tenancies secure, so that there should be' – she swallowed – 'no repetition of – I do not know what happened in the past. My father acted, as he thought, in the people's best interests. My brother-in-law worked for fourteen years assisting the Canadian settlers, and lost all by it . . . but . . . ' She searched Mr Macleay's face beseechingly. 'I want to help!' she cried.

He raised his head, his lips parted, his eyes alight. 'Thanks be to God!' he cried exultantly. 'By His grace you were led here. By His grace you will abound! Know, Miss Macdonald, know in your heart: every good gift and every perfect gift cometh from above! Let us pray together for God's blessing on you and on your work.'

They prayed together at length; or rather, he prayed fervently while she fretted over her aching weariness, his changeability, her cold feet, her lack of attention to prayer. She forced herself to remain seated for a few moments of silence after the long rolling phrases had ceased before rising to go.

Again Mr Macleay halted her by speaking. 'So you are quite without family, quite alone in the world?' he asked quietly, his prominent eyes intent on her face.

Issie could not say no. Yes was a lie and she could not lie on impulse; it required forethought and she had given it none. The blood rushed to her face and drained away, leaving her heart pounding.

'My brother-in-law may still be alive in Canada,' she prevaricated.

Sweating with confusion, she took her leave. Mr Macleay, in spite of her protestations, insisted on escorting her. She was afraid of another prayer, which she could not have borne, but he left with a hesitant bow and a low 'Goodnight'.

Issie slammed the door with unmannerly haste and sank down in front of the dying fire beside Dileas. He blinked old misty eyes at her, and nodded back to sleep, champing his stiff jaws and grumbling. She clutched his paw, the rough little hand that had comforted her through so many years. Her shawl under his belly felt damp and smelled rank: he had grown as leaky as a puppy.

'We'll wash it tomorrow, Dileas,' she promised. But he was unconcerned; he had little sense of smell left and snored comfortably in his malodorous nest.

She was slow and heavy with cold and exhaustion and with the deceit she had tried to throw off by laying other secrets bare. She rummaged in the bottom of her trunk for Augustus's journals and Miss Nightingale's *Notes on Nursing* and laid them by her bed with her Bible, as was her custom; but on this night their familiar presence gave no comfort. She opened the last of the journals and took out from between its flyleaves Helen's letter, with its mean Edinburgh address. She did not read it but sat with it on her knee, staring into the embers. She had not reread it in the four months since its arrival, but she knew it by heart: 'I kept my word while the child was alive. I have nothing. If you saw me, you would pity me.'

She had pitied her, even before she saw her; and had seen her, bent, gaunt, querulous, in a squalid room in a questionable street. She was at least more suitably lodged now – that at least could be done for her – but it was charity to a stranger, at best a pious tribute to a dear memory. Helen, the adored, the lovely, was no more alive to her than she had been for the past fifteen years. And Augustus: he had known all these years, had given his unfaithful wife what she demanded so as to keep his son untainted from her. Issie had misjudged him, thinking him a callous husband, a neglectful father. 'Forgive me,' she whispered to the dead man. She knew he was dead, somewhere in the northern forests.

She built up the fire for Dileas, undressed, and slid, shivering, into the damp lumpy bed. It was ice cold but she was too tired to be kept awake by it. Her closing eyes saw ice, frost: Major Drysdale in a beaver cape, striding quickly down the drive to Helen. She drifted further and the figure between the tall trees was Augustus, floundering in the snow. Helen was on the other side of the forest. She called that she had no money, and Augustus struggled forward. He had a heavy burden on his back. 'She must have this money,' he said. He walked deeper and deeper into the snow, till it closed over his head.

Mr Macleay allowed himself a candle to write his journal but it had almost drowned in a pool of tallow before he put pen to paper. He thanked God for Miss Macdonald's arrival, but somewhat coolly, as if constrained by some inner reservation. After staring at the partition between his former study and his present quarters for some time, he noted that it seemed satisfactory.

'Them teeth!' old Hector chuckled, slapping his long skinny thighs. 'Them teeth, boys! I'd know them anywhere.'

'Och, you'll not be saying to her, now. Don't you say anything at all, Hector. The poor soul is not wanting it known.' Annag spoke in his face and tapped his knee for emphasis, to be sure he understood. He had grown deaf and was inclined to ramble.

'Not a word, Hector,' Ciorstag added more threateningly.

'Och, not a word, not a word.' Hector shook his head, still chuckling, and packed his pipe, drawing on it with great satisfaction. There was always tobacco in the last few years, since young Hector did so well on the boats. 'I was with her uncle in Spain. I wouldn't be hurting the lassie.'

'Her father did ill enough by us, then.' John Blackie, whittling a spindle, cursed as his anger nicked a chip from it and swallowed the curse under Donald's eye. 'You didn't hear that one, Donald.'

'I'll hear the next one.' Donald did not smile, even in banter at the ceilidh-house. There were several there who, though they loved him, wished he would go home so that they could tell the old stories, of the brownie of Airidh Tobrach and Lachlan mac Iain's prophecies and the ghostly funeral that met Roderick's Hughie before his mother died. But Donald sat on, not smoking, just sitting. He had not smoked since he found the preacher didn't smoke. 'An indulgence we can do without,' he said now, eyeing John's pipe.

John's second wife Marsaili tossed her head, gathered her children, and tutted away home. She was a Port Long girl who had worked in the Big House and she knew there was a job for her there again, if she chose to be off: so she stayed, but wore her fashionable bonnet on Sundays, in spite of all.

'Ay, Donald.' John looked solemn. 'We can do without many things. We did without an elder on Fladday.' He had learned how to deal with his brother-in-law, over the years.

Donald was forced to smile after all, shamefacedly. After a pause he said, 'That's our wee dog she's still carrying.'

John looked up from his whittling. 'Never the same one!'

'Ay. With the one black ear.'

Annag repeated the conversation for Hector's benefit.

'Oh well, well. She must have liked it, then.'

'Ay. She must have liked it right enough.'

CHAPTER 17

Issie loved Dileas as a mother her dying child. She was under no
illusions: he was nearly sixteen, his senses were all failing, and
his tottery limbs often gave way. His stomach was large and his
appetite good, but his spine had begun to stick out. She could
feel it through his thick rough coat when she fondled him, more
knobbly every day. She had begun to stroke his sides instead so
that she would not be reminded; then his ribs began to be
perceptible as his fur became less thick. But Rona reinvigorated
him. It was a much more interesting place than the series of town
lodgings they had recently occupied, with smells potent enough
to attract even a dull nose. He had a day-bed in the schoolroom
at Issie's feet. She told the children he was an island dog and she
would have loved to tell them more, if it would not have given
away her secret. They, for their part, even the youngest, had the
discretion not to reveal that they knew his history. He barked
every time a child rose or sat down, with bright eyes and bristling
whiskers, so puffed by his new life that Issie began to hope;
though also to despair of ever making herself understood through
his constant yapping. But ten days after their arrival, while
waddling ahead of her up the hill, he fell over with a jabbering
yelp of pain and lay with half-shut eyes, his panting tongue
turning from pink to blue. She carried him home and sat with
him all night, trickling cordials down his throat from the store Mr
Macleay had entrusted to her for the relief of the islanders'
diseases. He slept fitfully and at last snored, almost in his normal
rhythm, but at dawn a second seizure took him. This time the
rigidity did not let go till his shallow panting ceased and his head
fell back slowly, with sagging tongue. Issie, who had soothed

and stroked him all night without a tear to worry him, burst into desolate weeping.

In the schoolroom the children assembled and after a time applied their ears to the intervening door. 'Oh, the wee dog! What a shame!' sighed John Blondie's Rebecca, the oldest girl. The big boys began to jeer, but she silenced them with a wave of the pointer: Miss Macdonald had made her top of the class at the end of the first week and everyone was impressed. Rebecca, Mary and Florann wept with their arms about each other's necks and the little ones followed their example, but all in undertones so as not to be heard next door.

'I'm off to tell himself,' announced Rebecca after a decent interval. 'She'll want him to say a wee prayer in her bereavement.'

'For a dog?' sneered Duncan, but had to duck from the pointer, though he was the elder's son. Rebecca handed over pointer and authority to Mary, and swept out on her errand of mercy.

Issie reminded herself of the waiting children several times, washed her face from the cracked basin on the table, and made determinedly for the door; but twice she caught sight of the poor limp body with its glazing eyes and crouched over it again in an agony of tears. The third time she covered it with her shawl, but that was worse, seeing the inert bumps that had been a living shoulder and haunch. 'Oh, where shall I bury you, where shall I bury you?' she sobbed, covering and uncovering the one black ear.

She had just made a fourth and most resolute repair to her face and hair when a hesitant knock came at the door. Thinking it was one of her pupils searching for her, she called 'Come in', and turned in sudden panic to the corpse, in case she had left it uncovered – or covered; either was exposure. She burst into tears again. 'Wait – wait for me in the schoolroom,' she gasped.

Mr Macleay cleared his throat.

'Oh!' Issie's screech expressed betrayal, nakedness. He backed for the door, stumbling against the table. 'Miss Macdonald, forgive my intrusion, Miss Macdonald. One of the children told me you were . . . indisposed. I came merely to enquire if I could – '

'Please go away,' said Issie, dully. Since the evening of her arrival she had scarcely seen him except at religious services, and these had made him even more of a stranger than their first acquaintance. With face averted she waited for the sound of the door opening and closing, but it did not come. She heard the creak of his heels rocking on the bare wooden floor. Trapped, she cowered silent in front of dead Dileas.

'Miss Macdonald, I see you are deeply troubled . . . very sad . . . ' He tried again. 'In grief of heart, Miss Macdonald, we must ever turn to the Comforter above.'

Issie mastered her voice sufficiently to say, 'My dog has died. Perhaps you would be kind enough to tell the children I shall be with them presently.'

The creak-creak-creak on the boards speeded up. 'Ah.' And ceased. 'You were extremely attached to the animal?'

'He was my only companion.' Issie forced herself to sit in a chair and face him. The sooner she appeared calm, the sooner he would go, surely.

Mr Macleay's protuberant blue eyes blinked at her. He means well, she reminded herself, trying not to turn from the insensitive fixity of his appraisal.

He cleared his throat again. 'Miss Macdonald, it is natural you should sorrow for the loss of your pet. Natural, but unworthy, Miss Macdonald, unworthy of a Christian. Even the great grief we feel at the loss of a dear friend or a beloved parent – even such grief is unworthy, except insofar as we fear for their souls and ours before the Judgment Throne: for they have but gone before us to the bosom of the Father, where is neither sorrow nor crying, and where God shall wipe away all tears from their eyes. Is it not idolatry, so to grieve for the creature, when we should rather glorify the Creator?'

He paused. Issie hoped he had done, and tried to appear attentive. A frown of perplexity crossed his features. 'But' – he laboured back to the unusual point from the usual formula of consolation – 'but, Miss Macdonald! If it be unchristian to mourn a fellow human soul, think how much worse – how great the sin – to grieve for a brute beast which has no soul – '

Issie rose. She was a tall woman, and anger pulled her an extra two inches up from her habitual stoop. Mr Macleay stopped in mid-cadence.

'How dare you! Who are you to decide where God has or has not placed a soul?'

'Not I . . . not I, but the Scriptures . . . '

'The Scriptures!' Issie was not exceptionally well read in Scripture, or retentive about it, but there was one passage at least over which she had pondered frequently: 'Don't you know what it says in the book of Ecclesiastes? "All are of the dust and turn to dust again. Who knoweth the spirit of man that goeth upward, and the spirit of the beast that goeth downward to the earth?" '

Mr Macleay was silenced, not so much by any inherent unanswerability in the text as by someone having dared, or even desired, to challenge him to scriptural battle. His silence brought to Issie's notice a faint scrabbling behind the schoolroom door: so eleven pairs of ears had heard him discomfited. She felt an upsurge of angry laughter, which turned before it surfaced to half-repelled pity for the poor man, who was all in bits and pieces; and then before she could steel herself, she had begun to weep again in bitter loneliness. She got herself quickly under control. By that time Mr Macleay was praying, but not at his usual length or volume, asking only for the blessing of the knowledge of the love of God as a sovereign remedy for all ills; to which Issie managed to concur 'Amen' without rebellion.

There was an awkward pause. Issie felt obliged to speak, lest he take it as hostility. 'Mr Macleay, don't think I rail against providence. I thank God for the dear companion I have lost, as for the others I have lost before. I have had my share of grief and I know what the best cure for it is – it is work. And I shall work. That is my offering to God, Mr Macleay – my work. That will be my comfort and I shall be thankful for it.'

He nodded vigorously, his round eyes blinking at her with great enthusiasm. 'Well said, Miss Macdonald. That was very well said. May God bless you for it.'

Still he did not go. 'There were certain matters I wished to discuss with you to do with the children's lessons.'

'Tomorrow after school,' said Issie firmly.

After he had gone she wrapped Dileas carefully in her shawl. The body had cooled and stiffened and that finality put a distance between them which made it easier to bear. Later, the big girls brought a spade and helped to bury him on a knoll just outside Issie's window. They gave him a dignified funeral, being well used to mourning and the decorum grief requires to assuage it. Rebecca, very softly, sang a song committing him to the kindly Christ of the free blessings, 'Because I don't think it would be right to sing a psalm, miss.' Whispering together, they made a little cairn over the grave: 'If Mr Macleay is asking, you should be saying it is to stop the other dogs digging him up, miss.'

Issie put herself to work. There was no lack of it. School, as the children were used to it, extended from dawn to dusk in the winter, and ceased altogether in summer, when their labour was required on the crofts. There were no slates, no paper, no writing implements, and no books except for Bibles and catechisms. Mr Macleay had chalked the alphabet on the grey plaster wall, together with numerals from one to ten and the English metrical version of the Twenty-third Psalm. The children sat cross-legged on the floor. For Issie there was a rough table made of driftwood, scrawled with the burrowings of marine worms, and a stool that was too high to allow of writing at it.

For the first few days none of her shy pupils would speak at all, except to give answers to the catechism, questions 1 to 107, according to age and aptitude, or to chant back at her portions of Scripture. Mr Macleay had impressed on her the necessity of using English as far as possible to encourage proficiency in that language, but when one child, on being asked his name, reeled off the Beatitudes, and another delivered the hundredth psalm in lieu of the two-times table, Issie decided it was best to use her own discretion on that point.

The two-times table was in any case an optimistic request. Multiplication in its strictly numerical form does not enter into the Bible; and so Mr Macleay had not wasted time in teaching it. Some of the children could read, though how well was difficult to ascertain, for they knew such vast tracts, such interminable wildernesses of Scripture by heart. The older among them could speak, as well as recite, some English, but they uttered the very phrases of the Authorised Version. 'Unto us a child is born,' announced Katie's boy, Archie, excusing his lateness on the morning of his little brother's birth, shocking Issie momentarily by his blasphemous familiarity.

From the first day she longed for Georgie's picture books, yet she could not bear to surrender the few she had kept as treasured mementoes to these rough, dirty peasant children: children with lousy heads and runny noses, who stared at her woodenly from eyes ringed black with peat smoke, on whose faces smiles seemed as rare as sunlight on their native hill-side. She wrote at once to the Society in Scotland for the Propagation of Christian Knowledge, asking them to send whatever was possible to furnish a schoolroom, but before she had even contrived to send off the letter, she had re-lented on the subject of Georgie's books. They stared at them woodenly, too. She closed them hastily, shrinking from their indifference; but there was a ripple, small hands reaching out, exclamations and pushing, and at last smiles, wonder over the big, easily traced letters and the pictures of sleek children in pretty clothes.

'These things are pleasing unto them, miss,' confided Rebecca, who was almost a woman and the only one prepared to speak before she was spoken to.

Issie set to on the lousy heads and runny noses, treated coughs and scabs and dysentery and worms, with variable success. At first a crawling scalp or an accidental pool of diarrhoea on the floor made her stomach heave, but she reminded herself at such times of the redoubtable Miss Nightingale, whose portrait she carried inside her Bible, beside the text, 'Whatsoever ye would that men should do to you, do ye even so to them.' Dirty limbs, once handled, lost their anonymity: they became Neil, or Bell, or Drina. The children began to be hers. Every day she awarded them marks for clean hands, faces and feet, and for combed hair. 'Clean' was perhaps overstating it: she was ready to accept a black tidemark at neck, wrist or knee as earnest of good intent. A child with four marks got a sweet at the end of the day. When her small store of Everton toffee was exhausted she substituted a piece of butter dipped in sugar and sent to the merchant's across the water as soon as possible for one-and-sixpence-worth of aniseed balls. They did not last as long as they should have done. There was always some grubby forlorn one who had forgotten, or slept late, and then it seemed unfair not to give to the middling dirty who had remembered but been less than thorough.

Other than aniseed balls, her one extravagance was tea. For the rest, she lived frugally in her one room, cooking and cleaning for herself, both to keep herself busy as a defence against unhappiness and to avoid the expense of a servant. The meagre income that had descended to her from her mother she had diverted almost entirely to Helen's use; she could not spend a penny on herself without a pang of guilt for the sick woman's straitened circumstances. And indeed she found she could live on very little. Every day Mary, whose mother Sara milked two cows, brought a quart of milk. Others came with butter, cheese, or eggs, with a string of herring or a creel of peats. No payment was asked, and Issie, being Highland-bred, knew better than to offer it, had she possessed a thousand times the scanty sum in her purse.

But tea! When the quarter-pound she had brought from the mainland ran out she tried for a few days to follow Mr Macleay's abstemious example, drinking only milk or water; but so great was the longing for her usual beverage that on the third evening she went shamefaced to young Hector's house to ask him to shop for her when next his boat put in at Gnipadale. Sara, on hearing her errand, made her sit by the fire while a cup was brewed in her honour. 'Ay, we've all got a liking for the tea nowadays,' she said, tossing a handful of the leaves directly into a black iron pot bedded in the embers. When the mixture had boiled to her satisfaction she dipped it out into a cup, and finished it with sugar from a bag wedged in the rafters between the hens, and a squirt of milk from the udder of one of the cows, in for the night and warming her steaming rump at the hearth. Issie took the cup appreciatively, though scarcely with relish. Sara pressed a package on her as she left: 'Till himself can get more for you.'

Back in her room Issie boiled her kettle and made a brew exactly to her liking, with grateful, guilty delight. As she drank it, she reflected humbly on Mr Macleay's remarkable self-discipline in the matter. To sit over his books in his bleak room all the long dark evening, without succumbing! Warmed and soothed, she encouraged her heart to expand for him. During her own days of enforced abstinence her lack of liking for him had degenerated into real antipathy. She smiled at it now, drinking her beguiling potion, but at prayer meeting the previous evening she had felt almost ready to shout at him, for his joyless concatenation of unlike Scripture proofs. How could Acts 20, of the young man

197

who sank down with sleep when Paul was long preaching, be related to Daniel 5, MENE, MENE, TEKEL, UPHARSIN? But Mr Macleay had related them, and had threatened thereby the wrath of the Almighty on poor devout old Barabel, who had nodded off during the sermon on the preceding Sunday evening.

'Well, we mustn't mind when he's absurd,' Issie, comfortable at her fireside, remarked to Dileas; and blinked back sudden tears, remembering. Resolutely, she turned her back on the empty place before the hearth, poured herself another cup of tea, and promised inwardly that when next the preacher tried her patience she would think of his virtues: the next occasion to be expected being probably the following afternoon.

Since the day after Dileas's death, scarcely one day had passed without Mr Macleay's ponderous presence at the schoolroom door as the children departed. It appeared that he found much that was ungodly in the manner and matter of her teaching, from the unbecoming mirth he detected as he approached the door, to the graven images in Georgie's books. Issie, finishing her second cup of tea, resolved that on the following day she would neither argue with him nor cut him short with the excuse of an urgent poultice required in the village, but hear him out and ponder his reasons with the respect due to one who, after all, treated his flock with less harshness than he did himself.

The sin discovered to her on Friday afternoon was to have taught the hymn 'All things bright and beautiful'. Mr Macleay, pale with emotion, gestured at the incriminating words chalked on the wall, caught in a rare shaft of golden afternoon sunshine.

'Unscriptural, Miss Macdonald. Oh, how I have laboured on this island to wipe out such vain ditties, to instil in the people due reverence for the psalms of David, which are revealed in the Word of God as alone fit praise for Christians to sing! I beg, Miss Macdonald – rather, I command – that you will erase those words and teach no more such frivolities.'

Issie, biting her lip, said nothing in defence, remembering her resolve. 'Bright' had died almost in the fiery brightness striping the dull cracked plaster. Outside, brightness flamed upon the sea and lit the grey rocks to gold and amber.

'Very well, Mr Macleay,' she said at last, 'I shall do as you wish. But I confess I cannot understand your objection. The hymn is not a paraphrase of Scripture but it contains nothing offensive to the Protestant faith. It seems to me appropriate to thank providence for the bounties we enjoy, and' – her gaze travelled over the shining sea with its scatter of jewel-coloured islands to the shadowed summits of Boreray – 'the purple-headed mountain,' she said softly. She turned to him, determined to be humble, to say what she felt even though she knew it would meet with a disapproval that would not in the least convince her of her own error. 'Spring is coming on. I saw primroses yesterday. And they have begun to dig the fields. I want the children to be thankful for such things. The world is very beautiful.' As she said it, she was astonished: Rona, grim Rona, had become beautiful to her. When, and how?

'The world!' exclaimed Mr Macleay. 'Miss Macdonald, do not forget, do not for an instant forget, who is the prince of this world. Oh yes, we must thank God for His mercy, that He manifested Himself even in this sinful, fallen world to our redemption – but it is to the world to come we must look. Let us not rest our eyes too long upon what you call beautiful, which is perishable and deceiving, but look to that which is above – which is immortal. "By their fruits ye shall know them." Consider, if the fruits of your teaching should be to set the children's eyes upon the things of this world rather than the next, oh, how you will then be convicted! Remember, Miss Macdonald, the words of the Gospel: "Whoso shall offend one of these little ones which believe in me, it were better for him that a millstone were hanged about his neck and that he were drowned in the depths of the sea. Woe unto the world because of offences!" '

Issie sighed, soundlessly. A longing to escape pressed upon her, to elude the inhibitions of his heavy dark figure, his fixed gaze with eyes rounded by continual revelation of terror, his hortatory exclamations; to be away, too, from the sour-smelling classroom and from the smoky fetor of the village, to run up the sunny hillside and walk on the clifftops, in the fresh breeze from the sea.

'I think you exaggerate but I shall follow your advice,' she said wearily, aware suddenly of how tired she was after her day in the classroom, of how her throat ached with careful enunciation and her back with perching on her high stool.

'Thank you, Miss Macdonald,' he replied heavily. His voice had dropped in pitch, volume and confidence, all at once, as often happened after one of his exhortations.

'Thank you,' he repeated, almost inaudibly, rocking. 'Miss Macdonald, you will understand, I hope you will understand, what I have just said is of course my true belief, but uttered not to offend you ... to encourage you. I am grateful for your labours, very grateful. I thank God, Miss Macdonald, every night I thank God in my private devotions for your presence here and ask His gracious blessing on you ... on your work.'

'Thank you, Mr Macleay. I'm not easily offended.'

'Is that so?' He peered into her face, with neck thrust somewhat forward. 'I'm glad to hear it, very glad.'

Poor man, he's very short-sighted, Issie realised, and wondered how she had failed to notice it before. So perhaps he could not even see the purple-headed mountains. The golden light striped across the wall was softening to copper. She bowed and made for the door.

'Very glad,' he repeated, following her, so that there was no civil option but to stop. 'I must say, Miss Macdonald . . . I would like you to know . . . I would not have been so stern with you today if I had not been appealed to on this matter.'

Issie started. 'Do people complain of me?' It was an unpleasant surprise. She had been received in all their homes with such apparently unfeigning gratitude and welcome.

Nervous throat-clearing preceded his reply. 'Yes . . . in a manner. Mr Macdonald the Elder objected to his children learning these verses. Also to stories . . . fictions. You see, Miss Macdonald, a strict regard for truth is not compatible with made-up tales.'

Issie was stung by the sheer absurdity of it. 'But they are children! How can they apprehend truth, except in a simple language? Do you really think, Mr Macleay, that little Morag, the elder's daughter, understands "the truth" about predestination because she can rattle off a long sentence about it from the catechism, in a foreign language? Yet by this harmless little hymn which her father condemns, she is learning a truth more fitting to her age – that her Creator is all-powerful and all-loving.'

'Yes . . . yes, I see that you meant no harm. I know that your intention was good, Miss Macdonald. But misguided, misguided! The children who learn, as you put it, to rattle off truths that they do not understand will by God's grace come to a revelation of these truths in due time. But if what they learn is lies – '

'Not lies. Truth spelled out in common language. I do not teach or tell lies – I do not!'

'I did not accuse – '

'You implied it.' Issie was prone to agitation, but not to anger; it passed through her mind now that she had twice been angry with Mr Macleay, that for a second time she had pulled herself up before him, so that she looked fractionally down her nose at him. And what a beaky nose, and what a silly way to behave, she chided herself, sagging with a sigh of exasperation.

'Miss Macdonald . . . ' Mr Macleay's voice had lost its firmness again. 'I beseech you, do as I ask. If Mr Macdonald turns against you, it will severely undermine your position here. All your good work, your assistance to me . . . '

'Are you afraid of him?' Issie was astonished: the question popped out before she had time to consider it. 'Of course not,' she answered it hastily herself, but admitted inwardly that that, at least, was something very like a lie. Mr Macleay's eyes bulged in unmistakeable fright.

'The elder is a man of religion, of the highest Christian principles.' He was a little stiff: Issie's tactless question had evidently not gone unnoticed, even in his consternation. 'If he finds you wanting, Miss Macdonald, he will withdraw his children from lessons, and then – ' he paused, rocking unhappily – 'then so will everyone else – everyone. And that will be the end of your work here.'

Comprehension was not instant. 'I understand,' she said, when she was sure she did. 'Please tell the elder I am sorry to have caused concern, but that if he has any further complaint against me, I should prefer to hear it from his own lips. That would be more neighbourly, wouldn't it?'

'Oh, there will be nothing further, I can assure you, Miss Macdonald. Nothing further.' His eagerness quickly drooped. 'There is one more thing,' he admitted, despondently.

'Then what *is* it?' Issie cried. The glow had faded from the wall: the room was a grey prison.

'His son Duncan – the oldest boy in the school. Mr Macdonald is concerned that . . . I believe you give out conduct marks – that one of the older pupils is made top of the class on merit each week.'

'Yes, Rebecca. It has been Rebecca every time.'

'But not Duncan?'

'No.' Issie's heart thudded at the drift of the conversation.

'May I ask – why not? Does Duncan not still learn his lessons well, as he did for me?'

'Very well. But he is not helpful to me or to the other children. I have seen him make his little sister cry; he is unpleasant to poor Neilie, who as you know stammers badly.' Issie's own voice had begun to shake in dread of the inevitable conflict.

202

'It might be better . . . more just . . . if . . . '

'No!' Issie shouted. It was the word 'just' that brought on the outburst. 'I will not – I will *not* favour a child who is surly and a bully over one who is good and kind, for fear of his father. And I shall go now this minute and tell his father so – '

'No!' Mr Macleay's negative was equally impassioned. He stepped in front of her hastily to block her exit, flapping his arms as if she were a sheep or a chicken. 'You're quite right, Miss Macdonald. You *are* right.' His arms dropped uncertainly to his sides. 'You really are right. I'm sorry.'

A man all in bits and pieces, thought Issie. A short-sighted man who can't see the beauties of nature, who is afraid, absurdly afraid of a village despot. But there is something more there, or was.

'I'm sorry too,' she said. They shook hands on it.

CHAPTER 18

' "And what shall I do, what shall I do with my wee baby?" the woman was saying. She was keeping him a while, see, but he got bigger and bigger.' Morag slipped a spoonful of milk into her sick sister's mouth, taking swift advantage of the child's rapt attention. 'He cried louder and louder,' she elaborated, inspired by the short squawls of their own baby brother. 'He was howling that loud, the neighbours were saying, "Where's that noise coming from?" They were all jealous, see, because their own babies was all killed.'

'That's not in the Bible, you bad girl,' Auntie Effie reprimanded, sniffling on the bench by the fire. 'Oh my head, it's my head keeping me from watching her,' she moaned defensively: she was often prostrated by headaches, which brought on her a black depression in which she quaked before the Almighty, and could do no work.

'Take the medicine the lady was giving you. You should be taking it, now,' Barabel urged.

'Medicine! There's no medicine for me. There's no cure for sin, Auntie.'

'Och, your sins are no' that bad. You're past the age now, anyway. You should be trying the medicine.'

'It's sin is bringing sickness on this house. The wee girl's sick, the baby's sick.'

'Och, now. Maybe not the baby.' Uneasy, the old woman shuffled across to the corner where Chrissann lay on a bed of heather. Morag, watchful, trickled a spoonful of milk down her throat whenever her teeth parted, but most of it ran out from the corners of her mouth. Barabel peered and shook her head.

204

Morag, whispering her tale after her aunt's rebuke, raised her voice again, to blot out Barabel's look, which said 'hopeless'.

'You know what she did? She put the wee boat in the water, off the rocks. In the seaweed. She put a rope on it and the baby's sister took the end in her hand and hid. Then there was this princess went down to the shore. It was a hot day and she went in for a swim and found the wee boat. "What's this in here crying," she says. "Is it a bird?"' A spoonful of milk went down. '"No. Is it a lamb?"' Another spoonful. '"Is it a wee baby?"' A third spoonful dribbled down the child's burning neck. '"Yes! It's a bonny wee baby, and I'll have him for my own," says the princess. She was awful glad, she was wanting a baby a long, long time, she thought it was the fairies brought him – '

'That's enough of your stories.' Mór, with the infant at her breast, crouched down and took the bowl and spoon from Morag. 'You nurse the baby and leave Chrissann to me. And remember what your father said.'

But without the story the spoon met only an averted cheek, flushed and mottled. A grating whimper rose in the child's constricted throat.

Morag, who had carried the baby out to the open door, scampered back with a warning. 'The lady's coming!' There was a scuffle of complaint and preparation: Morag shooed the hens out; Effie vacated the bench and wiped it with her apron; Barabel pulled her mutch over her bald head; Mór straightened up, fastening her bodice.

Issie met their polite curtseys in kind. In most households she was greeted with kisses and Celtic endearments, but the elder's family always kept their distance. Enquiries after health on either side were answered affirmatively, in a customary contradiction of truth so honoured by tradition as to go undetected, even in the elder's punctilious house.

'And the medicine you were giving her is very good,' Barabel added, prodding the migraine sufferer.

'Yes, very good, I'm sure,' Effie echoed.

Issie guessed it had not been tried. 'Really, it is very effective. My sister used to obtain great relief from it.' She turned to Mór, holding out a second bottle. 'I hear that Chrissann has a fever, Mrs Macdonald. Mr Macleay thought this might relieve it. It's often – '

Mór, silent, stepped aside from before Chrissann's bed. Issie had come nervously, expecting hostility, or at least embarrassment, from the mother of the slighted Duncan, whom she had passed over in favour of Rebecca, but there was no obvious resentment in Mór's dark melancholy eyes. Yet something brooded there so sombre that Issie broke off in mid-sentence.

'She's sleeping now,' said the mother softly.

Issie bent over the child. 'But very feverish. Have you tried to get the fever down, by bathing her?'

'We put her in the sea, then back to her warm bed.'

'Oh, but that's too extreme! You must be careful . . . sponge her down where she lies. I could show you.'

'We did it how my mother has always done it.'

Her voice and eyes were unanswerable. Issie, flustered, began to prattle. 'It could be scarlet fever, or measles. The symptoms are so alike at first. Or simply a very bad cold. All fevers start so much the same, it's very difficult . . . What does your mother think, Mrs Macdonald?'

Abruptly, she shut herself off. Her own unmusical voice, too loud, jangled in Mór's profound silence. Chrissann's breath rasped beneath it.

'Yourself can ask her,' said Mór drily, turning to the door.

Annag had just entered. She embraced Issie kindly, but Issie was too agitated to ask her anything: Annag's secrets were her own and would be only her daughter's after her. To Issie, expressing interest in her decoctions of roots and leaves, she had been always bland but uncommunicative. 'Your medicines are the best ones, I'm sure, my dear,' was all Issie had heard of her lore, though she had enquired often.

Routed, Issie handed the bottle to the grandmother, who thanked her warmly.

'Indeed, it will be very good,' Annag said gently, almost pityingly. Her dark intelligent eyes were very like her daughter's.

Issie's escape was hindered by the arrival of the elder, whom she had hoped not to meet, or not, at least, within the confines of his own house. His greeting was more a stiff nod than a bow, but his voice was mild, enquiring after her health and happiness on Rona with dignified civility, and at some length.

His sons had come in behind him. He gestured at Duncan. 'And how do you find my boy at his lessons?'

There was pride in his face, but no rancour, Issie saw, with a lightening of heart, almost with gratitude: yet she protested inwardly at the ease with which she too had toppled to the elder's innocent dignity, as she replied, 'Duncan learns his lessons very diligently.'

Mór's lip curled. Issie saw it, with a shock of surprise. At whom? Her sombre eye had flicked over Duncan, and Duncan's did not meet his mother's in complicity. His sullen head bent lower.

A divided family. Issie's mouth opened to blurt out some compensatory kindness to Duncan, but she collected herself, thinking ahead to the next week, when she would try harder to be friends with him.

'You came to see my wee lass,' said Donald. 'We are grateful to you for your attention, Miss Macdonald.'

She noticed that the elder boy, young Donald, lanky and awkward, had sidled round the room to squat by his little sister. The mother and grandmother bent beside him. She realised that the elder's words were a courteous dismissal, and left expressing hopes for the child's speedy recovery.

'If the Lord wills, she will be restored,' said Donald, imperturbably mild.

His words irritated her as soon as she was out of his presence. The little girl was plainly very ill: a father should not be so meek, so resigned. Outside she hesitated, aware that she had failed. She should not have left till she had identified the fever, and then, on Mr Macleay's authority, she should have insisted on appropriate treatment. As it was, she had no idea what was wrong with the child. The week-old baby of Norrie and Neiliann had died not long before of lockjaw, after terrible suffering, but Mr Macleay had assured her that though very common among the newborn, he had never known the disease to attack older children. Issie, still hesitating at the door of the elder's house, recalled the poor infant's contorted face and limbs, and winced.

She started as something dragged over her foot. Looking down, she saw a black and white cat, limping on three legs. One hindleg was horribly mangled, stripped of skin from the haunch, the blackened paw hanging from a thread. Crying out with pity, she bent towards it, but it dragged itself into the passageway leading through the thick house wall to the door, and struggled through a gap at the jamb.

'Get out, you!' She heard Duncan's voice, and the door grating to, then a feeble mewing in the dark passageway. Stooping, she reached for the cat, which this time did not resist. A sickening stench of purulence made her gasp as she straightened up with the animal in her arms. She stood undecided for a moment, started back to the schoolhouse, stopped. Something required to be said. It was not clear to her why that was important, why she could not simply carry the cat off to her own quarters and tend it there, but the impulse was strong enough to force her back to the elder's door, with hot face and leaden knees. She knocked, and little Morag pulled the door open. Issie stooped inside, catching her breath on the smell of rotting flesh as she ducked her head over the cat.

The elder was seated by the hearth, with the Bible open on his knee, and his family grouped around him in readiness for the reading.

'Excuse me, Mr Macdonald, do you know whose cat this is?'

He looked at her gravely. The other heads remained bowed in the presence of the open Book. 'The cat is ours.'

'Oh, I see.' Issie could not think how to continue. Her voice was untrustworthy under stress: she tried to speak quietly. 'She's very badly hurt.'

'Ay. A dog got hold of her, maybe.'

The boys were beginning to squint at her, screwing their necks round. Morag stared, wide-eyed.

'Couldn't . . . could I tend her for you? I'll bring her back when she's fit again.'

Mór sat up straight, watching her husband. He shifted in his chair, so that his good eye was intent on Issie.

'She'll never be fit but to drown.'

He signed, with a nod of his head, to young Donald, who rose and approached Issie. She had almost opened her arms to give up the cat when she realised his intention.

'No! Oh no, I'm sure she can be made better. I'll try anyway. If she is no use to you any more, I'll keep her. I shall be glad to.'

Every head turned towards her.

'Not that one, Miss Macdonald. I will be pleased to get you another cat, a good one. But I'll not give you that broken thing out of my house.'

Issie did not notice the precise moment at which the elder's features turned from mild to terrible, without the twitch of a muscle, but her skin felt suddenly cold.

'I'll take this one,' she insisted, shakily.

Donald's ice-cold eye fixed her. 'If you take the animal, you will be stealing, and breaking a Commandment.'

'Oh!' Issie's indignation burst into loud speech. 'If I leave her, you'll drown her – how can you talk about Commandments?

209

Don't you think God will be grieved with you for tormenting his creatures?'

'The Lord has given us dominion over them.'

'Dominion, yes, but not . . . not to treat them like sticks and stones. I've seen what you do here – starving your dogs, leaving poor beasts unmilked on Sundays – oh! How *could* you leave this poor cat in such a state? And to say it's God's will! That's not what is meant, not to be cruel tyrants . . . '

Every face in the room stared at Issie, impassive and implacable, even little Morag's. Her breath and courage failed her. She blundered out of the door, cracking her head on the low lintel, and fled for home with her pitiful burden.

Annag stood up as soon as Issie was out of the door. 'Oh well, indeed, and it's cruel, cruel, and it's not the way we were doing with the creatures of the good God in the old days. I'll not stay to hear you tonight, Donald.'

Her quiet voice was almost lost in the babble of resentment following Issie's departure.

'She's taken our cat!'

'Oh well, the cheek of it!'

'Stealing the elder's cat – '

'That's heathen.'

'Huh, that's nothing, wasn't her father stealing our land and our cattle?'

'Didn't that man steal our very lives from us,' said Mór bitterly.

'Be quiet, all of you.' Donald had not moved except to cover his face with his hand. 'Be quiet. There is more to try us here tonight than the life or death of a cat.' He opened the Bible at the Gospel of Luke and read to them of the healing of Jairus's daughter.

The story about the cat was the talk that evening in the ceilidh-house, how the chief's daughter had raged into the elder's house when he was at prayer and had blasted the ears off him before he had time to open his mouth. All were resentful, and all were glad.

'Quite right.'

'Ach, them gentry. They're all the same. Talking about starving beasts, was she? Maybe there's some here knows more about starving than she does.'

'Oh, but haven't I been wanting to say that to him for years!'

'That's stealing, that.'

'Well, and couldn't he have given the cat to the poor lady?'

There was another story later. Ciorstag came home from a visit to her niece to say that she had seen a shroud round the sick child, right up to the neck, and that Annag had reported two sparks from the embers had jumped out on Mór's sleeve that morning when she was making the fire. There was a murmur of commiseration.

'So that's the baby as well. The eight-day sickness.'

'Ay. It's coming on him tonight.'

After that, sympathy was entirely with the elder and the company broke up in a subdued mood.

'Them bottles herself is giving us,' grumbled John Blondie's mother Catriona, heaving her arthritic limbs painfully up on her stick. 'No use – just no use at all!'

'You have lost two already. How is this one different?'

Mór spoke tonelessly, without looking at him. He had come from the bed to crouch beside her at Chrissann's side. The child could no longer hear them. Her jaws were locked and her body twisted by intermittent convulsions.

He passed his hand over his eyes, breathing hard.

'How?' she persisted.

'Mór – ' His voice was pleading. He tried to lay a hand on her arm.

She drew away from him. '*How?*'

'The others were . . . they never lived hardly, Mór. Just new-born babies. This one, she's a lovely wee girl, she'd be always climbing on my knee, laughing at my shut eye . . . '

'Job lost them all, remember?'

'Ay . . . Oh God, but not this one!'

She stood up, looking down on his heaving shoulders. 'The others. My babies. Your offerings to God, Donald. I died with each of them, when you were saving your soul.'

CHAPTER 19

Thinking the cat would not survive, Issie gave her no name, in a vain attempt to prevent herself from becoming attached to another pet, but as a Hebridean cat would not know English, she addressed her as *piseag* rather than puss. And Piseag throve. After two days Issie came through from the schoolroom to find her purring in the warmth of the fire, and by the next day she was grooming her three remaining paws, shaking her head at the Epsom salts Issie had applied to draw the pus from her wounds. The injured haunch healed wizened and dented, and almost bald: Piseag would never be beautiful, but she held her tail high and kept her white shirt-front immaculate. She would not enter the schoolroom after she spotted Duncan there, and Issie often had to hurry through to her living room, on detecting from the other side of the door that her milk jug had been tipped over or her work basket raided. Outside, Piseag followed her gladly. If she turned towards the village, the cat would crouch on the window-sill with narrowed eyes to wait her return, but if the walk was the other way, up the hill, she lolloped ahead with as much delight as Dileas used to show.

As the evenings lengthened, and some days at least did not bring rain, Issie found it harder to turn from the classroom to the cramped houses of the village, with her bottles and bandages and her unsought-for recommendations of soap and chimneys and floorboards. She could be sure, certainly, of warm hospitality and a polite hearing, but she became increasingly aware that the effect of her advice was negligible. She took great pains to present it clearly, recurring often to Miss Nightingale's terse dicta on sanitary matters:

There are 5 essential points in securing the health of houses
1 Pure air
2 Pure water
3 Efficient drainage
4 Cleanliness
5 Light.

Try as she might, vehemently or tactfully, she could not persuade people that the bronchial complaints which plagued the aged and the consumption which carried off the young spread in the warm moist smoky houses where all ages and species crowded together, or that the washing of bodies was a surer aid to cleanliness than the careful laundering of snowy mutches for Sunday. They had never heard of Miss Nightingale and were politely sceptical of her principles of hygiene, as expounded by Issie. 'Ah well, we were very healthy in the old days, my dearie. Times are not what they were, no, not at all,' the old admonished her gently, and the matrons concurred 'Indeed!', and sniffed. Only the young wives from away – John Blackie's Marsaili, Shonny's Dolina and Norman's Dora, a shepherd's daughter from Fladday, who knew how things were done elsewhere – paid any heed to her advice. Indeed, so glad were those poor exiles to find a sympathetic ear, that she was frequently embarrassed by their railings against the barbarous ignorance of their husband's families and found herself defending the old ways to them. There were good reasons: the soot-impregnated thatches and the trodden dirt and dung floors of the houses became the manure of the spring fields, making soil where there had been none between the barren rocks, and producing the crops without which man and beast would starve; and the babies who survived Annag's secret ointment grew up into men and women inured to cold and hunger, who could bear their own weight over again on their backs through mile upon mile of bog and rock. In a population of sixty people there were three aged more than eighty, all of whom looked fit for another decade. Issie could not in honesty call them unhealthy; and yet she saw dirt and disease where none need be.

From these perplexities it was a relief to turn to walks with Piseag. She made it her rule, and the more she doubted her success the more rigid the rule, to do her work in the village first; then, till nightfall, she was free, to stretch her limbs and her spirit as Piseag did. Scrambling up the rocky path, they met people coming home from the fields or down from the shieling with milk-cogs. Issie was glad of their friendly greetings, and gladder to pass the last group and to be up on the rampart walk of Rona, alone with the glittering sea on one hand and the bare hill slope pastel-misted by evening on the other, falling away into shadow. Sometimes she sat silent, her back to a day-warmed boulder and Piseag on her lap, gazing at the setting sun's cardinal progress across the milky water; with a posy of wild flowers in her hand and peace in her ears, the lisp of the wind in the hilltop grasses, the rise and fall of sea-birds' voices and the rise and fall of summer waves. At other times she strode the whole circuit of the island, with the wind tugging the combs from her unbonneted hair and her skirt hitched above the tops of her boots. She pounced and frisked with Piseag among the boulders of the south-end beach, and sang at the top of her tuneless voice, the ballads of sentiment Augustus used to sing with Helen, and the nursery songs and godless hymns she had taught Georgie.

Out there she was cheerful, undisturbed by either the bereaving past or the barren wilderness around her. It was not lonely: furry golden bees bumbled familiarly among sea-rocket and angelica, and cuckoos shouted their preposterous notes from rocky knolls. So Issie shouted too, glad of the opportunity to swell her unmusical lungs where her audience was only cuckoos, or the myriad fairies and gnomes and brownies banished by Mr Macleay's edict. It occurred to her before long, though, that her eccentric secret was unlikely to have rested with the fairies.

215

Someone would have heard her; an old woman out late stacking peat, or children lagging to play as they carried milk home.

'Well, they're welcome, Piseag,' she said aloud, picturing the innocent scandal an unseen listener's revelation would cause in the village. She was surprised to realise that she was unabashed by the prospect. 'I'll be a crazy old woman, alone with my cat,' she told Piseag between two verses of 'Over the hills and far away'. But if she saw anyone in the distance, she fell silent, out of respect for local decorum. It was rare that she did; only occasionally would the elder and his boys be working late, the ring of iron on stone carrying far on the lucid evening air as they laboured at the long walls that bounded the lower ground.

People said Donald had taken the death of his child very hard. The newborn's loss he would have stood, had it been all: he had buried two other such in the same plot without complaint. But for Chrissann he wept at the graveside, calling for his darling, the light of his eyes, the joy of his heart: calling, people told each other later, on the Father of Peace to take her in his arms, and what was more scandalous still, on white Michael to shield her soul.

'And that's Popery, near enough!' more than one exclaimed, in pity rather than in censure: for while the generality of sinners might cling to such forbidden comforts in time of need, without feeling too much more sinful afterwards, it was another thing altogether for the elect to succumb. For Donald the Elder to petition so, against the foreordained will of the Lord, was a sign of a breaking heart, a spirit racked beyond endurance.

'He's near enough out of his mind, poor soul,' Annag reported. She pitied him the more because her daughter, bitter in her own grief, taunted him with his lapse. 'Oh, but he's patient, patient,' she said.

He was patient. There was no further outburst against the dispensation of the Almighty. His way of life was as it had always been: industrious, sober and frugal. But something had changed. Donald had been a man who was the same all the way through, clear like a well-spring pool. You could look in his face and listen to his words, and that was what he was, and all he was, uncompromising and honest as cold water. No one had ever known him falter in the truth, or excuse himself, or pass judgement on others, not once in all the terrible time of famine and exile when most people had done things they were later glad to forget. But now when the trouble of his child's death came upon him, they said he was not himself, that they didn't know what he was thinking, that he didn't seem all there. His outward composure of speech and manner were as before, but the inner heart was clouded.

He worked most days, as he had for fifteen years, on the wall or inside it. They called it the Park now. Few families even tried to grow crops there any longer. They had tired of the constant heavy digging and draining in weltering wet ground that was required to keep it from reverting to patchy marsh. Instead, they used it as a sheep-run. The success of Eagleton's Cheviots on Fladday had led to emulation. For some time past, whenever there was a bit of money, people had been buying, not another cow, but five or six lambs, or a good big Roman-nosed ram to put to their small leggy ewes. Rona didn't suit them as well as the sweet grassland of Fladday, but years of draining and manuring had left the Park looking something like pasture. There was a wash of green over the basin in the brown hills. Harbottle had terminated his lease when the deer failed, first on Rona and then on Boreray, and the new proprietor who had bought a bargain lot of bankrupt islands had never ventured further than Port Long. Rona's increasing flocks could graze the whole island with impunity, and found, astonishingly, healthy forage and good shelter among the broken rocks and screes. They lambed in the Park and grazed it again in the latter end of summer; otherwise they roamed the hills and the richer pasture of Out End.

Donald alone kept no sheep, except the few required to provide wool and meat for the family. His beasts were never on the illicit ground outside the wall. Inside, where his neighbours' strips lay fallow green and their ditches gradually choked with rushes, his clean-cut plots were black and fertile between sky-reflecting ribbons of water.

Chrissann died at the time of year when the new rosettes of potato leaves unfolded on the tilled earth and the ditches shone yellow with kingcups between the green stripes of young corn. Donald left the weeding that season to Mór and the boys. 'We'll put sheep on next year,' he said. 'Where's the use of planting here, with other folk's beasts breaking in all the time?' But he still worked at the wall. 'A foot a year,' people had said jokingly, since everyone else but Donald had lost interest in it; and it didn't look much more than that in the acres of open ground. Donald, who had worked on it by himself without complaint in the spare moments of maybe ten years, began to urge its completion, without which it was difficult to keep the sheep in or out.

'Ach, the wee ones can mind the sheep,' they said.

'They're to be in school at their books,' replied the elder, sternly.

His neighbours grumbled in private but did as he asked and helped a bit with the last few hundred yards, when they couldn't think of an excuse. But Donald no longer talked of making the desert bloom.

The first time Issie found him alone on one of her walks, she forced herself to speak to him of the remorse she had felt after her outburst in his house. She rehearsed her speech somewhat behind a boulder before she approached him.

'I really couldn't give up the cat . . . I'm so fond of her and, you see, she's quite well now. But I have been very, very sorry for the manner in which I spoke to you when there was such trouble in your family. Please forgive me.'

'You are very welcome to the cat, Miss Macdonald.'

He took her proferred hand without hesitation, yet Issie left him feeling no easier about the affair than she had done before.

He showed no resentment and was conscious of none, yet somewhere in his clear mind had lodged the unclear thought that the woman who had flouted the authority of his God had brought wrath upon him, had robbed him not of a half-dead cat but of his daughter.

10 JULY 1862

The elder today came with a complaint as to the conduct of Miss Macdonald; he takes it amiss that he often hears her singing songs which are frivolous, unbecoming in one who is engaged to teach the young. He would have me resume the conduct of the school myself, but this I cannot do, both for lack of time and because I do not wish to discourage the lady, who gives her services for nothing, which I pointed out to Donald. He appears unconvinced; I am uncertain how best to proceed and pray God will guide me to a wise decision.

As to Miss Macdonald's singing, I have heard her myself through the wall. This is unavoidable, the connecting door (though boarded) is not very thick. There is no doubt her songs are light and vain. Some I recognise as those my dear mother sang to me when very young. I wonder if there is much harm here, or is it not becoming in a woman to have that tender maternal disposition which so expresses itself? I believe she sings to her cat, which she has made a great pet. She does not keep a tune perfectly, nevertheless, I consider her voice pleasant.

I shall take the first opportunity to mention the matter to her, unless I am otherwise led in prayer tonight.'

Mr Macleay's bedtime devotions, close to the boarded door, were interrupted by 'I love little pussy' and a game of tag. This he took as a sign of divine permissiveness, having resolved that if he heard sobbing, as was sometimes the case, it should in the circumstances be interpreted as the working of grace upon a guilty conscience. Miss Macdonald's conscience was apparently unassailed. His relief and gratitude were great and kept him long in prayer.

Piseag was new and present, cementing Issie to her new life. Augustus's journals gathered dust, till, remorsefully, she dusted them, read for an evening of his strenuous farming life on Huron and his hopes for his son's future, and kissed the pages, weeping; and put the volumes aside while she consulted *Black's Medical Dictionary* on the subject of kidney stones, with difficulty between Piseag's mischievous paws.

CHAPTER 20

'What's this he's taken into his head, bringing down his own peats? Isn't it myself has carried his peats for him every day of all the days he's been on Rona!' Barabel, red with indignation, on her way down from the mission house, paused at Ciorstag's door with her complaint.

Ciorstag winked at her sister over her thrumming wheel. 'Och now, he'll be thinking you're getting up in years, Barabel.'

'Giving you a rest, dearie.' Annag never looked up from her knitting.

'I'm not the one for needing a rest. Here's me as strong as ever I was. If that's what was doing, he'd be getting one of you young ones to go instead of myself.'

'I'm no' feeling so young at seventy.'

Barabel was not distracted from the point she was determined to make. She leaned closer to her hearers. 'It's the woman. What else is taking him up the hill? He's looking to meet her.'

'Oh, do you think so now?' Ciorstag's thread flowed evenly through her hand. 'Well, she's no beauty.'

'Beauty, who's talking about beauty? What's she traipsing about up there for? It's not Christian, that. And gentry, too.'

'She's all right, poor lass,' said Annag, equably. 'Let her catch a man if she can.'

'But the preacher!' Barabel's dark wizened old face gathered to such a scowl that the other women burst out laughing.

'The preacher's flesh and blood.'

'Remember John of the Rock's Peggy, years past.'

Annag shushed her sister, but not quickly enough. A long rumble of woe sounded in Barabel's throat. 'Oh, if Donald had heard what Lexy saw that time.'

'Just as well he didn't. It would only be upsetting him,' said Annag, with unusual asperity. 'That's all long ago now, and the poor man has repented, I'm sure.'

Barabel departed, grumbling and shaking her head.

'It would be a good thing,' said Annag.

Ciorstag grunted. 'Ay, a good thing for him. But what about her?'

Mr Macleay had considerably less knowledge of the drift of his affection than his congregation, and Issie had none at all. It irked her, at first, that she met him so frequently as she returned from her walks, but when the increasing distance of the meeting point from home at last revealed it as no coincidence, pity curbed her irritation. He must be very lonely to find her company congenial. She was aware that preachers are flesh and blood, but quite unaware that such flesh and blood might be stirred by a buck-toothed stalky old maid of unorthodox persuasion and superior ancestry. It surprised and touched her that he made such efforts to be pleasant in conversation, keeping clear of any religious discussion that might provoke argument. Yet this very reticence left little to talk about, since everything, to Mr Macleay, had for so long been a matter of dogmatic certitude, and awkward silences frequently succeeded their greetings. Issie, being aware of his wide-ranging definition of vanity, scarcely liked to enthuse over the beauties of nature, which was what most filled her mind on these excursions. Indeed, when on the third or fourth evening of their meetings he gestured towards the rose-washed mountains of Boreray as a 'fine prospect', she felt concerned lest by her presence she had drawn his severity down to the common compromise of small-talk. She had no doubt he had spoken merely to please her: apart from any other consideration, eyes

222

that read the big pulpit Bible at nose-length could scarcely have distinguished clouds from mountains or mountains from water.

He must have felt her hesitancy, for he added, a little stiffly, 'I was once very fond of outdoor pursuits . . . too fond, which is why I foreswore them. But now, with increasing years, I think I may take out-of-doors recreation, as health requires, without fear of excess.'

'I am very pleased to hear you say so. I have often thought of the long hours you spend in study and wished you might have some relaxation.'

'Have you, Miss Macdonald?'

'Yes,' replied Issie, without guile.

She drew to his attention the posy of wild flowers she had picked, ragged-Robin, clover and hound's-tongue, which could be held up close for examination, and on his agreeing that they were miracles of creation, felt emboldened to suggest that on his next visit to the mainland he should have himself measured for a pair of spectacles.

'Miss Macdonald showed concern for my health,' Mr Macleay confided later to his journal, 'which has strengthened my resolve to take more outdoor exercise, in order to remain fit for all that duty may require. She is a lady of remarkable personal qualities.'

On their next meeting he went so far as to enumerate some of these qualities, referring to the compassion towards children and the sick that shone forth in her work.

Issie, surprised, confided some of her difficulties. 'People are set in their ways, Mr Macleay. I cannot urge change too vehemently without appearing to slight the aged and wise, and so I fear that I give in too easily. For I know, if I could overbear them, that observing elementary rules of hygiene would ease suffering and even save lives. Newborn babies need *not* die of lockjaw: there is something in Annag's method – but she is a dear good woman, and in many ways very knowledgeable.' The second baby of the year, Sara's, had recently died. Issie sighed. 'In any case, you will say that these deaths are the will of the Almighty, I suppose.'

'No, no!' He was animated. 'I fear you have misunderstood me . . . certain things I may have said in the past. No, Miss Macdonald, God requires us to minister to the sick and needy, to do our utmost to salve bodily suffering, to save life – as you do, Miss Macdonald. In due time God will bless such work with success. Do not lose heart.'

Issie was, in fact, greatly encouraged. There was no one else in a position to appraise her work; Mr Macleay spoke very sincerely and since he must know the people better than she, after such a long sojourn among them, she could hope that his judgement was correct.

'Miss Macdonald's hopes and fears for her work of mercy,' he wrote later, 'remind me much of the sensations to which I myself was opened when I first came to Rona. How well I remember the joy I felt in first drawing tears of penitence, the despondency on first noticing backsliding. O God, renew in me the spirit of charity, which shall cover the multitude of sins!'

Finding his interpretation of the divine will more genial in this respect than she had supposed, Issie was moved to question him on other serious matters. It seemed to her a failure in frankness, if they were to be friends, to avoid points of difference for fear of arguments. She reopened, one by one, the vexed questions of their first acquaintance; but no argument resulted. In each former case of disagreement, it seemed, Mr Macleay had expressed himself more violently than he had intended, or she had misapprehended his meaning, or he had since reconsidered his position and now felt somewhat differently, or even, her eloquence had so affected him that his previous convictions had changed. In particular he confided to her that her kindness to the brute creation, which no whit undermined her duty to humanity, had deeply impressed him.

'For example, I can no longer regard it as the will of a beneficent Creator, even on His Holy Day, that domestic animals should suffer from lack of attention. "A merciful man regardeth the life of his beast." If life, then surely aids to life – health and comfort.'

Issie was overjoyed. The sight of those milk-animals who did not have young at foot, with their udders painfully swollen, had cast a gloom over Sundays for her.

'Oh, if only you could change that cruel tradition of not milking on Sundays. Could you exhort them to leave it off?'

'That would be difficult,' he said, seeming preoccupied; but at her expression of disappointment he said, 'I shall pray for guidance.'

'And if your prayers are answered as I believe they must be, will you preach a sermon about it?'

He hesitated, rocking to and fro, so that she thought he would give some reason for refusal, but instead he gave his promise that he would, gladly.

Over a month, in daily rations of quarter of an hour, half an hour, an hour, Issie found that the distance between them, the dizzying gulf between the elect and the unregenerate, had almost closed. She no longer groaned inwardly when she caught sight of his stocky figure plodding up the brae. 'There he is, Piseag,' she would say, smiling at the earnest out-thrust of his peering head above the ungainly crow's flapping of his old black frock-coat. Once, when the day was too wet for walking, they took tea together in her room. She scarcely recognised the forbidding figure of her first arrival in this round-faced comfortable man with Piseag on his knee.

'You have wrought great changes in this room, Miss Macdonald. You have made it a home.'

'The curtains have made it prettier, I believe.' She blushed a little, bending over the kettle. She had contrived the curtains from a beribboned cotton petticoat that she had found unnecessary for her new way of life.

'The curtains are charming,' he agreed, examining them closely, wistfully, she thought.

'If you would like, I could make some for your sitting room.'

'No . . . oh no, that would not be suitable at all . . . ' He put his cup aside. 'Your offer is very kind – yes, I would be most grateful, Miss Macdonald.'

It afforded Issie secret amusement stitching the preacher's curtains out of her old petticoat. She shared the joke with Annag and then wished she had not, knowing how quickly and completely gossip spread in the small community. But when the finished curtains were received with innocent delight she concluded that she had misjudged Annag, from whom, after all, she had never heard a malicious word. She was as yet unaware of the tactful discretion always maintained towards outsiders. Annag, who had helped her hang the curtains while Mr Macleay was in his study, had no so much as hinted that the whole village, with varying degrees of enthusiasm, regarded them as a certain precursor to marriage, or that Ciorstag, being advised that they were white, saw in them an omen of disaster.

The ribbon-tied scraps of broderie anglaise billowed with impudent levity in that severe room, but Mr Macleay was pink with pleasure. He untied and retied, opened and closed them with gingerly care in his clumsy square hands. Issie's rising laughter foundered in a bleak realisation of how long it must be since anyone had made him a gift, not of the necessities of life with which his neighbours kept him well supplied, but of those tokens and remembrances which pass between friends. He has no friends, she thought. He is the preacher, not Duncan Macleay.

'Your sewing is very fine,' he exclaimed, holding up a hem to examine it.

I must be good to him, thought Issie, contemplating his friendlessness. Aloud, she said, 'Not fine, but I am competent.'

This modification was lost in his rush of reminiscences. 'Oh, how well I remember my dear mother, sitting by our bedsides, stitching the garments we had thought nothing of tearing at play during the day. Just her hands and the cloth in the glow from the

226

nightlight. What a beautiful picture of maternal tenderness and duty! I did not understand then how she laboured for us, how she alone made our poor house a home. She was always occupied, Miss Macdonald. As we hear in the Word of God: "She looked well to the ways of her household, and ate not the bread of idleness." How lovely such diligence makes a woman.'

Issie, who scarcely remembered her own, was warmed by his devotion to his mother, and questioned a little. The answers came fulsomely: 'She married late, and was widowed early. My father was an attorney's clerk and he left little provision for his family. She worked night and day, taking in sewing to earn a few pence. Even washing. I am ashamed to say it – would that I could have stood between her and such labour, but I was not seven years old. I used to try to cut the soap for her – how well I remember her remonstrances lest I should also cut my little fingers. My sister she would allow to help, but me she had already marked out for the vocation to which God indeed called me, with a mother's percipience. So I must keep my hands for writing, she said, and rest and eat well, so as to be fit for school – and at what sacrifice to herself. My mother, my dear mother, would often bring me my supper as I sat alone at my books, giving as her reason that I should not be disturbed in my studies. And I would have some childish treat – jam, perhaps, I was fond of jam. Or sugar in my drink. But from my sister I would hear later that they had supped on dry bread and milkless tea. Like Hannah, my mother was like Hannah, prepared for any sacrifice so that her son might be promoted in the service of God. And so it was. For like Samuel, Miss Macdonald, I heard the call. At the time I had been working for a year in similar capacity to my father before me, and this circumstance had cast a great depression on my poor mother's spirits. Her meagre income had provided me with books and necessaries for my schooling but proved insufficient to carry me through the university towards ordination, which was her one desire, for which I know she prayed every night of my early life, she who never asked a boon for herself, but gave all to the glory of God. She had hoped, had never doubted – such was her faith – that my fees might be paid by my sister's employment as a lady's maid. But as it chanced – no, as we saw it later, was foreordained – my sister was unpunctual and her employer dismissed her. Her next post, as a draper's assistant, was poorly paid, so that I had to persuade my dear mother that I must forsake my studies and earn my bread. Oh, it was not easy. She tried to prevent it, she even hid my boots, Miss Macdonald, on the first day of my employment, so great was her solicitude for her son. It was an unhappy time for my family; my mother lamenting the waste of my talents, and holding my sister in a sense guilty, so that there was acrimony – gloom, at least. Then one day, it was a foggy winter evening, I remember, and I was walking home from the office where I worked, a lady thrust into my hand one of the tracts of the SSPCK, which ended with an exhortation to young men to put their lives at the disposal of God, as missionaries of His Word. I knew, Miss Macdonald, at that very moment I knew, God put it in my heart, that it was to this work I was called.'

He paused, bright-eyed at his recollections. Issie was impressed and nodded encouragingly, her eyes shining, too.

A shadow sobered his brightened face. 'My dear mother continued to hope that I would enter the ministry, to her dying day that was her wish. She regarded my sojourn here as probationary, and assumed . . . but they have only agreed to keep me here in my original capacity. There is much study required and Rona is not the best place for it. Perhaps some day, if God so wills . . . '

'You came where no ordained minister would have come. You have done very well,' cried Issie, earnestly, remembering with sudden pain her father pleading for the lazy incumbent of Boreray and Augustus's contemptuous provision for 'missionary zeal'. They didn't know: neither of them knew. Suddenly, in that meagre chill room redolent of damp peat smoke and homespun, past and present collided. Her senses swam, between the other world, the gracious old world of the great house and gardens, with Helen lounging in the early spring sunshine on the terrace – then, then, that very moment, that was when it began to slide; no, it had begun before, but *then* it slipped dangerously, as a rockfall gathers momentum after the first slow trickle of pebbles and sand. Helen, rising, shrank from the husband who had mastered her, and Rona was slotted into its place in the management of the estates, in Augustus's confident hand in his leather-bound book, and no one dreamed of worrying about it. And now this world, squalor, poverty, strangers: and guilt, for not knowing enough, not knowing soon enough, not knowing how to help, how to expiate.

She caged the fluttering memories and left Mr Macleay to his own recollections. When she had gone he picked up his favourite Bible, that given him by his mother when he left home, and set it down again, frowning. He crossed to the bookshelf and took out another, one of the many provided by the society, and let if fall open at random. His eye lighted on 'And Joshua rose early in the morning, and they removed from Shittim, and came to Jordan, he and all the children of Israel.'

Finding this obscure, he tried again. 'Return, ye backsliding children, and I will heal your backslidings. Behold we come unto thee, for thou art the Lord our God.'

Once more, he let the Book fall open. 'For this cause shall a man leave his father and mother, and shall be joined to his wife, and they shall be one flesh.'

Straightway, he clasped his hands in grateful prayer.

During the following week, which was the last before his annual absence, Mr Macleay's reminiscences continued with scarcely a pause for Issie to ask politely, 'And what happened next?' His talk wearied her by its sheer volume, and yet, poor man, he had no one else to talk to, so she must listen patiently. Piseag miaowed, vying for attention, and raided the work basket, and Issie listened to that patiently too, for she could not break off in the middle of a heart-rending account of his mother's last days to say, 'Excuse me, I must save my knitting.'

But gradually she became aware that his talk was not just the spilling over of a lonely man's memories. There was a preoccupation, a focus, which at first she could not grasp, but when she did, she reddened and choked on her tea and wondered how she could have been for so long so blind. Mr Macleay had been speaking of his sister's undutiful conduct towards their mother and of how harshly he had judged her marriage, so that he had broken off relations with her. 'But now . . . yes, I deplore her weakness. Her first duty was clear, she should have been patient. Nevertheless, recently I have come to understand her longing for the married state. I trust she is happy in it. I am resolved to seek her out and give her my blessing, to make a brother of her husband. They have three children, nephews and a niece I have never seen. I *shall* see them! "Happy is the man that hath his quiver full of them." I shall be reconciled, and see Agnes a happy wife and mother – as I hope some day to see another – ' Here he looked at her very intently.

The choking fit interposed. Young Hector knocked with the mails, saving Issie further embarrassment. Mr Macleay departed to read his clerical journals, leaving Issie with her letter.

She recognised Helen's hand, but the poignant mixture of dread and affection that usually made her tear open her sister's infrequent letters at once was lost in the more urgent turmoil of her recent discovery. Her first astonishment gave way to dismay, and again to astonishment, on different grounds: Besides, I am a chieftain's daughter. He knows that. Almost as the thought formed, she shook her head at it, bewildered, for that was so long ago. Presently she persuaded herself that she should be flattered and grateful, even pleased. She was thirty-three, plain, penniless and friendless, and she was fond of him. 'We're fond of him, aren't we Piseag?' she said, stroking the cat. 'Poor man.'

Next day was Sunday. Mr Macleay preached the sermon Issie had been waiting for. People left the mission house as decorously as usual; only the closest associates saw each other's sly winks or little shrugs, but everyone saw Donald's steel-bright eye and pinched nostrils.

'Look out,' whispered Ciorstag, nudging her sister.

Issie, when they met on Monday for the last time before his vacation, expressed her delight at this respite for Rona's animals. He declared that he had seen it as his duty to preach as he had, but she knew him well enough, now, to see that he was worried.

'The elder has already remonstrated with me on this matter, which he says will cause desecration of the Sabbath. That is a serious charge – very serious.'

'But I'm sure you are right. Mr Macdonald is . . . ' She paused. 'He is a very upright man. But so rigid. He does not have the benefit of education or of seeing how things are done in other places. Surely he must come to agree with you, in time. It is only that the idea is too strange – the idea of kindness to animals, I mean. But nowadays it is considered a very serious matter by many eminent for their Christianity. The queen herself, you know, has given her patronage to the Society for the Prevention of Cruelty to Animals.'

Mr Macleay sighed heavily, trudging through the puddles. It was a blustery day of flying showers and rainbows. He paused in the shelter of a boulder, clearing his throat nervously.

'Miss Macdonald . . . it may be time I spread my wings. I take this disagreement with my elder as a sign – a sign that my work on Rona is complete. As I intimated to you recently, I once had other ambitions, to enter the ministry. Perhaps the time is coming when I must look to that, if I am spared. Indeed' – he paced on a few steps, and paused again, rocking on his heels – 'indeed, Miss Macdonald, were it not for one consideration I should have applied this summer to leave. That consideration is yourself, Miss Macdonald. Yourself. I do not ask for an answer now . . . ' He floundered, perhaps remembering that he had not asked a question. 'I shall say nothing more . . . we won't speak of it till I return. I merely beg you to consider it – consider it prayerfully.'

He set off at a lumbering trot through the mire, neither looking back nor slackening his pace till he had escaped from their privacy of rocks and air into protective earshot of the first house.

'Poor man,' said Issie to Piseag again.

He was a poor man. It did not even occur to Issie to refuse him, if he should ask. His need for her was its own answer.

CHAPTER 21

'Any old island will do! Dammit, they're all the same, anyway, miserable god-forsaken rocks. Sheep eating the natives, and chiefs who live in London clubs selling them for slaves. Or dog meat – turning 'em into polony, probably.' Aeneas Gibb, late of Gibb and Son, flourished his right arm above his uptilted profile and downed a dram. 'Another!'

The landlord poured silently.

'That's how it was,' continued his customer. 'Don't suppose it's changed. I was there, I've seen it. Island called Boreray – Boreray and Rona. Oh my God, Rona! Heard of it?'

'Yes, sir.'

'Could I get there?'

'You could, sir.'

'That's where I'll go, then. You just point me in the right direction.' He pointed emphatically at the landlord's nose lest there should be any confusion.

'Tomorrow, sir.'

'Tomorrow! What's wrong with tonight?'

The landlord tactfully excused himself to attend to another customer. Gibb settled grumbling by the fire, and lit a cigar. 'When I've smoked this ... Then I'm starting out. Can't wait any longer.' He increased his self-satisfaction by sprawling as he had in the railway carriage, with his hat over his eyes and his feet on the seat opposite, jauntily regathering his youth around him with the careless folds of his Inverness cape. 'Dammit, thirty-eight! I'm not old,' he remarked. 'Can't wait any longer, though,' he added, as he drifted into fumy sleep.

He had come back to fight the fight for the oppressed Highlanders; but rather late. His tardiness was not entirely to his discredit: he had gratified his father with more than a decade of daily duty at the office, confining his more sprightly activities to those hours when the old man, godly and oblivious, snored in their pink sandstone villa behind sober laurels. Respectability and benevolence to employees by day, by night (for there was ivy convenient to his bedroom window at the pink villa) Dionysiac capers. This dual life caused him no discomfort; indeed, its success in utilitarian terms confirmed him in his high regard for his own opinions. He dispensed charity, with fine judgement, he sowed wild oats and considered others privileged to harvest them. He did his filial duty to the Daddy-o, and when the old man croaked, he sold out of Gibb and Son and headed for Edinburgh to set up 'A. Gibb, Radical Publisher'. 'For the underdog – the oppressed – they can speak through me. I shan't fleece 'em,' he declared in salons occasionally, in taverns very frequently. But radical publishing was not what it had been fifteen years before. Gibb sat in his new office for six weeks enduring plain young Sunday school ladies and hideous old animal protection ladies, and on the Monday of the seventh week he called it a day. 'Dammit, what about the Highlands?' he cried. He locked the office, threw some clothes into a portmanteau, and leapt stylishly onto a moving train at Waverley. It went no further than Haymarket, but some sixteen hours and five changes later he had reached the end of the line at Dingwall, in the Highlands, indeed.

'It's the No-Hat Man, all right. He called me "wee Kennag". Kissed me, too.' She pulled a face. Having crossed on the same boat as Gibb from Gnipadale on one of her rare days off, she was first with the news. 'The merchant's near doubling himself in two bowing and scraping, remembering what he spent last time. Mrs Calum is going round like this.' Kennag pursed her lips in an arch smile, clasping her hands before her bosom.

Neiliann and Dora laughed at her performance. 'Though you'd need a cushion in your bodice to look like the merchant's wife,' Dora pointed out. She was a strapping girl herself, compared with those of her generation who had grown up on Rona. 'What's he here for, anyway? It's not much of a place for a pleasure trip.'

The two sisters became vague, busying themselves with young Kenny.

'What's he want?' Dora insisted, obstinately. She was touchy about Rona's silences, which marked her off as an outsider.

'Och, nothing. Old stories.'

Neiliann jumped down from the house wall to fetch another bundle of wool for spinning. Kennag tossed her nephew in the air till his chortles drowned Dora out. None of the young, who as children had eaten sand and slept among the bare rocks, liked to remember too much.

'A terrible day that was for us, as true as I am sitting here.' Old Hector's voice quavered with emotion. The old, at least, were pleased to reminisce. Barabel and Catriona sighed a low 'och-och-och' of Celtic mourning.

'A terrible day! Oh, the grief it was to see our little children crying and the stranger's sheep eating our corn. They put our houses in a blaze, they fired the roofs over our heads. Ay! There was the old bard carried out with his clothes all in a blaze . . . they left us in the snow, without a rag to our backs – '

Ciorstag tapped his shoulder. 'Not here, Hector,' she said firmly. 'That was over on the mainland some way.'

Gibb threw his pencil on the ground in exasperation.

'Och, was it? My memory's no good. Oh well, sir, it was much the same here.'

Annag trod on his toe to shut him up. There was no good offending strangers until you knew what they were after. Hector took the hint. 'Well, no. It wasn't so bad here. Not too bad at all.'

Gibb stabbed at his notebook impatiently. He had heard Hector's story in at least three places. Not that that would have stopped him using it, but someone else had done so already, with circumstantial local colour. 'Come on now, old chap. Give me a bit of a tale – I'm sure you know plenty.'

But they had seen his uncivil impatience and they distrusted his notebook. Barabel and Catriona ceased their murmurous mourning and bobbed their spindles tranquilly up and down. Hector shook his head. 'No, no, sir. We didn't do bad. Just a wee bit at the beginning, maybe. It's just grand here.'

That was all he got. They directed him to the elder's house. 'He's a man of learning. Yourself will be finding his stories better than ours.'

Silently, they watched his swishing cape down the village. A sad moan rose again from the two oldest women. 'Terrible days were on us then,' said Annag softly. And to each other they told over the old heartbreak, with the loving embellishment and elegant phrasing which had set order on a grief that, undisciplined, would have turned to madness.

The elder and his family were working on their potato patch above the village. They sent their daughter running for bannock and buttermilk to refresh Mr Gibb, and enquired courteously after the other gentlemen who had helped peg out the walls. The elder invited his visitor to view the finished result.

'Tomorrow,' said Gibb hastily; he recalled it as a bit of a tramp. He explained what he had come for: to collect evidence of the sufferings of the people, to make grievances known, to put old wrongs to right by forcing political action. He gave a flamboyant account: he remembered how they liked fine language. The elder listened politely, then asked an unexpected question. 'Are you a man of religion?'

Gibb flannelled. 'Well . . . you could say that, I suppose. I'm a man of high principles, principles of conduct to our fellow men. Christian principles, yes.'

Donald fixed him with his one steely eye.. 'I asked if you were a man of religion, a God-fearing man.' He did not, however, wait for a second answer, but went on: 'I could tell you stories, Mr Gibb, but I will not. I will say only that what befell us was the working of God's purpose. There was ignorance and superstition with us in my father's day and my grandfather's. In our folly we thought we were safe. But you never know the day or the hour, Mr Gibb. Our sins found us out. The sins of the fathers were visited on the children, by chastisement to draw them to salvation.'

'The divine plan,' agreed Gibb, scowling.

The elder's wife remarked that if he wanted to hear some sense he should speak to the lady at the school.

The lady at the school exceeded his best expectations. He was ferried back to Gnipadale fairly hugging himself with glee, whistling loudly, to the unease of the crew. 'What a gal!' he exclaimed, bowling his hat on to the pier ahead of the rest of him.

Calum the Merchant, whom he knew for a staunch ally and a very discreet fellow, was taken into his confidence after a dram or two.

'I can trust you, Calum. You won't say a word. She's the old chief's daughter.'

The merchant was indeed a man of perfect discretion. He stretched his eyes, with a long low rumble of well-timed astonishment.

'Yes! Macdonald of Drumharg's surviving child, masquerading as a dull little schoolmarm. How are the mighty fallen, eh? Now, keep it to yourself, old chap. I swore I wouldn't tell a soul, of course. Got it out of her quite by accident, too. There was I, bashing away at the whole rotten parasitical bunch of them, recalling the beastly mess I saw last time I was here, and suddenly she turns very red and says, "Pardon me, sir, but I must tell you that the man you are so maligning was my father." Well!

237

Embarrassing, eh? I felt sorry for her – almost. I got a lot out of her, all about what was going on up at the Big House when these kiddies were starving. Shooting breakfasts, supper parties, balls. It stinks.'

The merchant shook his sagacious head expressively.

'I got a lot out of her, and I'll get more, by God. Much more. What luck!' He broke into falsetto song: ' "The rich man in his castle,/The poor man at his gate,/God made them high and lowly/And ordered their estate" – damn' nonsense!'

Issie sat up all night with Augustus's journals. Sometimes she leafed page over page in a distracted blur, sometimes she read a passage carefully, moving her lips. Fever-glints of memory shot her brain: her father among his tenants, Georgie and Dileas in the rose garden, Augustus handing Helen into the carriage with the early morning mist in the rhododendrons. Augustus's words, the very cadences of his loud firm voice: 'It is proposed to further improve their condition by supporting the placement of a missionary among them, who may by his preaching and example bring the light of the Gospel into those all but heathen lives, besides educating the children, who are entirely illiterate . . . The settlers are for the most part sober and industrious, of simple piety and showing great solicitude to one another. Such germs of social virtue are deserving of every encouragement, both moral and material . . . Though the massive investment which has taken place of recent years has proved insufficient, it would be both a shame and a folly to grudge more: shame, because of the fortitude shown by the settlers, and folly, because the natural advantages of this land must eventually prove it profitable.'

'Oh, he was a good man. He was!' Issie cried aloud, warding off Gibb's revelations; but they rose on every side, insidious as foul vapours, poisoning all her memories. He had seen starving children tearing at a rotten seal carcass, a wizened hand protruding from the sand where people had been too weak to dig the grave properly, a woman brought to labour among the rocks where she had fallen gathering limpets.

'We didn't know,' she whispered, 'none of us knew', repeating what she had said to Gibb. She did not doubt him – not enough to make any difference. He was frank in his manner, his intentions seemed generous and praiseworthy. He had been profuse in his apologies when he discovered her family connections, and yet he had sworn he could deny none of what he had said. And the present confirmed the past: the squalor of the houses, the fatalistic acceptance of disease and death. They thought themselves well off if they could afford half a pound of sugar. 'But why, why haven't they told me?' she begged of Piseag, of the shadows. 'I've asked and asked about the past . . . I was always afraid . . . ' Her voice and thought shrank before the damning admission. She had been afraid, because she suspected the truth: suspected her father's account, Augustus's account. 'Oh, poor Father,' she cried, sobbing out an inarticulate prayer for the old man who hadn't known, whose world had changed too fast for him; for Augustus, who had put improvement before the clan: the one too old, the other too young, too impatient. She riffled the pages of the last volume desolately. It was different from the others, not a polished account but bald daily entries, some in an uneven hand that betrayed a writer no longer young, but exhausted, despairing and ill. 'Worked all day at the sawpit. They are short of hands, as many sick. Bitter frost. Tomorrow I intend to go north to assert our trapping rights against French interference.' It was the last entry. When Mr Gibb saw it, even he surely could not doubt that the debt had been paid, that Augustus was a good man. He had given everything, all that vital energy. His health, his means, even his son's fortune had been invested in their Canadian lands. Issie closed the book, cradling it in her arms. She did not want to show it to a stranger: the other volumes, yes, but not that last terrible year, beginning, 'News of my son's death reached me today.' Yet she must show

239

it, to vindicate him. There was still so much that could not be said, of the man who had supported his unfaithful wife, who had kept her from disgracing their son, who had loved the son such a wife had given him. The memory of Helen's recent letter, the shame and pathos of its crazy mercenary drift, brought bitter tears. Issie buried her face in the open books before her, kissing the pages with quivering lips.

By morning she was calm. Her duty was clear: to exonerate the dead as far as possible and to help the living. Mr Gibb (Alex Gibb – he did not admit to Aeneas) returned that day, and on most others during the following week, to learn what he called 'the whole truth about this beastly business'. Issie rushed, as she thought, to tell it, to lay before him Augustus's journals and all the trivia of life at Drumharg, where her father had been so loved by his tenants, so amiable among his friends; stalling only when it came to what was not truth, Helen's death in Rome. She blushed, stammered and fell wretchedly silent.

'I see your sister's death is still very painful for you,' he said, watching her steadily; but he did not refer to it again. He was sympathetic, interested in all she had to say. 'But tell me more about yourself,' he demanded several times. 'What was it like, growing up as Miss Isobel Macdonald of Drumharg?'

He was direct – too direct, vulgar, shocking. Yet she liked him. One fine afternoon he suggested 'a tramp', and they walked round the island together. Issie, chattering in response to his questions, suddenly realised that she was enjoying herself, enjoying the brisk walk and her account of Georgie's christening party. She stuttered to a halt. He eyed her enquiringly, raising an eyebrow as if they had known each other for years. That made her laugh; he was like a swaggering ill-bred dog, bounding and confidential. He asked about her girlhood pets and on their return she showed him Dileas's grave. After he had gone for the evening she busied herself late in the village, trying to keep from her mind a disloyal comparison with Mr Macleay, who walked like a rather slow duck and never showed any interest in her personal affairs. She had tried several times to cap his reminiscences of his past with some inkling of her own, but he had scarcely seemed to notice the interruption. At least, she thought, he does not care for me because of my family connections; indeed, he was remarkably innocent of such worldly considerations. She assured herself that this was an excellent quality, that his dwelling on his own past was the result of years of pent-up loneliness.

On Gibb's last visit he asked her to let him take Augustus's journals back to the mainland. They might be suitable for publication, with judicious editing.

'Oh, no, I couldn't . . . ' Issie's startled exclamation tailed off in uncertainty; Augustus, after all, had always intended to publish his observations and had reworked them, all except for the final year, to that end.

Gibb perhaps mistook her hesitancy. He leaned towards her over the tea-table. 'That sort of thing can make money, you know. And forgive me for saying so, Miss Macdonald, but I can see money's none too plentiful with you these days.'

'Oh, it's not that . . .' Issie hardly noticed the offensiveness of the remark, if offensive it was.

'What, then? Come on, you can trust me.'

'I . . . ' she swallowed, aware that her face was working uncontrollably. 'They are my last link with . . . home, and everything. They – I treasure them, Mr Gibb.'

'Why, dammit – pardon me, Miss Macdonald – don't you worry a bit. I'll treasure them too. You'll soon have them back – and the satisfaction of seeing a nice book made out of them. We'll have some engravings done – that's if I *can* publish: I shan't promise, now. But do let me try.'

Issie dithered. There was Helen, too, pleading for more money. 'Oh yes, yes, I'm sure he would have wanted it. You may take them, Mr Gibb.'

'Splendid. What luck!' exclaimed Mr Gibb rather unexpectedly, but she had become used to his impulsive manner and smiled as well as she could.

But she could not keep smiling. Her lips felt like lead as she watched from her window for his boat tacking across. The canvas-wrapped bundle was under one arm. He waved the other in exuberant farewell and blew a kiss; it would have made her laugh if she had not been so sad. Even from the dead, the parting was bitter. 'I loved you,' she whispered into the curtains. 'I'll never, never love another so much.'

Piseag twined round her legs, demanding. Issie blew her nose and told herself she had said a wicked thing. If she was to have a husband, she must love him. 'There's so much to do for him, Piseag,' she said, searching for milk and saucer. But before the one was in the other she was sobbing again, remembering Helen, and that love cannot be constrained, yet need not be happily bestowed.

Yet she was very glad of her admirer's return. At first he was distant with her, ponderously sulky. The elder had told him that she had so far forgotten her reputation as to keep company, in his absence, with a man of doubtful morals and known atheistic convictions.

Issie did not excuse herself. His plight was too apparent; it was time to put him out of his misery.

'Are you jealous?' she asked gently. 'If so, you need not be.'

He blinked, open-mouthed. When he could work his jaw again, he proposed, and she accepted. He had brought a ring from Glasgow. It was a little tight but she didn't tell him so.

'Isobel, I am the happiest man on earth,' he exclaimed.

She saw, wondering, that it was true.

'I am very happy, too,' she said, sincerely.

CHAPTER 22

They had intended to marry in the New Year but in November Helen died. The letter, from the housekeeper Issie had engaged for her, reached her one day just as she was dismissing the children. She perched on her high stool in the dusk, with the page in her hand, remembering that other letter long ago, remembering grief. There was none now, only pity, almost relief that the misery was over: regret at not having been present in those last days, but not remorse, for Helen in her few disjointed letters had expressed no desire to see her again, no desire for anything except the luxuries she could no longer afford. While not insane, she had not been of sound mind. She had become like a very old woman – apathetic, forgetful, fretful as a child, but with none of a child's affection. Issie, quiet in the dusk, sat till all that fell away, till she remembered her lovely youth, the promise so soon wasted. Then she wept, though not bitterly. 'Because that was the real Helen. That is the sister I shall meet in the next world,' she tried to explain to Duncan later. He looked doubtful, as if he suspected heterodoxy.

She had told him something about Helen, but not all, only that she had a sister whose irregular life estranged her from the family but who was in ill health and required financial support. He was incurious, as in most things not directly concerning his own affairs. If he had probed, she would have been glad to tell him more, even all she knew. But Helen's death removed the unease she had felt about his knowing so little of something that had so much affected her own life. Now there was no more tension between her two loyalties. Helen could rest in peace, unexposed, and Duncan in ignorance.

For the first few weeks after the event she experienced a loneliness more profound, if less anguished, than anything that had come before; a mirror of Helen's last days, a drop-off into nothingness, a darkness where something twittered feebly, alone without knowing it. At nights she woke on the edge of it, with Helen's name choking in her throat. Twice she woke reaching for Augustus's journals, confused between the one loss and the other, her hand tapping along the empty shelf by her bed in obscure anxiety.

Her isolation was compounded by Duncan's blindness to her state of mind, but in the end it was his very insensitivity, his immersion in his own and their joint concerns, that brought her back to the everyday. She settled in to a happy engagement but insisted that their marriage be postponed for six months out of respect for the dead. He was loath to agree.

'The work we have to do here can as well be done single as married,' she pointed out.

He grumbled about the indelicacy of their daily proximity, she threatened him with Barabel as a housekeeper. He gave way, because she would not. 'But in all other things, I shall strive to be an obedient wife,' she assured him.

The striving had already begun. She was well used to putting her own interests below another's: she knew no other way to live. But the conforming in habits of mind was new and difficult.

I am too old for it, she sometimes thought to herself during Duncan's sermons, or even during his private harangues, when force of will and affection had proved insufficient to stifle inward rebellion. But she bit her tongue on it, knowing that he, too, made efforts for her sake. The sick could now skip services with impunity. Girls working away, coming home on a visit, flaunted coquettish hats under the very pulpit, unreproved. Rona's congregation, though as frequently urged to repentance, heard less of damnation and more of salvation.

The change was not entirely welcomed.

'What's got into that man?' Barabel exclaimed after a particularly benevolent Sunday. 'There's Kirsty Mary near stuck that parasol-thing up his nose, and not a word about vanity, not a word. Them sermons, they're hardly worth hearing these days.'

She was not alone in her reservations. As a spectacle, preaching had become somewhat disappointing, but for the most part people joked good-naturedly enough about the cause. The elder, however, took it to heart and openly reproved the preacher's laxity.

Duncan began to talk again of leaving Rona, perhaps to resume his studies for the ministry. Issie faced problems in her work, too. The school, insofar as it went, was successful, but the islanders' steadily, if modestly, increasing prosperity would soon render them capable of supporting a schoolmaster. As for her medical assistance, tradition was too strong for her. The direst need for improvement was in midwifery: not in the delivery of babies, for Annag and her daughter had skill enough for even the most difficult births, but in the uncleanliness which Issie blamed for the fevers so commonly fatal to mother or infant. But though people took her cough syrups and castor oil readily enough, and extolled their virtues, she was never admitted to a woman in childbed. The house was in too much of a mess, it wasn't fitting for an unmarried lady – resistance ran through kindly deprecation to strained excuse to outright refusal, from mother, husband, midwife, or all three. Issie had given up any expectation of success.

She and Duncan discussed the possibility of going elsewhere. Their plans drew them closely together. Duncan prayed incessantly for guidance, but better than that – he hoped. Issie could see it; a more youthful light in his eye, a changed timbre in his voice, even the hint of a smile, once, after one of the elder's more preposterous reprimands. Preacher and elder had come to the schoolroom to catechise the scholars. All went well, with a little silent mouthing from Issie behind the men's backs; but as the children rose to their feet at the visitors' departure, a new india-rubber ball, an inestimable treasure, bounced out from under Archie's jacket, with slow direful plumps beneath the preacher's very feet. Eleven pairs of horrified eyes followed its progress. Mr Macleay, feeling something impeding his ankles, peered down at it short-sightedly, stooped, and with surprising accuracy lobbed it back to its owner. The smallest children broke into shrill giggles, and hushed abruptly, seeing the elder's face. Issie, escorting her visitors to the door, had seen it too. Not that it changed much: but steel entered his eye. As she struggled to close the damp-swollen door against the wind, she heard the elder's mild and measured voice. There was steel in it, too. 'Games are for children, Mr Macleay. A man's life should be work and prayer.'

Duncan told her about it later, smiling. 'But I can still throw, can't I, in spite of these weak eyes? What fun I had when I was a boy, throwing a ball with my cousins in the country.'

Issie vowed inwardly that he should have fun again, if not in that boyhood countryside, then somewhere more like it than Rona.

But in February changes occurred that made her waver, if only privately, in her enthusiasm for the move. Annag had taken influenza, which lingered on and left her weak and chesty. Everyone knew (because Ciorstag had told them) that it would be the death of her before the year was out. Issie did not at all like such prescience and would not allow herself to believe it, but it was apparent, nevertheless, that the old lady would be unfit for her work as midwife for some months. Her daughter Mór was herself far advanced in pregnancy and, for the first time, ill with it. The younger women of the village saw the excuse they needed. One afternoon, Issie opened her door to a unwieldy deputation: Neiliann, who had lost her third baby at two weeks, Dora, who had kept two and wasn't taking chances with the next, and little Dolina from Port Long, the bride of John Blondie's son Shonny, expecting

246

her first. Issie was astonished at their request that she should assist at their deliveries, and even demurred, asking weakly what Mór thought about it. But they were clamorous: they had only been waiting for a chance; if their babies lived, Katie would be the next to consult her; Mór had just the same old nonsense as her mother; they didn't want the babies to die. Dolina began to cry, wishing she was home on Boreray, and Issie gave in.

Two babies arrived within the week. The new midwife was singularly fortunate; she knew little enough about her trade, but in each case there was an aunt or a granny to help, the infants popped out head first, and then it was only a matter of soap and hot water and clean white linen to swathe the baby. Mothers and children all throve.

Vastly grateful and relieved, but still feeling guilty, Issie called to see Annag, who was confined to bed. 'Have I been doing things right?' she asked.

'Oh, just right, my dearie. I'm hearing good things about you.' Annag's kind deep eyes, enlarged in her wasted face, brimmed with gladness. She was incapable of malice. She patted Issie's hands. 'It's what you're putting on the cord, I'm sure,' she murmured, drifting into sleep.

Issie, pondering this remark, reflected that whatever Annag had been putting on the cord all those years, it would be better if the recipe were lost to the world.

Mór avoided all reference to her rival's successes and politely ignored her textbook suggestions for the easing of her headache and dizziness. What caused Issie more concern was Duncan's lack of relish for her activities.

'I consider it unseemly, Isobel, very unseemly. Such things are best left to married women.'

'But the work is so necessary. The only thing that has been missing here is cleanliness, but that is vital. I have told you about Miss Nightingale's principles of hygiene. I cannot refuse to help, Duncan, when I know I can be of use.'

'I have a good mind to forbid it. The elder considers that I should.' He spoke very pettishly, as was his habit when he was anxious.

'Forbid it?' Issie jumped up, reddening. 'It is life-saving work. It is my work for God.'

'Where is your promise of wifely obedience, Isobel?'

Issie forced herself to sit down again and did not speak till she was sure of sounding mild. 'I must attend Dolina, as I have promised. After that, there are no more babies expected till after we are married, except by the elder's wife, who will not want me. When we are married I take it you will have no objection.'

He agreed, sulkily, to let it go at that, but the affair cast a shadow that both felt, a chill of difference, of unlike minds.

One spring evening Kennag truanted home from the Gnipadale shop with a pamphlet under her shawl. 'Something the No-hat Man sent to the merchant. Quite interesting! Here, the old miser made me pay for it. Keep your grubby hands off!'

Knots of people gathered around her as she proceeded up the street, dispersing and re-forming with shocked exclamations and an occasional guffaw. When she reached the ceilidh-house, which had been home to her all her orphaned days, she kissed Ciorstag and Lexy and thrust the paper under their noses. It was headed *How Nero Fiddled While Rome Burned*, and subtitled *an account of a Highland nobleman's jaunts and jollities, undertaken while his peasantry starved during the removals of the 1840s, and of his salutary fate, by a 'Son of the Gael'*. PUBL. A. GIBB, EDINBURGH 1863.

The pamphlet passed from hand to eager hand, in a confused babble of amusement and distress.

'Thirty horses! Old Drumharg had thirty horses!'

'Oh well, that daughter of his, a scarlet woman!'

'Look here, Neiliann, this is you he's meaning.'

'Oh, terrible days, terrible days!'

As the evening wore on, distress and indignation were uppermost. Everyone knew the stories, and more, and worse; but to see them there in black and white lent them a new dignity. They had passed from the realm of private sorrow to an outrage the world should share. People who had slept for a whole year under an old sail without complaint wept at the written statement of their plight. The chieftain who in life had drawn little worse than a shrug or a wry jest from the tenants he had abandoned was reviled by them in his grotesque printed effigy. His daughter's three-hundred-pound wedding gown brought groans of hatred, her illicit amour a gabble of execration.

It was Donald's voice, seldom raised but never ignored, which stilled the hubbub. It rang out jubilant, as they had not heard it since the death of his daughter. 'Thanks be to God! He has put down the mighty from their seat. Oh, who among us can forget that day, when they turned us from our land and burned our homes? We rebelled then against God's will, but see now that He was testing us, He had not forgotten us. We had learned to live where He sent us and striven to walk in His ways when He sent the woman among us to try our hearts. We knew her parentage but did His will, we bore her with meekness and patience, with love instead of hate. Poor fool, she came to remedy the evil deeds of her father. In her arrogance she thought to do it by her own will and her own deeds. Oh, how vain is such a hope for any sinner! But now we see that God made her an instrument to justify us, to show us to ourselves, forgiven in His sight. For through her the traitor who exiled us is put to public shame, here, in this paper. Now all may know the judgment of God on the tyrant. That man's life was cut short, his lands were sold to the stranger, the wrath of God fell on his children and on his child's child for his iniquity. Where are his thirty horses now, his flower gardens, his daughters' jewels and fine gowns? The Lord has dashed them in pieces. "Vengeance is mine, saith the Lord. I will repay!" The Lord's will be done.'

There were murmurs and exclamations of assent.

'Oh, the good Lord saw our sufferings,' called out old Catriona, and began to weep, with penitent relief: for many years it had seemed that He looked on them only to visit them with punishment. His passionate wrath, dispassionate judgment had been testing them, trying heroic metal in furnace heat till it ran like water. Now some bowed their heads and sighed 'Amen' with tears; others squared shoulders, confident of proven favour.

'Praise be to God for His justice,' cried Donald, alight.

The kindly Christ of the free blessings was banished with the fairies. If Annag had been there, she might have said, 'I'll not stay to hear you tonight, Donald', and some would have remembered that the rich, too, can suffer; but she was too weak to leave her bed.

Issie had been up on the cliffs to watch the sun setting. For the first time that year it had swung far enough west to drop behind the tip of Fladday. She came down the hill full of peace, glad to have snatched half an hour of solitude while the elder was closeted with Duncan. She had ceased to feel guilty for sometimes enjoying a solitary walk. They had different requirements for refreshment; she had come to think of her own silent contemplation of nature as in a way comparable to Duncan's long hours of private prayer. She had not put this idea to him, not yet: it would be difficult for him to understand. But surely when they were married he would see it, in the unfolding intimacy of twenty-four-hour days, seven-day weeks.

As she neared the schoolhouse she saw him waiting at the door, in his familiar black frock-coat, and another dark figure, the elder. Like a couple of old ravens, she thought, smiling, then quickened her steps, seeing something amiss in Duncan's mien. As she reached the level he caught sight of her and ran towards her, waving a paper.

'Isobel! Is this true? Can it be true?'

Her heart clenched, thinking it was news of another death. As he thrust it at her, she said, 'Oh, it's only a pamphlet . . . ', and saw what pamphlet. It took perhaps half a minute – it seemed a long time to Issie: Duncan was babbling, she could not make sense of the print – to realise how she had been betrayed.

'Is it true? Isobel, is it true?' Duncan whimpered at her.

'I dare say.' Her voice shook: but it had been her own fault. She drew herself upright. 'I trusted Mr Gibb, which was very foolish of me. But I should have to read it through to see if it is all true. Please don't be angry with me, Duncan. I told him nothing which could discredit you – or me – and I see he has used false names . . . '

She could not go on. She had seen enough in her brief scan to realise that her frankness had been repulsively perverted. She held out her hands to Duncan in appeal. The elder brushed past him and took the pamphlet from her. He turned over pages, and pointed. 'Is this true, Miss Macdonald?'

The words were a jumble to her. The phrase 'a military lover' stood out. Slowly, the rest coalesced around it. Gibb had done his tracking thoroughly.

'Is this true?' the elder repeated.

'Yes.'

Duncan moaned. She tried again to catch his hand but the elder stood between them. He turned the page and pointed.

'And is this true also?'

She looked, and at first it made no sense. But she had read of such a disease before she came to Rona, when she had been studying all she could to improve her medical knowledge. She had seen no connection then: now every detail of Helen's illness fell into place.

'Yes,' she whispered. 'Dr Ross wouldn't tell me,' she added, as if it explained something, remembering Georgie, and the way the doctor had sometimes looked.

'Isobel, you don't ... can't ... understand ... ' He was pleading, blustering. 'Say no. You must say no.'

'Yes. I did not know, but yes, I believe it to be true.'

The elder drew a long breath, a breath, it seemed, of freedom, as if a burden had been lifted from his back. 'An adulteress punished for her sins,' he said quietly, almost tenderly.

Duncan's face had changed: Duncan had gone. The preacher of the pulpit raved at her. 'You lied, you deceived me! It was revealed to me, God has revealed it to me in time – through your own obduracy, you are condemned, I am saved. By God's hand I am snatched from the burning – God made her delay our marriage, we would have been joined by now, that honourable state of matrimony into which ... She delayed for mourning, mourning for such a sister. O Lord, her sins have found her out!'

He had ceased to speak to her directly. He spoke to the elder, or to his God. Issie stared at him in shivering amazement, and it amazed her too, the thought passed clearly through her mind, that she would not stammer or cry, but would speak quite distinctly.

'She was my sister and I believe God has mercy on her. And if I had known all I know now, I should still have supported her and mourned for her, even more, if I had known how truly pitiable she was. And I have never lied to you Duncan, except once. I told you I was ... alone in the world, and I ... was not, in the way you meant.'

Her composure dissolved as she reached the end of her defence. She found her way, somehow, blindly, through the ranting voices into her quiet room.

She did not know what to do, so she attempted to do as she had always done in times of crisis, to carry on as usual. Next morning she entered the schoolroom and waited, but no children came. She forced herself to go outside and look down the village. A child pointed up at her: it was Neilie. The few women in the street disappeared indoors.

As she turned back to her own door she saw that the white curtains had gone from the mission house window. She sat in her room and waited, no longer feeling or thinking. The elder knocked to deliver the note from Duncan and told her that a boat would call for her next morning at sunrise. She folded Duncan's letter after one glance and placed it on the table under her engagement ring. It passed through her mind that she should have asked the elder how his wife did, she was over her time. But now she would never know, and would never know if Annag recovered, or if 'her' babies throve, or if Rebecca became, as she wished, a teacher. In the strangeness of it all she stood lost, shaking her head.

At last she turned to packing, and lined a basket with moss to carry Piseag. In the evening she heard people go into the mission house for prayer-meeting. No one walked past her window. She heard the elder's voice, even and vibrant, and Duncan's, rising and falling in the tortured cadences of penitence, of castigation. Poor man, she thought.

There was a timid knock at the door. It was Morag, staring with wild scared eyes. She pulled at Issie's gown, hardly able to utter for fright, her looks darting towards the mission house.

'Come quick, miss. It's for Mam.'

'Oh, she won't want me, my dear.'

'Yes, yes, it's you she wants. Dad said you weren't to come, he called you a woman of sin. Bring the baby quick, miss, before he comes home. Please, miss, hurry!'

That it would be quick, Issie guessed from Mór's previous history. She snatched a bottle of chloral from the medicine shelf and an armful of clean linen from her open trunk, and raced down the hillside after Morag.

It was over sooner than the prayer-meeting. The baby was already in Mór's arms when Donald and his sons returned. Morag, timid little Morag, took a woman's courage, and stood at the door to keep them out. 'You menfolk can't come in here!' And custom decreed that they could not.

Mór, drowsy, laughing, called out, 'You would rather your son had died, Donald, and your wife, too.'

Issie turned to hush the terrible words, but the hatred in Mór's dark eyes silenced her protest. She had borne him eight children: it could not always have been so between these two. Issie baulked at the threshold of the bitter past, of the cankered years she had tried and failed to redeem for these and for all the outcast remnant of her father's people. She thought of Augustus. Her exhausted mind floated outward in a drift of snow among trees, to a fox and two rabbits sheltering under the cedar branches. The charm of shelter, of somewhere to hide, crept over her and withdrew, leaving her bleak and full of pity.

'I'll go soon and the poor things can come back,' she said to Morag.

Mór called her to the bedside. 'I knew the baby was coming this morning. I kept it hidden. I wanted you.'

'Why?' Issie searched her face, baffled. Perhaps to spite Donald, merely.

'That is what my mother wanted. What will you do when you go way from us?'

'I shall find some useful work,' quavered Issie.

Mór smiled and took her hand. 'God's blessing on you. You are a good woman.'

The Boreray boatmen came up for her bags themselves. Though her disgrace did not concern them very closely, they were silent out of embarrassment. The sun was well up, and Rona should have been stirring: but all the doors were closed as they walked through the village. Issie remembered that they had been closed when she arrived. She had felt then that these would never be her friends; but they had been friends indeed, though now they were not. Mentally she saluted, as she passed their homes, Annag, Mór, Rebecca, old Hector and young Hector, Neiliann, Katie – and everyone, everyone who had suffered and been exiled, because of whom, now, she was suffering and exiled. She had paid recompense, though not in the way she had intended; but perhaps it was in some manner right.

She clambered into the boat, with Piseag mewing in the basket under her arm. The men looked curiously at her burden. She fixed her eyes on the little grave cairn above the schoolhouse till distance swallowed it up, then took her Bible from her pocket and opened it where Miss Nightingale's portrait lay.

1 8 8 4

CHAPTER 23

Young glowing Ranald and faded Issie had talked small-talk for half an hour about Rona's prosperity, good fishing and good wool prices. 'He's keeping very well', 'She passed away last year', his shy answers to her enquiries had filled the gaps between mouthfuls, as his big hands found their way carefully round thin crockery and thin bread and butter. Now they had run out of things to say. Three floors below, in the dingy evening, Glasgow traffic rumbled and clattered. They eyed each other, under cover of growing dusk. What a fine strong lad, she thought, of her last Rona baby; and Mam said she was a big strong woman, but she looks real poor and thin, he thought, of the grey stooping figure in the austere uniform of an infirmary sister.

The cat jumped from her lap as she rose to light the gas-lamp. It gave Ranald an idea for something to say.

'Is the cat a kitten of the one you had off us that time?'

She started. 'Oh, you heard about that?'

'Ay.' He blushed, half smiling, though.

She smiled too. 'Well, I suppose it was an infamous theft. No, she isn't her kitten, but a great-granddaughter. She is Piseag, too. My Rona cat I called Piseag, you know.' She hesitated, resettling the cat on her starched white apron. 'Tell me, Ranald . . . is there still a cairn just above the schoolhouse?'

'Ay. Your wee dog, Dileas.'

'You've heard all about me. I'm glad it's still there. He was an island dog, you know.'

An innocent country grin beamed between his young black moustache and his too-tight, too-stiff collar. 'Ay, I know. It was my father brought him to you at Drumharg.'

259

'What? Oh, I wish I had known. I should have remembered faces – but I was so startled at the time when the men brought me the puppy. And then many years had passed, and, of course, I didn't want it to be known who I was.'

Ranald was still smiling. He leaned back and crossed his legs, suddenly relaxing. 'Och, they all knew who you were, Miss Macdonald. They didn't say anything, they thought it would spoil things for you.'

'Oh . . . ' Issie's exclamation tailed off in an incredulous laugh and then into sad silence. But a long-unsatisfied curiosity revived her. 'Then . . . the girl who put her blue ribbon on the puppy – your father's sister – was that Effie? Oh, but of course you wouldn't know about the ribbon. I forget how young you are, my dear.'

'Ay – och, everyone knows everything in them places. That wasn't Effie, that was Eilidh. She was going to Canada.'

'Was she the mother of your cousin who came back? And shall you see her when you go out? I have kept her ribbon all these years. I should love to send it back, with a letter – '

The closing down of the boy's frank smile stopped her eager chatter.

'She never reached there. She . . . died.'

An old grief oozed its chill between them. Ranald tapped his fingers on his knees, as if he would rise in a moment to go.

Issie could not look at Eilidh's nephew but managed to say, more statement than question, 'On the ship. What terrible things were done . . . that can never be undone.'

'Ay, terrible.' He had picked up his hat and was turning it over, in the embarrassment of the young before the sadness of the old.

'I must not keep you. You have much to attend to, I know,' she said gently.

'Ay, I'd better be going.' He half rose, relieved, but saw her wistfulness, the quivering soul behind the colourless face and hair. He sat down again. 'It wasn't all terrible. There's my cousin, now, that I'm going out there with: his father's got five hundred acres there, ten men working for him. Well, he'd never have done that at home. There isn't the land to go round. Good, productive land, too, and plenty more to spread out on. Ay, they're doing well out there. And I'll tell you something my cousin John was telling us, Miss Macdonald, about Mr Green, your sister's husband. Well, I know on Rona they're all against him, but John said his father and the rest of them were making that man a hero, for the way he worked for them. Oh, he was pushing them hard, right enough, but if he hadn't, they'd never have made out. They used to say the devil was driving him, but they were joking. When he saw they were trying so hard, in the early days, when things were so bad, he just worked along with them every step of the way. And two men died looking for his body – yes, that's how much they thought of him. There's ten or twelve fellows in Macdonald Settlement called Augustus after him, John says.'

She was silent for some moments, but her face expressed gladness. 'Thank you for telling me,' she said, at last.

Ranald rose again. 'I'll be off now, then. I'm much obliged to you for your hospitality, Miss Macdonald.'

'And I to your mother for sending you. You can't imagine how – never mind. You're in a hurry. God bless you, and I wish you the greatest good fortune in your new country.'

'Och, it'll be a great life! It's a grand place to go if you're young.' His dark eyes brimmed with excitement. 'My cousin John, he was looking at that wall at home, you know, that my father was always at. You'd have thought it was the Garden of Eden inside it the way Dad worked at it. Well, John looks inside of it and outside of it, and says to me, "Where's the difference?". That's just about it on Rona.' He flexed his arms ebulliently. 'No more of that for me!'

Suddenly he was not so full of it. How you will miss your home, thought Issie. He met her compassionate glance with a sheepish smile.

'Well, it'll take getting used to. Miss Macdonald, would you . . . my cousin's father, that's Ciorstag's son Alasdair, he was the one who went out with Eilidh. After she died he never married for, oh, fifteen years. He couldn't forget her, see. There's a song he made about it. It's a lovely song indeed, I wish I could sing it for you, but I'll have to run for that train. I was wanting to ask, though, if you would give me that ribbon you were telling me about, to take to Alasdair?'

She was no time finding it. She leaned over the banisters as he clattered down the dimly lit stairway, till his bright upturned face and the blue ribbon in his waving hand were hidden by the last turn.

Slowly, she went back into her room. 'How lovely, Piseag!' she said, closing the door behind her.